Praise for Learning How to Fly

Learning How to Fly is the inspiring story of a fellow activist who has hung in there through thick and thin for all of the 32 years I've known her. Fighting vivisection is a hard road and it takes both courage and incredible patience to stay in the battle. But Britt found a way to stay on course and still fulfill her passion for acting. Readers will find this book entertaining and humorous, but it's also her journey that provides guidance on how one can find their own way to a meaningful life.

With Respect for all Life – Chris DeRose - Founder and President -
Last Chance for Animals and author of an autobiography -
In Your Face

As a young starlet, Britt Lind was a beauty who was cast in a Clint Eastwood movie and found happiness being married to a television producer and acting and raising a baby girl. But in a flash, her marriage ended, riches vanished, the house was foreclosed on and her career crumbled. Britt's story of disappearing success is poignant and unforgettable, and by the time she is beaten down in Hollywood and heads for New York with visions of Broadway, you cannot help but cheer for her and the animals she has dedicated her life to saving. This is a heartfelt, timeless story of shining on to create a life filled with love, beauty and triumph.

Janette Turner – Writer, director and author of the forthcoming memoir *Magazine Crush: My Life as a Cosmo Addict.*

These are the adventures of an innocent young girl from Norway, thrust into American culture, driven by a passionate ambition to be an actress in a ruthlessly unpredictable and sexist industry. Britt navigated through a life of obstacles, betrayals and disappointments with courageous resolve, a resolve deeply rooted in a firm moral foundation and strengthened by a deep compassion and a fiery desire to end the suffering of animals.

Captain Paul Watson – Founder of *The Sea Shepherd Conservation Society* and author of several books including: *Sea Shepherd – My Fight for Whales and Seals, Seal Wars - Twenty-Five Years on the Front Lines with the Harp Seals* and *Ocean Warrior – My Battle to End the Illegal Slaughter on the High Seas.*

Learning How to Fly

Learning How to Fly

A SPEED REEL JOURNEY
TOWARD LIFE'S PURPOSE

Britt Lind

ISBN-13: 978-1-64704-129-8

Cover Watercolor Painting by Howard Tharp

"Daffodils" by William Wordsworth

"Turn Your Eyes Upon Jesus" by Helen H. Lemmel

To my forever husband, Nick
my incredible sister, Irene
my beautiful daughter, Erika
my BFF, Georgia
my soul sisters Diane, Helen, Jeanette, Kathy, Marlena, Rosemaria,
Sandra, Susan and Sylva
my faithful agent, Carlyne Grager
and
all my beloved animals, past, present and future

Table of Contents

Foreword

I HAVE KNOWN BRITT FOR many years, since she first started training with me in my classes, and I saw her work evolve into fine experiential acting. When she asked me to write the foreword to this book I was delighted and honored.

Britt is a woman "for all seasons." She is an accomplished actor and writer and has a singing voice that the angels envy. When reading the book, I was taken aback by the sheer honesty expressed on every page. She willingly and courageously exposed and shared her incredible journey throughout. Her passion to act and the difficulties all actors experience on that journey, full of rejections and disappointments, never deterred her from getting up when she was knocked down and continuing the journey with renewed vigor. Her love and commitment to animals reflects the soul of Albert Schweitzer. Her activism, even at the cost of her own safety never stopped her from working to end animal experimentation. As an autobiography, this book stands out as a totally truthful account of her life. Without compromising the privacy of those who might be hurt, she never resists her truth even when she takes responsibility for her mistakes.

I lovingly call her "the cat lady" because of her love and her relationship to the cats who supported her through the good times and the bad. This is an important book for all artists to read because it parallels what all of us experience and feel on our journey, a journey that still continues for her with the same unbending commitment that she started out with. It is one of the best autobiographies that I have ever read. I was affected emotionally throughout the entire reading experience and I hope every actor, singer, writer, painter and musician who needs some inspiration to keep on going will read this book.

Eric Morris – Acting teacher and author of several books including *No Acting Please, Being and Doing* and *The Diary of a Professional Experiencer*

Introduction

THERE ARE MANY TALENTED PEOPLE in this world who had a dream, pursued it passionately, with persistence and hard work, but never reached their ultimate goal of success and recognition.

All I ever wanted out of life was to be a working actor. Since grade school I knew that was where my talent lay and was what would make me happy. When I finally moved to Los Angeles, I would have happily lived by myself in my tiny apartment in Studio City for the rest of my life if only I were granted my wish of earning my living as an actor and never having to get a "real" job ever. The possibility of failure was so unthinkable, so horrifying that I would rather have died if by age 40 I still hadn't "made it."

What I didn't know then was that even though my passion was acting and it was all I ever wanted to do, my real mission in life was actually still out there, somewhere, waiting for me – a mission that would make my life meaningful in a way acting would not. When this calling suddenly appeared and kept hitting me square in the face, time after time, I resisted like crazy. This mission was difficult; it was an impossible challenge but finally there was relief in giving in. And yes, it may be frustrating not to be working constantly as an actor, but I wake up every morning knowing I have a God-given purpose in life.

For all of you who may think you have fallen short of your goals, don't give up on them, ever, and know that there is something important you are supposed to contribute to this world. Depression sometimes may threaten to overwhelm those of us who have a fervent unfulfilled ambition, be it in the arts or elsewhere, but we can move through that, knowing that as human beings we are here to not only make our own lives happy and rewarding but to share our talents for the greater good.

This is not an autobiography that details every single thing that has happened in my life (which would be of no interest to anyone but my friends and they know everything anyway). Experiences that helped shape me but would reveal personal things that would hurt innocent people by being exposed, I left out. They can tell their own stories if they wish. This is a blueprint of sorts to show you that if someone as singularly focused and fanatically dedicated to her goal as I was can find the way to a special little niche in this world, anybody can. It's in your heart already. Just listen and do it.

Speed\sped\
Swiftness or rate of performance or action

Reel\'rel\
A revolvable device on which something flexible is wound

For actors, a speed reel is a compilation of past work, lasting no longer than two minutes, which is shown to casting directors in order to convince them we are brilliant actors. Casting directors have short attention spans and are easily bored, so even if you have more talent than a triple Oscar winner, if the reel is longer than two minutes, their eyes glaze over, your headshot and resume go in the round file and, as they say in Brooklyn, "You can tell your story walking backwards." You're done.

Hence, be brilliant, be brief and let them know that *you* are perfect for the job. All you have to do is accept that and remember no one can do it better than you.

CHAPTER 1

They Like Me! They Really Like Me!

I WAS IN A DAZE over what had just happened. It still hadn't quite sunk in. Looking straight ahead, I slowly walked down the pier and barely noticed that the sun was shining and gentle breezes were creating a perfect September day for all the tourists who were wandering through the shops and restaurants on the Monterey Wharf. The laughter of children and cawing of the seagulls hardly penetrated my consciousness. My brain was still too busy processing the fact that after years of waiting and hoping, I was finally on the road to fulfilling my goal of becoming a working actress; it *was* going to happen.

As I neared the parking lot, my steps quickened and I allowed myself to believe the miracle; I was going to be in a movie with Clint Eastwood. Yes! He wanted me! Yes! I ran to my car so I could hurry home and tell somebody, anybody, the incredible news. My dream was actually coming true; a dream I had had since grade school when it seemed completely beyond the reach of a little girl from Norway who had parents who believed that what meant the world to me was a mortal sin. I could exhale. Finally.

It was a terrifying moment. Seven years old and still learning English, I was seated in the first row right under the teacher's nose as she introduced herself to the class. I looked up at her and strained to understand what she was saying. She wrote something on the blackboard that I couldn't read because I was extremely near-sighted and could only see clearly about six inches in front of me. No one knew this because I had never had an eye test so the glasses I so desperately needed were still years away.

Unfortunately, before escorting me to the classroom, the principal had not shown me to the little girls' room – an oversight that now threatened to become a tragic mistake. I felt the pressure building as the teacher droned on and on in a language that was nothing like my native Norwegian. Even if I hadn't felt strangled by timidity, I did not know the correct language or proper protocol to enable my escape from this room in order to find relief, and then, where to go after that?! Meanwhile, do I raise my hand? Then what? I wouldn't know how to put the words together to make the request. There had to be another way. Maybe I can hold it until the class is over. But how long is that? Thoughts jumbled around my head at the speed of light, some in Norwegian and some in English, and as I procrastinated, the pressure grew. The outcome was inevitable and I began to weep. There was no way out for me. The pressure became unbearable, the spigot turned on and overflowed – more liquid than I knew I had inside me. It seemed to flow endlessly as my tears joined the lake forming on the floor. The teacher looked first at my face and then underneath my desk and registered surprise and pity. The other kids in class followed her gaze and giggles turned to laughter as the teacher reprimanded them. But her stern warnings only made their howls louder until they swept over me in a tidal wave of humiliation.

That was my first live appearance and even though it was a boffo performance and garnered mega laughs, I cried all the way through it.

The next year my English had improved considerably. I was a voracious reader and loved poems and fairy tales, so when we received the assignment to pick our favorite poem, memorize it and recite it in front of the class the next week, I already knew which one I would choose. Alone in my room, I memorized and rehearsed until I felt ready to share it with the class. The big day came and I listened to the other kids recite their poems and was appalled. Their delivery was flat and monotone, interspersed with face-rubbing, nose-picking, the girls lifting up their dresses and showing their underpants, staring out the window and in general having no connection with the material whatsoever. And this was their own language they were mutilating!

My turn came and I walked to the front of the class and faced the 25 kids staring at me, many of whom who had laughed at me the year before and probably would remember me for my shame the rest of their lives. But all fear and shyness fell away as I started to recite my poem with all the emotion in my young, tender heart – "I wandered lonely as a cloud that floats on high o'er vale and hills, when all at once I saw a cloud, a host of golden daffodils. Beside the lake, beneath the trees, fluttering and dancing in the breeze..." I finished my poem to a hushed classroom. The other kids actually looked at me with awe and admiration. My teacher had tears in her eyes. "Yes," she said, "yes, that is how it is done." She sniffed a little then pulled herself together, showered me with more compliments and told me that I was to go around to the other classes and recite it for them.

I was a hit! And I was taking my show on the road! I was so elated basking in all this glory if I had known there was such a thing as an Oscar I would have started composing my acceptance speech then and there.

So how, exactly, had a little Norwegian girl ended up thousands of miles away from home, having to learn a new language and finding out a good review was worth all the abuse that came my way from classmates for talking and looking "weird?" Two years earlier, in the early 1950s, my father, Elisar Wessel Fredriksen, had dragged the whole family kicking and screaming to America. Actually, he went there a year ahead of us to find a job and a place for us to live in Seattle, Washington. My mother, Johanna, and my sister, Irene, were not overjoyed at leaving our beautiful house in Sauda, Norway, which was nestled in the foot of the mountains at the very end of Stavanger Fjord. My sister had many friends and didn't want to leave them or her school and my mother hated the thought of leaving her sisters and brothers behind for a strange country where she didn't know a single soul. But my father was the boss and I learned early on that the man makes the decisions, and since you can't live without them, you do as they say. Why my father chose to leave behind his four brothers and one sister and start all over again from scratch, I have never found out. Maybe it had something to do with the war.

During World War II, the Germans invaded Norway, marching right through an accommodating, neutral Sweden (giving birth to the Norwegian expression, "He pulled a Swede on me") and occupied Norway, including our little town. I wasn't around yet but I know it was an extremely difficult and tragic time for Norwegians, even more so for countries and people bombed into oblivion and the millions who lost their lives in the Holocaust. Businesses were destroyed, opportunities for higher learning put on hold and never regained, talents wasted, homes occupied, and not to mention, lives lost and, worst of all, a few Norwegians betraying their own countrymen. Jews had to hide in the mountains assisted by people willing to risk their lives, while many young men like my father became slave labor. My mother and sister were allowed to remain in their house but I can only imagine the fear that permeated the existence of my mother during those years, a fear that turned her into a woman who spent the rest of her life worried and anxious about almost everything. At the airfield where my father worked, the Nazi pilots used to think it was great fun to swoop their planes down as low as they could over the men working on the runways, forcing the workers to throw themselves on the ground to avoid being hit and killed just for laughs.

After the British came to the rescue of Norway and rid the country of Nazis, the personas of both my parents became irrevocably changed. My fun-loving, dancing, movie-going, party-loving, carefree parents abandoned the standard Norwegian Lutheran Church to become Pentecostal.

Why they were drawn to this rigid, dogmatic way of thinking and living I have no clue. It was not something that they would ever discuss with me. I still remember when, as a little girl, I would stand beside my mother in church and look up at my parents as they stood stock still, staring straight ahead as the noise and fervor of their fellow believers swirled all around them – two stoic, intensely private people who had joined a denomination that encouraged unbridled displays of emotion of which they never partook. It made no sense to me at all. Nevertheless, their conversion resulted in no more fun, no more dancing, no more movies, no drinking (not even my Lutheran uncle Fredrik's delicious, home-made wine) no nothing – only rules and regulations that were to be strictly adhered to or risk burning in hell. So maybe it was memories of the war or maybe it was the religious conversion that set him apart from their families that made my father want to leave. I'll never know because my parents never told me, no matter how many times I asked.

My first memory is when I was about 2 years old, sitting on the path that led to my house, screaming as a rooster pecked at my eyes. I remember my father came running, grabbed the rooster and went to the back of the house and chopped off its head. I'm sure blood was running down my face as my mother took me inside. That poor dead rooster must have pecked deeply because I still have scars around my eyes from that ordeal.

The next clear memory is of my mother heating up my little potty by the space heater so it wouldn't be so cold on my bottom. Our bathroom was downstairs in the cold, dark, dank basement and I had to put on wooden shoes when I got to the bottom of the stairs before shuffling into the gray bathroom which had a cement floor and was surrounded by cement walls. The water tank was high above me on the wall and I had to pull a chain to flush the toilet. To save me from that entire trauma, my mother had a little pot for me to use upstairs in the kitchen. But this time, when I plunked down on that potty it was as hot as a stovetop burner and it sizzled me for about one millisecond before I flew straight up in the air howling in pain.

My poor mother was devastated and cried when she saw what she had done. I had to sleep on my tummy for a few weeks after that and decided it was time for me to start using the real bathroom no matter how cold and scary it was down in the basement.

My next misadventure happened two years later when I was having fun with my friends treating my parents' bed as a trampoline. I jumped as hard as I could to get higher than anybody else and bounced right off the bed, onto the floor and broke my collar bone. Nothing can be done for a broken collar bone, so I had to be very still for a long time to allow it to mend.

Other than that, life in Norway was ideal for a child. I have memories of my mother sitting at the sewing machine and me standing on the chair behind her, with my arms wrapped around her neck, watching intently as she worked the fabric under the needle. She treated me almost like a pet; warm and affectionate and calling me silly names like "bamse," Norwegian for teddy bear. It wasn't until later in America when life became hard and my parents had to scramble to pay bills that she became more stern and distant.

My very first pet was a goat named Snø Kvit (Snow White). I loved him so much I brought him in the house one day where he promptly relieved himself on my parents' bedspread. I felt very sad when he disappeared after that and constantly searched for him up in the mountains where all the other goats roamed but I never found him. It never occurred to me that my parents would have taken him away from me on purpose.

I loved to play in my yard with all my friends in the summer, and in the winter, build snow houses and ski down the little hill by my house. I would sing to myself as I walked up and down the hills of Åbødalen, oblivious of the fear and hardship my fellow Norwegians had suffered only a few years ago at the hands of the Nazis. To me it was a childhood paradise where I wanted to live forever. But the desires and opinions of my mother, sister and I were of no consequence and off we went to join my father. I hoped we'd come back soon.

CHAPTER 2

Animals, Debbie Reynolds and Me

OUR FIRST HOME IN SEATTLE was a tiny garage apartment in the back of a large house near Greenlake. I began my American education in a grade school that was right across the street, and felt very special when the teacher sat me on the floor in the middle of a circle of my classmates and they asked me questions about Norway in a language I could barely understand. School was mainly arts and crafts and recess so I got along fine. Play is play in any language. That first summer in Seattle was very warm and my father and I used to walk down the hill to the lake and swim in Greenlake. The first time we went he told me to go out into the deeper waters and swim; no lesson, just do what he did. I followed his instruction and managed to stay afloat. We rented a bicycle in a rental shop nearby and he told me to get on it and ride. He never taught, never held on to the bike or considered that I'd never done it before, and since he expected it, that's what I did. I rode like I'd been doing it forever. His motto was just do it. He had Nike beaten by a few decades.

I had barely started making headway with my English at my school when we moved to a house so small it could barely hold the four of us. And then moved again to the home where I ended up attending the grade school where I started my show business career. My sister was very shy and, like me, barely was able to speak or understand English. She decided that she would rather work than go to school and found a job at Sears, wrapping packages in the mail order department. She briefly joined the Salvation

Army and bought herself one of those huge bonnets you only see now in productions of Guys and Dolls, thinking that this would be the center of her social life. She was disappointed to find out that in America, the Salvation Army is not an organization of Christian young people like in Sauda but mainly people who pick up furniture and other belongings to sell in their stores to help the needy.

My father worked at Hostess Cupcakes and my mother at a sewing factory. Since we didn't have a car, both my parents took several buses to get to work. They had to get up early in the morning, stand at the bus stop in the cold and rain every day, while my school was close enough for me to walk. In those days, no one worried about kids getting snatched by perverts. I walked up 45th Street from Stone Way, a very busy street in the middle of the city, several blocks to Interlake Grade School and no one thought anything of it. Some of my friends walked twice as far. On our way home, we stopped by the pet store to snuggle with puppies, by the fire station to talk to real fireman and spent any change we might have at the candy store which was filled with a myriad of tasty delights.

So far, I knew for a fact life in America was not better than Norway. Not by a long shot. My parents left Sauda for this grueling (for them) existence? The house we finally ended up in (these days called a Mid-Century Craftsman and very expensive) was in a lower middle-class neighborhood populated with Norwegians, Ukrainians, Italians, and Jews. All of us were house-proud and all of us kept our properties up immaculately. None of the families had much money but the neighborhood was lovely. These days, in the Wallingford area, dandelions and other weeds sprout up on everybody's property unimpeded. Back then, that would have been unacceptable.

My parents worked long, hard hours and sacrificed a lot to be able to buy that house and to support my sister and me. Inevitably, wherever my father found work, the union would go on strike and he would have to move to another job. Finally, he found work as a carpenter/handyman at Northwest

Steel Rolling Mills, where he stayed until he retired. Whenever the steel-workers' union went on strike he would work temporarily as a longshore-man and if he was laid off from that job, my mother would carry the whole load doing piecework as a seamstress in a sewing factory. Life for my parents in our new country was grim for the most part but they did find time for car trips in the summer and to get together with Norwegian friends and enjoy life a bit. But my mother was far away from her family, my father's dream of higher education or being a musician died during the war, and, because their new religion demanded they be constantly reminded of imminent hell and damnation if they strayed off the path, their existence was far from happy and carefree.

I wanted in the worst way to try out for our grade school play, *The Princess and the Pea*, but I couldn't do that because my parents had told me being in plays was a sin, even if you were just nine years old and had only vague notions of what sin was. I knew drinking, smoking, dancing and going to movies was very bad but having fun pretending to be someone else in your own school with your own friends? I didn't get it. After the auditions, the role went to the daughter of the president of the PTA (nepotism is everywhere). I snuck in at lunchtime one day to watch a rehearsal and was again terribly offended by the lack of acting professionalism in my schoolmates. The girl who played the princess didn't bring one ounce of believability to the role, and to my complete horror, instead of actually crying, merely *said* "boo hoo, boo hoo" when she was supposed to be crying. "Boo hoo?!" I covered my face with my hands and agonized over the unfairness of it all. She did not deserve this starring role, but why should it affect me so? I was not even in the running to begin with.

Dancing was, of course, strictly forbidden, as it could lead a young girl directly down the road to ruin (where was that?). So when all the other kids trooped down to the gym for an hour of square dancing, I was left behind in the classroom to sit alone wondering how my parents even found out about the dancing in order to tell the principal I couldn't partake in this particular sin. Except for my mother, who came once, they never visited the school. After my sister married, she and her husband Jim came to school and played my surrogate parents on visiting days. But somehow my parents managed to nose out the disgraceful square dancing and make sure I spent that hour alone, appreciating the fact that I was not committing an offense against God by stomping around the gym to country music, laughing and having a good time like everybody else.

I was a latch-key kid like every other kid in my neighborhood and, in those days, who the heck cared? It was normal and we all liked coming home to a house free of parents and their nagging for a few hours. I used to run over to my friends Lorna and Nancy's house to watch American Bandstand as soon as I got home. I knew this was flirting with damnation but the siren call of rock and roll music and watching the fabulous dancing of those kids from Philly was impossible to resist. We danced in the living room, imitating them as best we could and all thoughts that I was committing a transgression flew out of my head as Dick Clark flashed his ageless smile through the television set and beamed his approval on our clumsy, albeit enthusiastic, efforts.

I found it both shocking and fascinating that Lorna and Nancy's parents touched each other affectionately and actually hugged and kissed in front of other people. Wow! My parents *never* did that. In my entire life growing up I never saw my parents touch except when my mother took my father's arm when they walked into church. I assumed that they must have touched for me and my sister to exist but they avoided any kind of contact in front of us. I always figured a husband and wife touching must have been one more sin to add to the already long list.

All of us kids ran in and out of every room in Lorna and Nancy's house all the time, including their parents' bedroom. On their wall, they had a calendar with a picture of a naked blond women laying on a bright red cloth for anybody to see. Even I knew it was a picture of big movie star

Marilyn Monroe. Nobody in Lorna and Nancy's family seemed to think it was any big deal so I acted like it wasn't either. I just knew that my parents would no more hang a picture of a naked woman on their wall than orbit the earth in the next Sputnik.

One afternoon when I came home from watching television at Lorna and Nancy's, my father, who must have had a sixth sense that told him I was coming back from committing an egregious sin, was waiting inside the side door as I snuck in. He yelled at me for disobeying the rules, then grabbed me by the hair, shook me violently back and forth and tossed me down the basement steps like a sack of potatoes to the cement floor where I landed in a heap. He didn't bother to check to see if I were alive or dead before going back into the kitchen. In spite of, or maybe because of, the threat of bodily harm, I continued to find inexplicable joy and release in dancing to the music from hell. If Lorna and Nancy weren't at home, I daringly put a rock and roll station on our own hi-fi and danced by myself, keeping an eye out the front window so I wouldn't get caught. As soon as they came home, I'd switch radio stations, turn off the hi-fi, and run out the door to play, my parents none the wiser that their little daughter was flirting with disaster and loving every minute of it.

About this time, I started my piano lessons, which were not something I had asked for. I would much rather be outside playing than repeating boring exercises until I thought my brain would explode. My teacher was very old (at least 40) and her new husband was in his early twenties. This was scandalous at the time and much gossiped about, but I thought they made a cute couple. She was very patient with me all the years I took lessons from her, but she knew I would never make it as a musician. While my father could play any instrument he picked up and my sister played guitar and the accordion effortlessly, I had not inherited the gene that both of them were lucky enough to get and no matter how many hours, days, and years I practiced, it was just not going to happen. But I did love singing. I would buy sheet music of secular songs and play and sing when my parents weren't home. It was my great joy and my release from living in such a strict, religious atmosphere. As soon as my parents came home, I would slam down the piano lid and run downstairs. I still have that old Davenport piano, still play badly and still love to play and sing when I'm alone.

In spite of the austere atmosphere he created at home, I do have some positive memories of my father. Sometimes he would joke with my friends as we were playing outside, and when I was ten years old and going through a period of having horrific nightmares, he would help my mother calm me down. When I was very little he would take me to the zoo, and I loved sitting on the horses on the merry-go-round. I imagined they were real horses and I was riding across the plains like I'd seen on TV, but looking at the animals in their cages made me sad. I still remember seeing a huge elephant imprisoned in a brick building with a big window so we could watch him stand there swaying, with hardly any room to move. I knew even then that he shouldn't have been there, that he belonged in his home in Africa. How did he end up a prisoner at the Woodland Park Zoo? I wondered. I didn't know. But I knew it was wrong.

When I was around eight years old, someone gave me a tiny little gray kitten that slept in a box on a chair by my bed. My parents told me the kitten couldn't actually sleep with me in my bed and it made me sad that I had to keep forcing her to stay in her box. I wanted her right beside me on my pillow. One day I was down in the basement looking around for the kitten and couldn't find her. My mother's shrill screams penetrated the gloom of the dark basement, "Britt! Britt! Come up here!" I flew up the basement stairs and saw her standing in the doorway, horrified, staring at something and covering her mouth with both hands. I looked outside and saw a big Dalmatian in the driveway, backing away from us, and disappear around the corner of the house. My eyes were drawn to where my mother was staring at the flower bed of the next-door neighbors. I saw my little kitten lying in the dirt, her head bitten off with blood covering her body. I ran over to her, threw myself down beside her and screamed, "No! No!" I reached out, wanting to put her back together again, but was afraid to touch her. My mother dragged me away and took me inside to tell my father. They ordered me to go to the house of the dog's owners and tell them what the dog had done. I was so traumatized I could hardly speak but they told me I had to do it. So I walked alone up to the house where the owners lived and, completely disoriented, knocked on the door and told the boy who opened it up, that his dog had killed my cat. The boy called for his father and told him what I had said. Neither of them looked at me. It seemed like forever that I stood there waiting for someone to say something. But no one did. I turned around and walked back home. I saw that my kitten had been removed from the flower bed and I went inside to the bathroom and threw up.

My father used to let me listen in when he rehearsed in our living room with his church string band (he played guitar) and my little girl brain thought it was beyond hilarious that when they performed in church they would sing songs that spoke of praising God and rejoicing while looking as miserable and glum as if they were going to the funeral of their best friend (always a critic). My father was a good provider, a faithful husband and well-liked among his co-workers and fellow Norwegian émigrés but his insistence on keeping all of his fears and frustrations to himself brought on ulcers and back spasms that caused him terrible pain. I knew, even then, that considering how talented and smart he was, he had to have been disappointed in the way his life turned out. As the years went on, I admired his work ethic and diligence in striving toward his dream of building their own beautiful house outside of the city. And this they accomplished together with nothing but hard work and determination. If I have only a portion of their grit and persistence, it is a valued legacy.

One day, Lorna and Nancy and I heard the amazing, incredible news that Debbie Reynolds was coming to our neighborhood to open a shoe store right up the street from where we lived. She of the fan magazines we read at the drugstore who that awful Eddie Fisher dumped for that evil vixen Liz Taylor. A movie star of awesome proportions was actually coming to our humble, out-of-the-way bailiwick? Then we read that her husband Harry Karl (such a hideous toad of a man we couldn't believe she could actually touch him let alone marry him) owned the shoe store. We could hardly wait to see her and counted the days till she was due to appear. When the big moment came, we chattered nervously as we stood in line outside the store with hundreds of other people to get her autograph. When it was finally my turn, and she was actually sitting right in front of me, I couldn't believe how beautiful she was. She looked at me, smiled and said, "It's so hot today. I wish I were dressed like that," meaning my shorts. As she signed her picture I had to steady myself against the table to keep from fainting. Debbie Reynolds had spoken to me! But I was too shy and overwhelmed to reply. As we headed for home I thought, I want to be just like her, famous and a brilliant actress and singer, even though it would be impossible for me to ever be that beautiful.

But there was more to come! Lorna, Nancy and I were sitting on my front steps reliving our special moments with Debbie when a black limo turned the corner onto our street from Stone Way. A limo on our block? Driving by our very own houses? We had surely never seen anything like that before. But as it passed my house, the car slowed, the window rolled down and Debbie smiled and waved as the driver honked his horn. We stood up and waved back and yelled "Goodbye! Goodbye, Debbie!" and felt like we had just touched royalty. I didn't know then that Debbie would again touch my life years later.

At home, when I wasn't forced to sit at the piano and practice classical music for an hour, I spent most of my time in my room reading. I've loved animals ever since I can remember. I read my favorite book of all time *Black Beauty* when I was nine years old. Learning about the suffering of carriage horses as told through "Beauty's" narration made an impact on me that has lasted a lifetime. And eating animals never seemed right to me. As a little girl, I would see all this great food on the table and smack dab in the middle of it, an entire dead body or parts of a dead animal next to all the rolls and potatoes and vegetables, and it was not appetizing. But I was forced to eat meat (which took forever to chew because my parents boiled meat until it was tough as shoe leather) and later, as a good wife, I would prepare meals that included meat for my husband. It would be years before I would be on my own and feel emancipated because I didn't even have to have it in my house anymore.

I was very excited when my sister announced her engagement to Jim Hopkins, a man she met at Sears, and that I would be the flower girl at the wedding. My mother sewed a beautiful long white dress for me that had sparkles all over it and bought me a little basket that would hold rose petals for me to strew in the aisle in front of my sister. The day before the wedding I was playing outside in my neighbors' yard when I slipped through a hole in the ground and cut the top of my foot on a piece of glass. The cut went deep and I could see right down into something white inside my foot. My friends helped me home and my parents immediately took me to the doctor, where I had to have stitches and thick bandages wound around my foot. The next day my foot was still throbbing and tears ran down my face as my mother stuffed my foot into my new flower girl shoes. Even though I could barely walk, somehow, I made it down the aisle and through the ceremony and painted a smile on my face so as not to ruin my sister's big day. I could hardly wait to get home and take off my shoes and relieve the pressure. I look at the pictures of the wedding party now and you would never know the pain I was in. Brilliant acting, performed for my dear sister on the happiest day of her life.

When I was 11, my very best friend in the world was my cat, Taffy. She was yellow striped with yellow eyes and a purr as loud as a souped-up '57 Chevy. Since my overworked parents mostly ignored me and I had lost my sister to an early marriage, Taffy was my family. No one was closer to me than her. She slept in my bed, sat with me when I read, and listened to all my problems. So when my parents announced that my mother and I were going back to Norway for awhile while my father completely remodeled the house, I was happy to be finally going "home" but anxious about leaving my Taffy. I hoped my father, who rarely talked to me or even seemed to notice I was there, would pay a little attention to Taffy who loved and needed a lot of affection.

Back in Sauda I picked up right where I had left off. The day after I got there, my cousins and I headed straight for their cabin in the mountains and we spent our days swimming in the lake, running through meadows, rock-climbing and biking around town. For some reason, my friends wanted to hear me sing (I guess my parents had me sing in church when I was little), so I sang American songs for them right up there in the hills by the river and loved feeling special and being the center of attention. They asked about America and I told them I loved Norway much more than Seattle and wished I could come back but there was not much hope of that. But I continued to enjoy myself and eat gobs of the whipped cream-filled pastries so beloved of Norwegians until I gained five pounds and a noticeable spare tire. A boy actually called me "fatty" one day when I was in my swim suit and I realized I better stifle my appetite for sweets. Skinny little me a fatty? I was deeply offended but spurred into action.

Then one day, after a month of climbing, running, bike-riding and swimming, trying extra hard to wear off the spare poundage, I received a letter from Lorna and Nancy that said Taffy had had kittens! I was overjoyed and could hardly wait to hold them and feel their soft, newborn fur against my face, and as much as I was enjoying myself in Sauda, my heart ached to hold my Taffy again. I counted the days until it was time to go back to Seattle and finally my mother and I boarded the little boat that would take us down the fjord to Stavanger, where our New York-bound ship awaited us. But leaving Sauda again was wrenchingly difficult and I cried and waved at the people on the dock until I couldn't see the faces of my friends and family anymore.

During the crossing, I met kids my own age and we ran around the ship exploring every nook and cranny all day long. I don't know why my always-nervous mother didn't spend a minute concerned that we might catapult over the railing and be lost at sea while we were playing, but she didn't and neither did the other parents, so we took full advantage of our freedom.

My mother had a Norwegian friend who spent a lot of time with us on the ship. I didn't know it then but she was Jewish and had survived a Nazi concentration camp. One day I saw the tattooed numbers on her arm that were a witness to her ordeal and I asked her about them. She just smiled and said no need to talk about that now, maybe later, but we never did have that discussion. What I remember best about her is her incredible smile and unfailing sunny disposition. She was looking forward to going to America and filled with optimism about her future there. Later, when I found out what those numbers meant and what she had been through, I thought to myself, if someone can go through that much pain and horror and come out of it as kind and gentle as she is, always in a sunny mood, there is no excuse for me or anybody else to feel sorry for ourselves. Nothing I could ever go through could compare to spending years in a concentration camp, watching friends and family die, not knowing day to day whether you will be killed and thrown into a mass grave, then finally being rescued, emaciated and near death.

In the years to come, no matter what difficulties I was going through and how much I wanted to and did feel sorry for myself, the memory of her smile would remind me that the very least I could do is attempt to show a fraction of her strength and courage.

As soon as I got home I ran around the house looking for Taffy. I called her name again and again but she was nowhere to be found. Frantic, I ran over to Lorna and Nancy's house and, heart pounding and breathing hard, asked them where Taffy and her kittens were. They answered reluctantly that my father had taken Taffy and all her kittens to be put to sleep at the pound. "No!" I screamed. "That can't be true!" I ran back home and confronted my parents and demanded to know, "Where is she!?" Where is Taffy?!" I don't remember what they said or did. All I remember is they indicated she was gone and made no effort to comfort me. I ran around the house, still searching, not accepting, calling out her name, "Taffy!" Taffy!" And when I had exhausted myself tearing the house apart, I ran into my room and threw myself on the bed and had a nervous breakdown. My whole world had crumbled and my heart was broken into a million pieces. For days, I couldn't eat and couldn't sleep at night. All I thought about was my little Taffy and her kittens. Dead. Killed by my father. I hated him.

But life went on and I made it through the madness of junior high school in one piece, seeing as I spent most of my spare time in church. Years before, when I was in grade school, a neighbor lady had offered to take me to her Baptist church with her and her kids because I had told them the Pentecostal church which I had to attend with my parents scared me. All the screaming in strange tongues, arm-waving and carrying on was very disconcerting to me, not to mention the sermons that went on for hours while the pastor kept wiping gallons of sweat off his face with his big, white, floppy handkerchief as he gestured and threatened us all with the fires of hell if we didn't ask God to save us. I had already asked Jesus to come into my heart when I was younger because I believed he was good and kind, and I knew there must be a church that talked about all the wonderful stories and lessons he shared with his disciples. At Elim Baptist Church there was no screaming or arm waving and the pastor gave, thankfully, short sermons speaking in a normal quiet voice, and there I met other kids who weren't allowed to do much of anything fun just like me. Baptists didn't like movies or dancing either.

Everybody remembers where they were when they heard that Kennedy was shot. I remember clearly sitting in the library studying with my friend

Georgia and chewing and cracking my gum. Georgia, annoyed, looked over at me and whispered. "You're chewing your gum like a cow!" Seconds later the school librarian walked into the room with a radio and told us the President had just been shot. She turned on the radio and we all listened, hoping against hope that he wasn't dead. Then came the terrible news that he was gone. Every kid in school was in shock. We walked from class to class like zombies, not knowing what to say or do. The President of the United States had been assassinated and the joy went out of our lives just like that.

It was through friends at church that I met my very first boyfriend, Dave, the most handsome boy I had ever seen in my life – dark curly hair, green eyes rimmed with black lashes and over six feet tall. I was in the back seat of a friend's car when I saw him appear in front of the hood of the car as he walked up his driveway. I gasped. My friend Barbara, the pastor's daughter, kept pointing at him, hitting my arm and saying, "Look at him! Look at him!" And I, not talking my eyes off him, answered back, "I see him! I see him!" Dave apparently liked what he saw as well and he started hanging around Elim Baptist Church with me and all my other friends. It didn't take long, even though we went to different schools, for the two of us to become inseparable. When they saw how serious we were about each other, my parents, his parents, and people at church all worked overtime to break us up, insisting that we were too young to be with each other exclusively, we needed to date other people. Madly in love, neither of us could even consider being with anyone else, but the constant, insistent badgering would eventually have an impact on Dave.

I had a little terrier mix, Scamp, a rescue and my best buddy, whom I looked forward to seeing every day after school. One day, Dave and I came home and Scamp wasn't in the back yard or in the house. Ominous thoughts of what my father had done to Taffy crept into my sub-conscience but I pushed them away as Dave and I searched for my dog. My father came outside, saw us looking around and casually mentioned he had taken Scamp to the pound. My heart stopped. Not possible! Just like I had when I found out about Taffy, I screamed at my father, too terrified to accept it might be true, "No! You wouldn't do that!" Dave, who loved his own dog more than himself, or me either, for that matter, turned red and lunged at my father. They were scuffling, shoving and pushing each other as I yelled at the top of my voice, "When did you take him in!? Where is he?!" Dave managed to get the location of the pound out of my father, jumped in his car and tore out of the driveway to see if he could get there in time to save Scamp. I turned away from my father and ran up the street ten blocks into the woods of Woodland Park and flung myself on the ground under a tree and sobbed. Please, God, let it not be too late for Dave to find Scamp.

But it was. Dave got to the pound too late and Scamp was dead. Somehow Dave found me in the woods and sat beside me and comforted me. That was the last time my father would ever take a pet away from me. I would never again forget how, without a second thought, he was capable of snatching away from me what I loved most in the world. Distant, cold and cruel, his unfathomable rules and regulations and dark and gloomy view of life meant nothing to me anymore. And I knew that the God who graced my little Baptist church was infinitely more kind than the vengeful, disapproving being that ruled my father's life. But I will be forever grateful for what my father did inadvertently do; because of my suffering and the fear and pain that my Taffy and Scamp surely went through, the deep connection I have with animals was revealed to me at an early age, and a seed was planted that would grow into a need and a passion to do everything I must do to protect them from harm.

As for Dave, it was inevitable that his amazing good looks would attract hordes of eager, willing young females. He lived in the rich part of town and went to a high school with wealthy and upper-middle-class kids while I resided in what was considered the other side of the tracks by people in his neighborhood. So after the constant nagging of his parents telling him I was not good enough for him and because he was a weak, good-looking, teenage boy, he began to see other girls on the sly. Every time I found out I would cry buckets of tears and he would say he was sorry then go out and do it again. Our love was true and chaste, but when worldlier, more experienced girls seduced him away from me there was nothing I could do. After I saw him for myself holding hands with another girl at a football game, it was over. I stood at the top of the grandstand and wanted to fling myself down into the abyss to stop the pain. I didn't realize it then, but that's when the iron curtain went down and no matter how hard he protested or tried to make up for it in years to come, I was done with Dave. High school was supposed to be enjoyed and I didn't intend to let him ruin it all for me.

It has been said that people who are the "stars" of their high school never experience that kind of success the rest of their lives, and vice versa. But I don't believe that. Maybe because my senior year in high school *was* so very fabulous. My homeroom was choir, where I rehearsed with *Chanters* the best singing group in the whole city. I listen to our recordings now and I am amazed at how professional and adult we sounded. My first class at 7:45 AM was Ensemble, where I spent an hour singing with the *Chanter Trio*: Pam Bennion, Sally Orrell and me, accompanied by Carol Farnsworth on the piano. When we practiced our songs at my house we sang and laughed so much my mother accused us of being on drugs. Drugs?! None of us even smoked cigarettes, and Pam was a Mormon and even more pure than me. To my parents, especially my father, kids laughing meant there was something insidious going on that they didn't know about.

In high school, I had my first of four kidney stones. I had no idea of what the pain in my abdomen was. Only that it was the most excruciating pain I had ever felt, and by now I had already had a lot of that. My parents rushed me to the hospital and the doctors told us what it was and that they didn't want to give me pain pills because then they wouldn't know if the kidney stone passed or if they would have to do surgery. No matter how much I begged, the doctors refused me any kind of pain medication. For hours, I was in agony until finally, when I hobbled from my bed to the bathroom, the pain intensified to such a degree I felt that I was being tortured for the entire world's sins. I sat on the toilet hollering, and then, wondrously, it passed and the pain was gone. I was so grateful for the end to the pain I didn't know whether to laugh or cry. I didn't know that once you get a kidney stone it is very likely you will get them again. Four times so far, and every time I wished I had a gun and could shoot myself just to end the agony. Everyone who has had a kidney stone knows exactly what I'm talking about.

My mother was especially suspicious of my every move. Once, in my senior year, after I broke up with Dave, I snagged a date with the best-looking guy in our school, Wayne Levandoski. He was even more handsome than Dave. (He was also very nice. I wasn't *that* shallow.) On our first date, we went skiing up in Snoqualmie Pass and on the way home got caught in a snowstorm that was so blinding we could hardly see as we crawled along in bumper-to-bumper traffic all the way down the mountain. Cars were slipping and sliding in front and in back of us, and we passed cars that had been abandoned by the side of the road, and some that had gone off the road into the ditch. We were relieved to finally get off the mountain where the snow turned to rain. When we pulled up in front of my house, happy to be in one piece, my mother, instead of asking what had happened and being concerned about our safety, came charging out of the house, grabbed me by my jacket as soon as I opened the car door and shook me till my teeth rattled, the whole time screaming accusations regarding things Wayne and I had probably been doing (which we never had or would do). Wayne watched open-mouthed at my hysterical mother, completely out of control as she shoved me toward the house. He never called or spoke to me again.

During my senior year, when not singing in home room, I made brief appearances in my boring (math, history) classes until it was time to go to cheerleader practice where we learned new routines, mostly choreographed by my best friend since junior high, Georgia Miller. Getting permission to try out for cheerleader the year before was a minor miracle. I wanted to be a cheerleader badly and Georgia and I were both into sports and captains of our various softball and basketball teams during our junior high years and extremely competitive. We were determined to be one of the chosen six and not even my parents' narrow-minded views would stop us. We both begged and pleaded with them to no avail and I finally asked the youth minister at my church to come talk some sense into my parents. He dutifully came to our house and, after much persuasion, somehow convinced them that cheerleading was merely an extension of the sports program, playing down the short skirts and jazzy music (it's not really *dancing*) and sealed the deal when we all agreed that if they allowed this to happen, Georgia would come to church with me, which she did after I told her there were several cute Christian boys there she might be interested in. At that point I hadn't cut the cord with Dave yet so she was welcome to the others.

My senior year flew by too fast and by the time it ended, Dave and I had broken up and I had to start thinking of my future. My grades were good and I had been accepted into several colleges but would have to go to the University of Washington, which, in those days, was easily affordable. I knew I wanted to be an actress, but how to go about it, that was the question. School counselors at my high school told drama students that earning a living as an actor was impossible. Their advice was if you *have* to try to get work as an actor (implying it would never happen) get yourself a college education and have another career to fall back on when you inevitably fail as an actor. There was not an ounce of encouragement or support, just "It's a bad idea. Don't do it." But I refused to accept their negative predictions. I knew I was special and would be one of the chosen few who succeeded. There was no doubt in my mind. The prospect of having to do anything else in life to earn a living was unthinkable. The thought of being imprisoned in an office my entire working life gave me chills. And failure as an actress? Why, that would be nothing less than hell on earth.

I couldn't wait to move out of my parents' house after graduation so I found myself a roommate and a part-time job and registered for classes at the University of Washington. I signed up for drama classes, knowing I would have to know how to act if anybody in Hollywood was going to hire me, and registered for other classes I considered unnecessary for my chosen vocation but needed in order to graduate. I figured I'd get myself a degree in theater and head south to Hollywood where the work was. My parents' objections had become irrelevant the day they killed Scamp. I would do exactly what I wanted to do from then on. I would learn how to become a brilliant actress and set the theatrical world on fire while starring in a series. I wasn't exactly sure how I was going to make all that happen since I had no mentor and no one to tell me what steps I needed to take. I figured I would have to blunder forward on my own and learn as I went along. And, as it turned out, I wasn't far wrong about either of those.

Was there even a glimmering of the need to have a purpose in life at that point in time when I started college? Can't say there was. I had my ambition to succeed as an actress and yes, I did love animals very much, but as far as moving out of my comfort zone to do anything for anybody else besides my friends and myself, that was not anywhere on my radar. I thought of myself as a good person who didn't drink, smoke, or take drugs and belief in my Creator was always there. Whenever I had a special need or request, I would hit him up for a favor. I didn't feel it was necessary to go to church to talk to God, and I had noticed long ago that those who were regular attendees, like my parents, didn't seem to be kinder, stronger or happier for going there. On the contrary, often times those people were more pessimistic, more judgmental, and a whole lot meaner than people who had never set foot in a church. I resolved to find my own way and my own spiritual path. But, meanwhile, I had more important things on my mind than figuring all that out.

CHAPTER 3

Witchy Woman

FOR SOME REASON, EVEN THOUGH we were broken up, I was in the car with Dave the first time I heard the Sonics' "The Witch" on the car radio. I thought it sounded like hideous, deafening, discordant noise and asked Dave who the heck was singing, or rather screaming, that song. He was dumbfounded that I would even ask, "You never heard of 'The Witch?!' That's the Sonics, a Northwest band who made it big with their first record." He turned up the noise to further make his point. I promptly turned it back down to keep my ear drums from exploding. How could I have been so crazy about a guy who thinks this mad howling is music? Smokey Robinson, the Beatles, Frankie Valli and the Four Seasons, Dion and the Belmonts and my most favorite group of all, the Beach Boys, *that* was music. I banished all thoughts of the Sonics, and their caterwauling from my mind.

A couple of months later, I was sitting in the University of Washington cafeteria eating lunch and reading when another student appeared beside me and said he had a friend who wanted to meet me. I suggested that he tell his friend to come over and introduce himself if that was true. But this apparently wasn't possible, as his friend was very shy. I kept eating and said that was too bad. But the boy wouldn't take no for an answer and continued to beg and plead. I suspect he had been given this assignment on a dare or a bet and didn't want to fail. So I took the most fateful move of my young life, said yes, gathered up all my belongings and went to meet this "shy" person who *had* to meet me.

That's when I was introduced to the man who would pretty much decide my future in the next several years, Rob Lind – good looking with big brown eyes, black hair and very tall (6'4"). When he stood up, he seemed gawky and shy like many boys who grow up too fast, find themselves towering over everyone else, and don't quite know how to deal with it. He was seated at a table, surrounded by his buddies (turned out to be his fraternity brothers) and had Coca Cola dripping from his eyelashes. I asked him what that was all about, and he laughed, very embarrassed, and deflected the question. (I never did find out which one of his friends doused him with Coke.) We talked briefly, and as I was about to walk away, definitely not interested, one of his friends blurted out, "Rob plays with the Sonics you know!" I turned and looked at him and asked if that was him screaming the lyrics on the record "The Witch" but he gave that credit (or blame, as I saw it) to another member of the band, and said he played sax. He asked for my phone number, and because I had an inexplicable breakdown between my brain and my mouth, I gave it to him.

He called, and the courtship began. Dave, for some reason, wanted back into my life but, as much as it pained me to tell him, I could never trust him again and all we could ever be was friends. Rob and I met during breaks in class and before long, he became more important to me than my classes. We became addicted to each other, me more than him, and when he asked me to cut class or write papers for him, ignoring my own assignments, I would put all my energy into getting him the best grade possible so he could graduate with a degree in broadcasting. I used to watch him perform on video in class and he was amazingly good, an absolute natural and very funny.

During the early portion of my life (and still lingering effects of it cling to me) I was unknowingly afflicted with what someone coined, "The Cinderella Complex." A lot of us baby boomers had it and didn't even know it was a bad thing. We were taught and continued to assume that the man is the head of the household, that his needs come first while we take care of the home and children, and in return he takes care of us. Sometimes we even have a job to help out but that doesn't mean that he is not our Prince Charming to our Cinderella, and that we are very lucky for him to have chosen us to be his helpmate. We are the wind beneath his wings as we watch his career soar while we stand on the ground watching, content to adore him and spend his money shopping and making ourselves beautiful. At least that's the way I interpreted the complex. Nevertheless, I could see myself as a successful actress and his helpmate at the same time. We would fulfill both our dreams together!

Meanwhile, I had heard the Sonics play in person at a fraternity street dance and found out to my surprise that "The Witch" was an aberration – they were in fact a rhythm-and-blues band with a dose of pure blues thrown in for good measure. To say I loved their music and Rob's incredible sax playing is like saying Brad Pitt is kind of good-looking. They mostly toured the west coast and northern states and sometimes Rob, who had his pilot's license, would fly them to their gigs. But when they played near home I was there, front and center, soaking in the music and reveling in the fact that "I was with the band." I may not have been able to escape the fact that my singing voice was as white bread as my looks, but in my heart I was Aretha Franklin and longed to sing like her and my fellow soul sisters. I used to watch the Sonics as they played their rhythm and blues: Rob's wailing sax, Gerry Roslie's raunchy, screaming voice, Andy Parypa's pulsating bass, Larry Parypa's plaintive guitar, and Bob Bennett's drums pounding out the beat, combining to create the most explosive sound in Pacific Northwest band history. I considered them musicians talented well beyond their peers and in my innermost heart imagined singing with them and sounding like Aretha. Hey, Sonny had recorded with Cher and she could barely sing at all. But considering that my voice sounded more like Julie Andrews than Janis Joplin, that dream was dead on arrival.

My good friend, Anne, was going out with Larry, the guitar player in the band, and I still remember how excited she was to tell me about a movie she had seen, *A Fist Full of Dollars*. She swooned over Clint Eastwood, the star of the movie, and told me I just had to see it. I, ever the insightful critic, asked skeptically, "Clint Eastwood? The guy who played 'Rowdy Yates' on *Rawhide*? Him?" Anne assured me he was very different from "Rowdy" in this movie. If I saw it, I would understand what she was talking about. I was not convinced and it was years before I saw the movie and wholeheartedly agreed with her, not knowing what an important role Clint would play in getting my acting career off the ground.

Rob and I planned our future and it was glorious: after graduation, we would move to Hollywood where I would be an actress, he would be a film director and all of our artistic passions would be fulfilled. Meanwhile, he was moving toward graduation and I was cutting classes and failing, but that was okay, because I had been taught that the man is the boss and his needs come before yours. That is what the Bible teaches and that's just the way life is. Rob had also talked about possibly applying for Navy flight school because he was afraid of getting drafted, and in that case, our Hollywood dream would have to be put off for a year or two. I agreed that flying planes would be better than fighting his way through the jungles of Vietnam.

For a few blissful months, I gave Rob every ounce of love and affection I had saved up for that special person who would be my soul mate for the rest of my life. Life revolved around Rob and the Sonics and we were both happy with that. But I should have known it wouldn't last. Rob betrayed me in a selfish, cruel way that changed my life forever. He found a new girlfriend and left me to pick up the pieces and live with untold regret.

I tried to move on, past Rob, past all the unrealized dreams, and halfheartedly continued on with my education while fighting depression every waking hour. I still loved him in spite of what he had done and even though he was with someone else. But I was very young and inexperienced and I had no concept of the differences between hurting because you were in love, or because you needed a man to prove your self-worth, or because you had been rejected and your feelings trampled on big-time. My ego was battered and bruised and deflated like an old tire on a scrap heap of broken promises, but I still had that competitive spirit I was born with and nurtured by years of playing sports, so I was determined that nothing would stop me from getting him back. Meanwhile, what about auditioning for plays at school? What about planning a future alone without a man? Never entered my mind.

Since I loved Rob's mother and we had a great relationship, throughout the entire ordeal I kept in touch with her and, through her, Rob. He parked his car in front of my house one day but there was no sign of him. I left a note on his windshield and he called. There were more notes, gifts, apologies, excuses and explanations, while both of us felt the irresistible, crazy, whatever-it-is feeling that had drawn us to each other in the first place. I knew that he was the one that I was supposed to spend the rest of my life with. We stumbled and fumbled our way back together and decided we could forget the past and make this work. So we forged ahead and laid out our great plans once more.

What we hadn't counted on was the conflict in Vietnam still raging on with no end in sight. Protests had been growing in size and becoming more violent in the past few years. No one wanted us to be over there. Practically every person in the country knew or was related to someone who had died or been wounded in that pointless war. We had hoped it would be over by the time he graduated but that was not going to happen. Rob was ripe for the taking by Uncle Sam. He went ahead with his plans to join the Navy and go to flight school to avoid his worst nightmare of getting drafted and having to crawl around in the jungle getting shot at by Viet Cong. We figured that by the time he got his wings, the war would surely be over. Then he would be able to pick and choose what plane he wanted to fly and where he was stationed. Of course, that would be somewhere in Southern California, where I could begin my acting career.

Rob never failed at anything, so naturally, he was accepted into flight training and became an Ensign in the Navy. My mother, like me, was in total denial over everything that had occurred in the past two years and acted overjoyed that Rob and I had resolved our problems and were getting married. Being a Navy pilot was a respectable career, not lurid and scandalous like playing in a rock band or acting. She envisioned me as a faithful Navy wife, following my husband wherever his country might send him while at the same time she was fervently praying the war would be over soon. My father, as usual, said nothing to me and his thoughts and opinions about what was going on were as mysterious and unavailable to me as they had always been.

We were married in my parents' house and had a short honeymoon in San Francisco. A few days later, Rob flew to Pensacola to begin the rigorous physical training that preceded ground school. I stayed in Seattle and worked as a nighttime switchboard operator at a Catholic school, Seattle University. That was when I found out that men of God can drink as heartily as anybody else. The very friendly and jolly Jesuit priests would come by my ancient switchboard (one with all those little wires to connect just like "Ernestine's") pretty much blotto and let me know they were going back to their rooms if someone needed them. From their odor and dangerous swaying of their bodies I knew they would be asleep and unavailable in five minutes flat. Not all of the Jesuits enjoyed partaking of spirits at the end of the day; most were gracious and kind and stopped by from time to time just to say hello and see if I needed anything.

At last the moment came when I would join Rob in Pensacola. It seemed as if I had lived a lifetime already, one filled with just as many highs as lows. Now I was ready to start the new phase of my life where I would be the perfect wife for Rob and I could begin to think of future plans for myself as well.

When I first saw Rob after my plane landed in Pensacola I was shocked at his appearance. I had never seen him without long hair before and now it was gone. He seemed like a completely different person to me. The rock and roller I had known was now in a Navy officer's uniform and had a shaved head. It was awkward at first because we had to get to know each other all over again, but it didn't take long. We moved into an apartment complex in Gulf Breeze where all his Navy pals and their wives lived. We had constant pool parties and barbeques and to us wives, Navy life was a fabulous lark, while our husbands were sweating through ground school, hoping to get the grades that would secure them a chance to become pilots. Rob had no problem getting passing grades and, since he already had his pilot's license and many hours, easily mastered the Navy trainers, the T-3s.

Pensacola was very small compared to Seattle, but that's where we'd go for our big nights out for dinner and a movie. One night we were in town with two friends and decided to see a movie. Afterward, Rob and I, experts that we were in show business, gave our critique of the film, Rob first, said "The music was okay, even though I'm not that much into Paul Simon and folk music, and the acting was great, especially Anne Bancroft. But the lead was totally miscast as a college student and mumbled his lines all the way through the movie." I chimed in, "He has some appeal but he's not at all good-looking and has a big nose. He may get to do character parts now and then, but he'll never make it as a leading man." Our friends pretty much agreed with our assessment of *The Graduate* and Dustin Hoffman, who managed to carve out a name for himself in spite of our insightful predictions regarding his career.

Towards the end of our time in Pensacola, my friend and fellow Navy wife Neeva, who was born and raised in Louisiana, gave me a stern warning. "Under no circumstances allow Rob to choose jets over props. "Why?" was my obvious response, because the pilots with the best grades all wanted to fly jets. Flying propeller planes was for the poor saps with mediocre grades, and flying helicopters? Yech! Forget it! That was the bottom of the barrel. You could make your preferences known, but flying jets was for the elite and everybody knew that. Neeva was adamant. "If Rob picks jets you'll have to go live in Meridian, Mississippi and you don't want to be there." I didn't know what she was talking about. "Why is Meridian any different than any other part of the South?" She was hesitant, "I know people from Louisiana can be as bigoted as anybody but in Mississippi or Georgia it is downright dangerous to be black or to be as liberal as you and Rob. You will *hate* it there, believe me. Awhile back they dug up some northern civil rights workers just up the road from Meridian in Hattiesburg-Laurel who had disappeared a few years ago after being murdered by Ku Klux clan members. I'm telling Rick he has to pick props and we're going straight to Brownsville, Texas. Make Rob do the same."

But I couldn't make Rob eat his *vegetables*, let alone tell him what plane to fly, and there was no way he was going to pick anything but jets. We said goodbye to Pensacola and drove up to Meridian for him to begin his training there and where I would learn a few lessons myself.

CHAPTER 4

Conquering the South All Over Again

As soon as we settled into our apartment complex in Meridian, we found out that the black maid who cleaned the public areas of the buildings had been forbidden by the management to use the ladies room in the office and had been told to go out into the woods to do her business. The Navy wives who lived there had told her no way that was going to happen, she could come into any of our apartments whenever she wanted and use our bathrooms. Rob and I were immediately onboard with that and had the first indication about what we were going to face in Meridian.

While Rob immersed himself in ground school to prepare to learn how to fly jets, I was content to continue being the supportive, helpful wife my mother had always envisioned me becoming. But then one day, shortly after we had moved in, I had to face down the "Welcome Wagon" lady.

This bubbly, friendly, middle-aged southern lady breezed in through my door as soon as I opened it.

"Hi! Welcome to the neighborhood!" She carried a huge basket, full of "goodies" – cleaning supplies, coupons, packaged food and potholders, and held it up for me to see.

"I think you're going to enjoy all the things I've brought you."

I invited her to sit on the couch and she piled her treasures on my coffee table all the while keeping up a steady stream of one-way conversation in her

Mississippi accent. I found her utterly charming and knew we would become the best of friends. Then she began to fill me in on everything a newcomer to Meridian needs to know, just as bright and chirpy as a friendly Blue Jay.

"Well, first I have to tell ya'll a few things to get you acquainted with this town. I'm sure it won't take you long to get the hang of everything and feel like you've lived here all your life."

After hearing about the maid, I wasn't convinced of that but she continued on.

"The closest church is the Community Methodist, just about a mile up the road. You don't want to confuse it with the other church a few blocks up. That's where all the nigras go."

I wasn't sure I had heard correctly.

"The...the what?"

"They'd die if a white person ever showed up there, except for those nosy civil rights workers buttin' in our lives where they got no business being. And the noise those nigras make -- clappin', stompin' and carryin' on like they're wild animals or somethin'."

I had never thought much about racism in my teens. I was the typical self-involved teenager and was aware that black kids were being bused into my high school from another part of town but nobody thought it was much of a big deal. I was friendly with all the kids from different countries and ethnic backgrounds that went to my school but my world was pretty much limited to singing, cheerleading, and Dave. Listening to this woman talk, I was, for the first time in my life, being slapped in the face with the reality of deep-seated bigotry and as much as I detested what she was saying, I was strangely fascinated by the complete lack of awareness that she, as a "God-fearin'" woman, accepted her hate-filled existence as being completely normal. I stared at her as she continued on.

"Now the shopping center is almost across the street from here as you probably saw. But the market closest to you is the one you'll want to go to. The market on the other side is for the nigras. And be sure you notice which drinking fountains and restrooms are for white people. God forbid you use the ones the nigras use."

I was almost spellbound by the filth spilling out of her mouth and her obliviousness to her own degenerate self. I had to ask.

"Why? What happens if I go there?"

She laughed nervously.

"Well that's the craziest thing I ever heard! Nigras can work for us and cut our grass and all that but the rest of the time they go their way and we go ours. It's worked out fine for a hundred years."

She looked at me suspiciously.

"Why would you ask a question like that?"

"Oh, it just sounds a little strange to me."

"What do you mean *strange?*"

"Just...not right."

"Uh-huh," she said as her mouth puckered up and her eyes became slits.

"Where you from anyway?"

"Seattle." She had to think about that.

"Seattle? Isn't that way up in the corner of the country somewhere near Canada? Are you Canadian? I didn't think you could be in the Navy if you're not a real American."

I couldn't take anymore. I stood up and walked to the door.

"I'm sorry but it's time for you to leave. I have some important things I need to do right away like... organize my husband's underwear."

She was aghast.

"Well, you're just about the rudest Navy wife I ever met." She began piling her goodies back in the basket.

"You sure are ungrateful. And I was showing you all kinds of hospitality. Try to be nice to a *Yankee.*"

I opened the door wide.

"Actually, I'm *Norwegian*."

She gasped. "I don't know what that is but there's no need to forget your manners!"

As she hustled herself out the door, I couldn't resist one last shot.

"Where was that church again? The one I'm not supposed to go to? I'm feeling in need of some loud singing, stomping and praising the Lord!"

I smiled at her as I firmly shut the door on her horrified expression.

I dutifully reported her visit to Rob and he laughed nervously and warned me, no matter how sorely tempted, do not do or say anything that would reflect badly on him and the Navy. Like the good Navy wife I was, I assured him I would never even think of doing anything like that.

Our one and only car was in need of repair so I took it to a garage to be fixed. A black man who worked there gave me a ride home in his car. I started to get in the passenger seat and he panicked.

"No, no, ma'am! Get in the back, please!"

"Why?" I asked.

"People would see and they wouldn't like it. Please."

I reluctantly got in the back seat and asked him why he would want to live in a place that gave him so little freedom and forced him to live like a second-class citizen. He explained to me that he had visited family in Chicago once but hated the cold weather and missed his friends so came back to Mississippi. It was home.

I described to him how when I walked down the street and a black man was on the sidewalk heading in my direction he would cross to the other side of the street to avoid me. Nothing like that had ever happened to me before. I said I had half a mind when that happened again to cross the street and force him to walk by me. My driver just about swerved off the road.

"NO! You must not do that!"

"I don't know why not!"

"You want to get somebody killed? Is that it?"

"Of course not."

"Then don't be doin' somethin' that God-almighty, bone-headed stupid ma'am!"

He calmed down.

"Sorry ma'am."

I was an idiot, of course. I knew how dangerous it was for black men to have anything to do with white women. But in my northern white girl naiveté I wanted them to stick up for themselves! This mechanic could drive me home but only if I sat in the back. Any hint of impropriety and his life would be in danger. I felt as if I were living in the dark ages. Local television commercials told me "moonshine kills" so stay away from it, candidates running for public office didn't bother using correct grammar and had teeth missing, schools were supposed to be integrated but still were almost completely separate and civil rights workers disappeared and showed up dead a year later. Louisiana was no haven for black people but maybe Neeva was right, Mississippi was worse.

In Meridian, I started having nightmares whenever Rob was on cross-countries and one of my neighbors loaned me their Irish Setter to stay with me during nights when he was gone. But soon I found myself a German Shepherd puppy at the local veterinarian's office. All his brothers and sisters had died of some sort of disease shortly after being born. But this little guy seemed to be doing fine. His name was Hans and he became my best friend. He followed at my heels everywhere and cuddled with me on my pillow at night. He was sweet and loving and I knew he would give me a sense of permanence as we moved from place to place. Hans was there for me as I spent nights alone with Rob off on his cross-countries. One day, Hans seemed to be listless and tired. Terrified that he might be sick with the same disease as his siblings, I carried him in my arms to the veterinarian's office because Rob had the car that day. The vet was not encouraging. He gave me some pills to give to Hans and warned me straight out that Hans could die. All the way home I held little Hans close to me and prayed that he would be okay. But it wasn't to be. I saw that he was suffering terribly and I had to take him back to the vet to be put to sleep. I was devastated. I always seemed to lose what was most precious to me.

I read in the newspaper about auditions for *The King and I*, which would be performed at the Meridian Theater, and I decided to try out. I would never have presumed I was good enough to play "Anna," but I imagined I sang well enough to be in the chorus -- the director thought so too, and I was cast. Friends and family were invited to the dress rehearsal, and before the show I kept peeking out through the curtain to see if Rob was there. But he never showed up. Afterwards I found him at home playing cards with his friends. He thought he was being hilariously funny as he ridiculed my soprano singing voice by pretending to be Jeanette McDonald, an actress from old MGM musicals, and sang in a high falsetto, "When I'm calling youuu-hoo-hoo-hoo-hoo-hoo-hooo. Will you answer tooo-hoo-hoo-hoo-hoo-hoo-hooo?" His friends all thought Rob was a riot and laughed uproariously, while I felt so humiliated, I wanted to slap him. I wished I could run away and follow my own dreams in California and let him cry on somebody else's shoulder every time he got down and discouraged and thought he would fail. That would show him! Miss Ideal Housewife had a lot of growing up to do.

For Rob, jet training was a lot more stressful than learning how to fly the little T-3s in Pensacola. Flight students would have to fly with an instructor who taught them the various maneuvers and if the student didn't do them correctly they would receive a "down," which meant they flunked the lesson. If they received too many "downs" they would wash out of the program and end up…actually I don't know. I never asked Rob what would happen to us. Since he had never failed at anything, I just assumed he would make it through. Whenever Rob had to go up with a bad instructor (called "screamers") and received more than one "down," he would come home very despondent, near tears, sure he was about to wash out. With complete faith in him, I would sit him down and put my arms around him and reassure him that would never happen.

Much of the time, like the other students, he was filled with false bravado. They had to be to do what they were doing. They were forced to watch movies of horrific crashes after which they would tell themselves that could never happen to them. The causes of the crashes were usually attributed to "pilot error," and since that was something they could control, they convinced themselves none of them would ever make a mistake that would cause them to crash. At night, alone with their wives, their true feelings of fear and anxiety spilled out and we were happy to be a source of comfort and encouragement. But week after week, we saw their confidence grow, as they did more and more complicated stunts and maneuvers, flying in tight formation and generally making us proud we were married to Navy pilots. During the most stressful times, sometimes I had more faith in my husband than he had in himself and I like to think my unswerving belief in him helped him make it through.

One night when I was by myself, I turned on the news and saw that there had been a big shootout at a synagogue a few blocks away. The police had found out that KKK nightriders were going to try to blow it up for the third time. (These nightriders were inept as well as bigoted and murderous.) This time the cops were waiting and a volley of gunfire exploded into the balmy summer air. A Navy man who ran out on his front porch to see what was going on was shot in the stomach. One of the KKK nightriders was a young, female kindergarten teacher. I wondered if people in Meridian were totally insane.

A few days later, I was driving down the street and I noticed that in the ancient, battered truck ahead of me, an old black man with white hair was driving very slowly and it seemed to me as if his head was slightly sway-ing back and forth. As I slowed down and stayed behind him, watching, I flashed back years ago to when my mother worked in a sewing factory and her best friend there was an elderly janitor named James. She couldn't pronounce the "J" so she called him "Games" and for the longest time, that's what I called him too. Since my mother didn't speak much English and was very shy, James befriended her and made her feel not so alone at the factory. Not only that, James crafted a beautiful, glass-fronted china cabinet for her little girl, me, and a mirror-framed armoire for her dolls' clothes. One day my mom took me to the factory so I could thank him in person. James was my first black friend and no one ever said he was any different from us. He was just a good man who was nice to my mother.

So I was following this truck and suddenly the man slumped over and crashed into a telephone pole. I jumped out of my car, helped him out of the truck and set him down on the embankment. I ran into a gas station and yelled at the men inside. "Call an ambulance! A man's been hurt!" They all looked at me blankly and one of them said, "What are you so all-fired excited about? It's just a ------," and they used the "n" word.

I have no memory now of what I said. The blood must have rushed to my head in righteous indignation and I blotted it all out. I know if I'd had a baseball bat I would have wrecked their squalid little gas station and gone to jail. I called the ambulance and made sure the injured man was helped before I left but the whole episode is a blur. Afterwards, it made me happy that my friend James had lived in Seattle instead of this sorry excuse for a town.

Then I did what Rob ordered me specifically not to do, I shot off my mouth. I told every Navy person within the range of my voice and all their "precious" southern belle girlfriends what I thought of the state of Mississippi and everybody in it. I was becoming so evangelical about it, Rob had to tell me, "Cool your jets and zip it! A Navy couple had to move on base after having their front window shot out because he was white and she was black. I'd like to make it out of here in one piece!" So I made a sincere effort to do as he said and we made it out alive. And Rob passed his jet qualifications with flying colors.

Next, we had to go back to Pensacola for a short time to practice "touch and goes" (simulated carrier landings on the ground which I was allowed to watch), then on to Kingsville, Texas – landings on actual carriers out in the Gulf of Mexico, brutal survival-training, ejecting in the Gulf where you have to struggle out of your harness, inflate a boat and learn how to stay alive – and more fun stuff the guys get to experience and us wives had to worry about. So we packed up our car once more and headed for Pensacola for a few weeks, then it would be on to Kingsville for grueling training and the much-anticipated graduation ceremony where Rob would finally receive his famous Navy Wings of Gold, after which I would have a chance to earn my own...or so I thought.

CHAPTER 5

Wings of Gold

 ⸎

NEW ORLEANS WAS THE ONE city in the South where I really looked forward to spending time. I had seen Mardi Gras scenes in movies and television, and friends had told me about the fabulous restaurants and jazz clubs and all the history connected to the city. I hoped to spend at least three days there but Rob said no, that he wanted to get to his new base right away and check things out. So we only spent a day and one night in the French Quarter, which I found absolutely magical. We drank our "hurricanes," listened to jazz and ate amazing food and rich pastries. I'm sure I put on five pounds during that short time, but I loved every minute of it. Too soon we were on our way to Kingsville and the apartment complex we would call home for the next few months.

When we drove into Kingsville my heart sunk as I saw the small town where I would be doing my shopping and other housewifely duties. My first thought was that it looked like a movie set from the 1930s; one main street with old fashioned buildings and store fronts. Rob was stressed and worried and all I could think of was me and how I was going to pass the time in this backwater town. As I unpacked our things I looked out the bedroom window and saw miles and miles of flat nothingness. The King ranch and their long-horn Santa Gertrudis cattle took up a lot of prairie. But at least I had my fellow Navy wives to pass the time with, and to placate us bored housewives, the guys promised us trips to Padre Island, Corpus Christi and Nuevo Laredo when they had some time off. But they had more important things on their minds, like landing on an aircraft carrier out in the gulf, survival training and the possibility of getting kicked out of the program, which would be the ultimate humiliation. Earning the coveted Navy Wings of Gold was their singular goal and this was the last leg on that journey. Us womenfolk would just have to suck it up and be there for support when called upon.

Nuevo Laredo was dirty, noisy, crowded, smelly, exciting and fun. I loved how we had to bargain for everything we bought, and buy we did – all kinds of thick Mexican sweaters and household decorations that "everybody" in the Navy ended up buying. If you didn't have a miniature suit of armor standing in your living room you weren't with the program. A couple of years later we looked at it all and asked, why did we buy those horrible things? But at the time we wanted to be like everybody else and bargaining was addictive.

Corpus Christi, on the other hand, was just plain gorgeous. The homes along the gulf were breathtaking but only a few short years later would all be washed away by a hurricane. The homeowners always rebuild after every storm. I can *almost* understand why because the views are stunning. Padre Island turned out to be one long beach and we all baked in the sun, impervious to the hazards of too much of a good thing, and never thought we would ever wrinkle when we got old. Who got old anyway? We were going to be young forever. Being old was for our parents who had always been ancient. So we tanned to a dark brown and let the sun bleach our hair and knew we would never pay the price later.

Wives stuck together when the guys went out on cross countries and out in the Gulf. We comforted them when they needed it, but by then we were used to their false bravado and went along with it. None of us fully appreciated what they were going through and the hard work they were putting in. The guys wanted it to seem easy and maybe to some it was. As for Rob, by this time he was as self-assured as any of them. As I said before, he never failed at anything he did and I had total confidence that he would succeed.

Meanwhile, the whole experience did not, for the most part, bring wives and husbands closer together. The pilots, faced every day with a potentially dangerous occupation where student pilots had been known to crash and burn, bonded more closely with each other than with us. But we were young girls and this Navy life was all we knew so we found companionship with each other and that was fine. For me, I knew this was just a temporary existence. As soon as Rob earned his coveted Wings of Gold, he had promised we would be heading to California where I would begin my acting career. How I would do that, I still hadn't a clue. Nevertheless, Hollywood beckoned with the promise of better things to come. It was the center of my universe where my dreams would come true and I would earn my own wings.

One day, one of my friends rolled up her jeans and showed me the huge bruises on her legs. Tears welled up in her eyes as she described how her husband beat her and she didn't know what to do, who to talk to, or if she should leave him or not. I was shocked and tried to comfort her but had no idea of how to advise her. No one talked of going to women's shelters in those days. Men beat their wives and no one did anything about it. And divorcing a service man meant you would receive little or no alimony to help you get back home and start a new life. I was at a complete loss and felt that I, of all people, was in no position to tell her what to do. I hoped she would leave him, but I never did find out what happened to her after we left Texas.

It was in Kingsville, Texas that I had my first taste of fame. One of the wives, very excited, came running up to me at one of our get-togethers at the O Club and asked if I was a model. I told her no, but that I had posed for some ads in Seattle and I didn't know if they ever were printed in anything. She was bubbling over with enthusiasm when she said her husband had seen somebody who looked like me in his motorcycle magazines – could it really be me?! I was reminded of my short stint in Kathleen Peck's Beauty and Modeling Agency where we learned how to walk and move like "real models" and were taught make-up tricks, especially how to make our noses narrower by using a white concealer stick to carefully draw a white line down the middle of our nose, which only made us look like we had a white line down the middle of our nose. At the time, I thought modeling school would be my first step into show business even though, at 5'5", I knew I'd never be a model. I was excited at first when Kathleen sent me out to some photographers and I ended up in some home remodeling brochures and that was about it. Having my pictures taken was not a lot of fun for me because I considered myself a serious actress, and modeling I decided, after I had a little taste of it, wasn't really real acting. I pretended to the other Navy wives it was no big deal if the pictures in the magazines were me.

Of course, the next day I ran to the drugstore and rifled through every issue of every motorcycle magazine they had. Yes! There I was, in every issue: in my short, glittery gold dress and my glittery gold boots seated in alluring poses on various motorcycles with the caption "See anything you like?" I was famous! All of Rob's fellow pilots were impressed, the wives were envious and I decided, hey, modeling was a part of show business and having my pictures taken wasn't half bad. I started counting the minutes until the graduation ceremony when Rob would be assigned to Southern California, close to my mecca and everything that is important in this world.

The graduation ceremony started out with us wives trying to suppress our giggles as the high mucky-muck Navy officers came striding into the room. Clank, clank, clank; the noise was deafening. Their chests were covered in medals and with every step they took those medals bounced up and down and made such a racket it sounded as if a herd of cattle wearing cow bells had entered the auditorium. During this quiet, solemn ceremony it struck us as being so hilarious we had to hit each other to keep from laughing.

Later, at home, I waited with baited breath for Rob to tell me where we would be stationed – would it be Point Magu or Miramar?! Point Magu was closer to L.A. but Miramar in San Diego would do. He gave me the good news and the bad news; he was going to be stationed in Monterey as a test pilot. Monterey? I didn't even know they had a Navy base there. That's a few hours away from Hollywood so it was kind of a disappointment, but Rob assured me it would only be for a couple years and it was a beautiful place to live and it *was* California. But the even worse news was yet to come. Rob looked at me, bracing himself for my reaction; before going to Monterey he was to be stationed in Georgia for a few months of training. What?! Nooooo! I absolutely was not going back to the deep South where road signs say flat out, "The Ku Klux Clan Welcomes You to Georgia" and bumper stickers warn, "If Your Heart Ain't in Dixie Get Your Ass Out." Well my heart wasn't and no part of my anatomy was ever going back. Ever!

Rob waited for me to calm down and explained we would only be there for a few months before heading to Monterey. Surely, I could put up with the South for a little while longer? I was adamant. My answer was no. But Rob already had another solution for me; one of his buddies was going to be stationed near San Francisco just an hour or so north of Monterey. We could ask if I could stay with him and his wife for awhile and then Rob and I would meet up in Monterey when he was through with training. I immediately jumped on him and the suggestion. Yes! Yes! Yes! I'm free, free, free of the South forever! I'll be able to see mixed race couples walking down the street and not wonder how far they'll get before being shot dead. No more separate drinking fountains, restrooms and supermarkets! No more southern belles using the N word as if it were perfectly normal and passing their bigotry onto their kids who had been "forced" into private schools because of integration. No more listening to political ads with candidates who sounded like their IQs were in the single digits. Wow! I had become a reverse racist. It would be years before I could hear a southern accent and not dredge up memories that made me feel sick to my stomach.

So Rob and I said a reluctant goodbye and I told him I wished he were coming with me, but he was understanding and explained he would be buried in work anyway. We both looked forward to our new life in California then flew off our separate ways.

CHAPTER 6

San Francisco, Monterey and Clint Eastwood

I SETTLED IN WITH NAVY friends in Fremont, California, and at the first opportunity headed a few miles north into San Francisco to find an agent. I had looked up agents in a local actors' handbook and made some appointments. When you're young and pretty, even completely inexperienced, how easy everything is! I signed with Brebner, the best agency in town, had headshots taken, and started going out on auditions. I had starved myself down to about one hundred pounds because I had read somewhere that the camera adds ten pounds to your weight and the thought of looking fat horrified me. I landed a job, my first real professional job, almost immediately. I was on top of the world.

The job I booked was a commercial for a local news show. I was to play a secretary in the newsroom, typing at my desk behind the male anchor person as he is doing the news. While he explains to the audience that a giant gorilla has escaped from the zoo, the gorilla walks into the newsroom, picks me up and carries me away. Meanwhile, the news anchor declares that this station is on top of the story and will give viewers the latest updates. Very funny, ha, ha. But I was working as an actress and that's all that mattered. As I look back on it now, I figure, yes, I was cast because I was attractive but I was also light as a feather and they obviously wanted a small, skinny person for the role because of the poor man in the gorilla suit having to lift and carry me take after take. But I didn't think about that then. I must have been the best actress for the role or why else would they want me?

My next big acting opportunity was to appear in a feature called *The Strawberry Statement* which was being shot in San Francisco. My role was to portray a student protestor protesting something or other I didn't have a clue about, nor did I care. It probably had something to do with protesting the Vietnam war, to which I gave little or no thought except that, thank God, now that things were winding down, Rob probably wouldn't have to go there. I held a sign and chanted slogans along with about 20 other people. The fact that I was a mere extra didn't register with me. I was in my first Hollywood movie. There were cameras, a director, actors I'd heard of like Bruce Davison, and I felt like I was completely in my element. Everything I had visualized in my high school theater class was coming true. My high school career advisor was obviously full of crap. What I didn't know is that there were two people working on this movie who would feature prominently in my future, Alan Godfrey who worked in production and Tony Eldridge who had a "for real" acting job in it. It would be years before I met either one of them.

As anybody knows who pays the slightest bit of attention, this period in San Francisco was a time of sex, drugs and rock and roll. The flower children still existed but were now on a downhill slide into serious addiction problems, and Haight-Ashbury was not a place where you wanted to hang out at night. In my focused little world, all this was as if it never existed. The only rock and roll that was important to me had been Rob's band, the Sonics. Drugs, alcohol, Janis Joplin and the Jefferson Airplane never registered on my brain. I could have experienced Janice Joplin in her prime if I had wanted to, but risking life and limb in Haight-Ashbury at night and rubbing shoulders with hippie drug addicts in a dark nightclub was not an option for Miss Goody-Two-Shoes. I may not have been going to church every day but my ingrained radar for evil was alive and well.

The only real worry I had at the time was the Zodiac Killer. He was prowling around killing people in northern California at the time, and the cops couldn't seem to get a handle on catching him. He taunted them in his letters and to this day no one knows who he was. Roaming around the area always by myself, I avoided strange men like the plague. I had a vivid imagination and the Zodiac Killer wasn't going to get his hands on me.

Time flew by and Rob ended his training in Georgia. I profusely thanked my friends who had allowed me to stay with them and reunited with Rob in Monterey. At my first sight of Monterey Bay, I fell in love with the area. Then, when I saw Carmel, I never wanted to leave. I wished it were closer to Hollywood so I could make it my permanent home.

We found an apartment in Pacific Grove where thousands of Monarch butterflies lived in the tall trees in our complex. What an awesome sight to see them for the first time. Their beauty took my breath away. Deer lived in the nearby woods and wandered around the Pebble Beach golf course a few miles down the road. Fortunately for them, they were appreciated and loved by residents in Carmel and Monterey, not brutally murdered as is the case in the South and other parts of the country where I never want to live. The residents' love of wildlife made it an even more perfect place for me to be.

The occupation of "test pilot" had always seemed to me like something dangerous that you would not want your husband to be, even worse than being a Navy pilot and having to land on a carrier in choppy seas. If he had to test the plane, what if the test failed? That prospect frightened me. But Rob being Rob, made it all sound perfectly safe, and so I stopped worrying and decided it was time I worked on getting my college degree. I enrolled in Monterey Peninsula College and majored in Theater Arts. And while walking around Carmel one day I saw that they had a beautiful dinner theater there; I decided to audition for their next play.

The first play I auditioned for was *The Seven Year Itch* for the role made famous by Marilyn Monroe. My main competition was a girl who was so stunningly beautiful there was no question who would win the part. Alena

Johnston was almost six feet tall, had an alabaster complexion, perfect figure and was an exceptional actress. I played the 'French Dream Girl" and was happy with that.

Whenever I hear people knock dinner theater I think, why? It's an intimate venue and fun for the actors and for the audience. People eat dinner, have a little wine and are ready to have a good time and be entertained. I ended up playing the lead in two other plays at the Carmel Dinner Theater and not only did I enjoy it, it was a great training ground as well.

One of the plays I did, *Any Wednesday*, was especially enjoyable because I had the privilege of working with an incredible comedic actor, Rod Allison. After a few rehearsals, we had the kind of rapport actors usually don't attain until after they've worked together a long time. We immediately became friends and our friendship lasted through all of the ups and downs of life until his untimely death of a heart attack in May 2013. He left a hole in my heart that no one and nothing can fill, but his laughter and his enthusiasm when talking about acting and the theater are memories that will always be with me.

Alena and I also became friends and I was fascinated by her experiences in Hollywood and of her role as a "Ziegfeld Girl" in *Funny Girl* with Barbra Streisand. She told me whenever Barbra had a scene where she sang, people would come from all the other sound stages on the studio lot to listen. It was an incredible experience for Alena. But after divorcing her first husband, she came back home to Carmel Valley, where she had grown up, to an uncertain future. She was so beautiful, most women did not want to be friends with her but she seemed like a nice person to me, quiet and shy in spite of her beauty, so I unwittingly cast myself in what was to become my role for years, as Tonto to her Lone Ranger.

Meanwhile, I auditioned for *The Apple Tree* at college and was cast in one of the leading roles as "Passionella," a movie star. I got to sing and dance and wear gigantic boobs on my chest, which these days, wouldn't seem big at all. Compared to what Dolly Parton has, they were miniscule. My friend Rosemaria was cast in the other lead of "Eve." Rosemaria was a beautiful girl with shoulder-length wavy hair, wore long dresses and was the kindest, most gentle person I had ever met. To this day, I consider her to be my dearest friend and an angel put down on this earth.

I enjoyed all the singing, dancing and comedy in the musical but when the play ended was hardly ready for Broadway, so I immersed myself in the theater department; acting in scenes and directing several myself. I struggled through my non-theater classes, which I hated but had to take in order to graduate.

I was hired to work as a guardian to a child actor on a television movie, *The Harness*. The script was adapted from a short story by John Steinbeck and was to be filmed in Salinas. Lorne Greene, who had played the father on *Bonanza*, had the leading role and we became friends. One day I asked him the inevitable question would-be actors always ask famous actors: how do I make it as an actor? He answered without hesitation in his booming voice, "Go to New York! That's where all the serious actors are. Not Hollywood!" Of course, that was out of the question for me. Rob and I had everything all planned out. Our goal was now within reach: Hollywood, where I would act, he would fly, and when he was through with the Navy, he would become a famous director. Me going off to New York for years trying to make it as an actor was not a realistic goal.

While we were filming in a cemetery in Salinas I was watching the leading lady, Julie Summers, lip-sync a song during a burial scene and was thinking about John Steinbeck, who was the author of the story *The Harness*, and what a coincidence it was that I had just read his book *Cannery Row*. I knew that Steinbeck spent a lot of time in the area, especially along Cannery Row in Pacific Grove where I lived. After Julie finished her song I asked a crewmember if he knew if Steinbeck was buried in a cemetery in Monterey. He shrugged and said he didn't know and for some reason I happened to look down at the ground and saw I was standing right on top of John Steinbeck's grave. I immediately jumped off and was almost frightened by the weird coincidence.

One day, driving home from grocery shopping, I spotted a film company shooting in downtown Pacific Grove, all two blocks of it. I was so excited I almost drove off the road. A movie company right here in my little town! I rushed home to put away my groceries so I could drive back and watch. Maybe there was a big star working on the film! But when I got back to Main Street where they were filming, the company had already packed up and moved on. A few years later I found out that they had been shooting a show called *Then Came Bronson*, starring Michael Parks, and that the production manager was Alan Godfrey, who had also worked on *The Strawberry Statement*. Two times I had just missed him before finally actually meeting him when I was working in the production office of another movie in Los Angeles.

I saw in the paper that Clint Eastwood was going to make his directorial debut with a movie called *Play Misty for Me* and that it would be filmed in Carmel. I was excited. Maybe I would actually see Clint! He had a bar in Carmel, The Hogs Breath Inn, but no matter how many times I passed by there I never saw hide nor hair of him. Somebody in the cast of the play I was doing at the dinner theater told me a member of his company had seen the play. Maybe he would remember me. So I decided to be brave and I wrote a note to the local film office to ask if I could audition if there was any role right for me. When I got the phone call asking if I would like to audition for Clint and the producer I almost stopped breathing. I was actually going to meet Clint Eastwood – "Rowdy Yates," who I couldn't see as the star of *A Fist Full of Dollars* was now just about the biggest star in the world. I never thought I'd be fortunate enough to actually work with him but I would be breathing the same air as Clint for just a few glorious minutes.

At the same time that I was looking forward to meeting Clint, I had adopted a little kitten, who, as all my animals are, was everything to me. Rob had accidently knocked her off the couch after we adopted her and she had broken her leg. She had just had her cast taken off when she disappeared. I realized she must have snuck out unbeknownst to us when one of us opened the front door to go out. Rob asked the apartment manager if he had seen her and he admitted to Rob he had seen her, taken her in his car to the animal shelter but that she had escaped from the car on the way there. Rob was incensed. The manager had obviously taken her somewhere and dumped her. We looked in the animal shelters but she was gone. I was still grieving when I got the call for the audition.

I was told to go to the Wharf in Monterey where Clint and Jessica Walter were filming a scene in a restaurant. I walked down the steps to the restaurant, sat in a booth and was pretty much overwhelmed when Clint and the producer Bob Daley slid in across from me. Nevertheless, being in a play every night gave me confidence as an actress and I read my lines from the script they handed me. After I finished, Clint immediately said, "Go to wardrobe." He thanked me and they both went back to the set. Meanwhile, I was thinking, "Wardrobe? He wants me to work in the wardrobe department? I don't know a thing about that." I slowly walked up the steps to the wharf and down the pier before it dawned on me, "I'm not working in wardrobe, I got the part! I'm acting in a movie with Clint Eastwood!"

While thrilled to be in the movie, I was still mourning the loss of my little kitten and wondered why good things in my life always had to be accompanied by the bad.

My first day on the set was easy: walk up a street in Carmel while Clint chases after me, turn around and say my lines. But for whatever reason, all the commotion that went along with filming a scene confused me – people yelling out things like quiet, speed, rolling, action, etc. I asked Clint, "Could you just tell me when you want me to talk?" I can't believe now I asked him to do that! Any idiot knows you start saying your lines after "action." But Clint didn't mind. He was very nice about it. He'd say, "Action, okay Britt, now." I'm convinced that I influenced Clint in his directing manner because years later I read an article that explained how he talks to his actors after saying "action" to get them in the mood of the scene. Can this be true? Have I had something to do with his incredible directorial success? Probably not.

After we finished filming at the house on Spendthrift Road where Jessica Walter ends up crushed to death on the rocks below, Clint offered to give me a ride home in his truck. He was very considerate and courteous and asked me questions about what courses I was taking in school and such. I had the perfect opportunity to tell him that I intended to pursue acting in Hollywood and ask him for advice and help which I know he would have given. Instead, I was totally tongue-tied and hardly said a word. A lost opportunity never to be regained.

Rob was very supportive of my dream of taking singing lessons, and I studied with a dear and talented man, Dr. Marshall, who lived and taught in Monterey. For the first time, I learned how to correctly place my voice and sing as a lyric soprano. He introduced me to operatic arias and I gloried in singing them and reaching high notes I never knew I had. After a year, he told me what I would need to do in order to become an opera singer; I would have to move to San Francisco and study for two years and then it would be three years before I would be ready to perform on stage. As much as I could visualize myself going in that direction, it was impossible for me. Rob was headed for Southern California and that is where we both would live and fulfill our dreams. But I continued the lessons for my own pleasure and with the thought in mind that in the future, doing musicals was not out of the question.

While attending college in Monterey, I had told Rob and my mother I needed to get a job so I could buy a car. Having one car just wasn't working for us. My mother panicked at the thought of me possibly not graduating and sent me money to buy a car. Her generosity surprised me and I thanked her profusely. After looking at a variety of used cars I settled on a little green MG convertible. It was cute but, as I would find out, not very practical.

I earned my associate degree in Theater Arts and applied to attend UCLA. If they accepted me, I would go down to L.A. and start school and Rob would join me later. Our goal, our final destination, was at hand. I was readier than ever, now armed with a SAG card, thanks to Clint. I spent a few tense months waiting to hear back from UCLA and when the acceptance notice came, I was ecstatic. I figured I would go down first and Rob would join me as soon as his time in Monterey was up. Point Magu was our first choice because it was closest to Hollywood and Miramar in San Diego, the second, but either one was fine with me.

My friend Alena was being pursued like crazy by Max Baer, who had seen her in *Funny Girl* and fallen in love with her from afar. Max, who had played "Jethro" on the *Beverly Hillbillies*, had given up on acting and turned to producing movies instead. He managed to find out where Alena lived and used to come up to Carmel periodically and take her out to dinner. As a favor to me, she asked if I could stay in his guest house in Studio City until I got an apartment and he agreed. He would do anything to make Alena happy. She and some of my other friends had given me some show business contacts to call when I was settled in L.A., and Andy Sackheim, the son of the director of *The Harness*, with whom I had become friends on the shoot, had told me to call him as soon as I came down.

I packed my little green MG with as much as it would hold and Rob and I said goodbye, knowing we would survive this separation the way we had survived every other one, and I was on my way. I had an intense feeling of excitement and anticipation on the drive to L.A. The strongest feelings in my life were my love for Rob, my love for animals and my desire to work as an actress, a desire strong enough to temporarily wrench me out of my comfort zone as a taken-care-of Cinderella/housewife.

Coming to America

Our Home in Sauda

Birthday Age 9

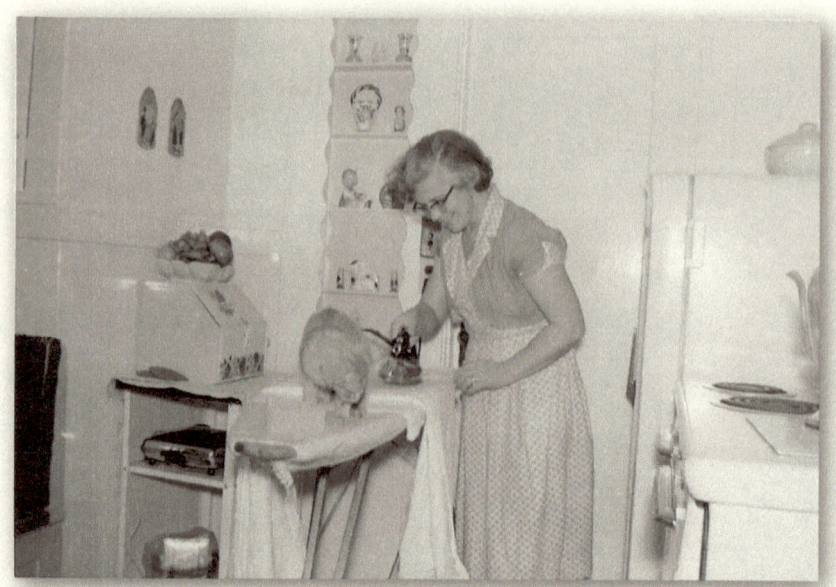

Taffy and Mama

First Job

Rob in Hollywood

On the Carrier

Watching Landings

In San Francisco

First Musical

My Friend Telly

Kevin in Makeup

The Beautiful Alena

Tony Eldridge, "the boy"

Alena, Amazon Queen

Alan, Erika and Me

Erika and Alan

Kitty

CHAPTER 7

Max Baer and Hollywood

As it turned out, when I arrived in Studio City at Max's beautiful home in the hills of Coldwater Canyon, I didn't stay in the guest house. Max warmly welcomed me with open arms and told me the roadie of the band he managed and his wife were living in the guesthouse so I would bunk down in the maid's quarters in the main house seeing as he had no live-in maid. That was fine with me. I unpacked and made myself at home and sat out by the pool with Max's dogs. He had three or four, one being a German Shepherd and the others were small dogs that he called "the babies." Needless to say, my first best friends in town were those dogs.

I called all the people on my list who I hoped would give me some help and direction in getting started finding acting work. Some ignored me while others promised to get back to me later. I looked forward to starting classes at UCLA and began the actor's life of waiting and hoping while being as proactive as the acting profession allows. Unlike being a doctor or lawyer or many other professions, an actor can't go out and set up shop and work on a television show or in a movie. We have to audition and are dependent on the powers-that-be to hire us. Having family and friends in the business gives an actor a huge leg up, and I didn't have that, except for Max who wasn't working at the time and Andy Sackheim, who it seemed had forgotten me, but I was determined and focused. An underlying feeling of depression was always with me and something I constantly had to fight against, but I believed with every fiber of my being that getting acting work would bring me the joy and peace of mind I longed for.

Max's band was called Pollution, which seemed like an outrageous name to me at the time but now seems pretty tame. The lead singers were Dobie Gray and Tata Vega, and naturally I got to go to their gigs and hear them sing all the time. Both of them were awesome singers and when I listened to Dobie I couldn't understand why he wasn't incredibly famous. He'd had a hit called "The in Crowd," but nothing since. His huge hit, "Drift Away" was yet to come. I drove him down to a gig in Orange County once when somehow, he got left behind. All the way down I drilled it into him on how he should push for his own single and how it would be a big hit. I knew so much about the music business (not!), he must have listened.

I had no idea of what a great career was in Tata's future. I only knew I wished I could sing like her. Listening to her belt out songs would be the closest I would ever come to hearing Janis Joplin in person. No popular female singer today can touch Tata. One of Max's band members had a cocaine problem, a drug I had never heard of. Max used to say this band member was really into coke and he wished he knew what to do about. I thought Max was talking about Coca Cola and wondered what the big deal was. I figured I better not tell him I liked Coke too since he seemed so adamantly dead set against it.

I registered at UCLA, bought my textbooks for the next quarter and sat by the pool waiting for people to return my phone calls, while communing with Max's dogs. Max, who had more energy than anybody I'd ever met, asked me one day what I was doing sitting around the pool all the time. Why wasn't I doing anything about getting acting work? He didn't realize that I *was* already doing everything I could think of doing, but, nevertheless, he wasn't going to let any grass grow under my feet. He set me up with his manager, who set me up with the best photographer in town, who sent me to the Charles Stern Agency who booked me for a role in a beer commercial without me even having to audition. THIS was the acting business that presumably was so difficult to get into? I hoped it wasn't a fluke.

On set, there were about 30 people who were going to be in the first shot. When the assistant director yelled for all those people to move to a certain spot, I moved with them. He stopped me and said, "No, no, you're not an extra, you're the principal, don't you know that?" He told me to join another actor over by the barbeque and wait for our cue. That actor happened to be a very handsome star of a television series who had a wife and several children. After the easy shoot, where we just held up glasses of Budweiser and smiled, he wanted to take me home (my home) and fool around some. I declined, telling him that I was married. It was the first of many such propositions by actors, agents, producers and directors, which in this day and age would be called sexual harassment and cause to take the offenders to court. Back then, it was merely an annoyance an actress had to put up with, or for some actresses, give in to, in order to get work.

Rob was actually proud of me for booking a job but my father saw me in the Budweiser commercial while he was watching a football game and just about had a heart attack. Both my parents wanted me back with Rob, safe and sound and acting like a proper married lady and this beer thing was just further proof that my Hollywood aspirations would see me ending up in the gutter. Other parents would have been proud. Mine mourned for weeks and were humiliated in front of their Pentecostal friends.

My first real theatrical agent, who I had managed to find on my own, was a very kind, good-looking young man who represented some well-known actors and former child actors who were now grown up and no longer so well-known. As soon as I signed with the agency he sent me to MGM to audition for a western. I had no idea where MGM was or how to get there so he enlisted the help of one of his working actors, Raphael Campos. Raphael lived in a not-so-nice area of Hollywood on Cherokee. I had seen

Raphael in movies, and wondered why he was living in such a rundown building. That was before I became intimately acquainted with the highs and lows of a show business career. Raphael had been married to singer Dinah Washington, whose voice I adored. I had a hard time imagining them together but one of his friends said to me, "Man, she loved that kid to death!" And since I found him lovable as well, I could see why she was crazy about him.

Raphael drove me to MGM and my first sight of the fabled studio just about took my breath away. I tried to act cool on the outside but on the inside I was thinking of all the big stars who had worked there in Hollywood's heyday. And I was about to walk in the very same gates where legends of Hollywood had been driven by their chauffeurs. Wow! This was magical. The audition is a dim memory and I didn't get the part, but I still remember the first time I laid eyes on MGM studios.

Max had a lot of show business and famous athlete friends. I met L.A. Rams players and baseball players and got to talk to baseball legend Mickey Mantle on the phone. But I was the most excited when Max asked me to pick up Rosie Grier at the airport. Rosie used to play football with the Los Angeles Rams, but I will always associate Rosie with the death of Robert Kennedy. Rosie was at the Ambassador Hotel protecting Bobby that terrible night I will never forget as I watched the unreal events unfolding on television. Rosie, like Max, was a bundle of energy, but a whole lot bigger. Who would have guessed he liked to do needlepoint?! I don't remember what we talked about, but when we got to Max's house he put on music and we danced. And what a great dancer he was! He made a half-hearted attempt to hit on me but I laughed it off and we just went on dancing. Years later, I met his cousins Pam and Rod, and Rod became a life-long friend.

Staying with Max was easy because he treated me like one of the guys. He only liked women with giant breasts, and since I did not qualify in that department, I could go out with him to various events and always feel comfortable and protected. Max had buckets full of charisma and was always the life of the party. It was impossible not to end up laughing hysterically when he told jokes. He was kind and generous to me and so much fun to be with I couldn't figure out why his wife would have divorced him to take up with George Burns, of all people, but he had jokes about that too, even though she had ended up with at least half of his *Beverly Hillbillies* windfall. But Max had another side that I never saw. There were signs of his temper in the bedroom wall, where he had made holes with his fists after getting angry at a girlfriend. And Dobie told me of violent temper outbursts directed at the band for reasons I never was privy to. But he never said a harsh word to me and his generosity in allowing me to stay rent-free at his house made me very grateful. And when he told jokes and funny stories about actors he knew, all my worries would drown in laughter that made my stomach hurt.

After the Budweiser residuals started coming in, and with Rob sending me a little money, it was time for me to get my own apartment, and I found the perfect one on Moorpark in Studio City, one block from CBS Studios. I loved that little apartment. From there I would walk up to Du Par's restaurant to meet my friends, right past CBS studios which was then MTM. Sometimes I would see Mary Tyler Moore sitting outside the studio door working on her needlework. I wanted to wave and say hello, but I was too shy.

I now had a life in Hollywood: I was attending classes at UCLA, had signed with an agent and occasionally was going out on auditions. All I needed now was for Rob to tell me when he was coming down and where he would be stationed. Every time I drove up to visit him the anticipation grew. I looked forward to spending time with him near whatever base he would be stationed at in Southern California and the rest of the time in my apartment until he was finished with the Navy and we were free to do as we pleased.

I'm still not sure of what really happened and why our lives ended up being turned upside down with all our plans permanently de-railed.

All I remember is that, on one of my visits to Monterey, Rob told me we were going to be stationed back up in Washington State, in a place called Oak Harbor, so far north of Seattle I had never heard of it, on an island in the middle of nowhere. I think that he had requested to fly a certain plane that flew out of that Navy air base and for several months out of the year he would be out on a carrier and I would be stuck living up somewhere near Canada in the rain and snow and cold by myself while he was gone. He had no problem with the fact that this move would be a cataclysmic disappointment to me and it would put my life on hold indefinitely.

I have little memory of how I reacted the moment I received the news, but I know it must have been intense. I was in shock and so completely caught off guard I could barely believe it was happening. Going back to live in Washington State was almost as bad as going back to Mississippi. Did he request to fly this plane? Did he know we would have to go to Oak Harbor for him to be able to fly it? Did he not even request Miramar or Point Magu? I only remember snatches of the conversation so I can't say for sure. But Rob seemed happy with the move to Oak Harbor, while I was so stunned I felt like I had been sucker-punched. Events from the past and never-resolved resentments rolled over me and reminded me that to him, everything to do with his own life was more important than what happened to me and I, ever the "good wife," had always agreed to put him first. This time would be different.

Rob flew up to Oak Harbor, which was situated on Whidbey Island, while I contemplated what my next move would be. I had fervently wanted things to work out for us. In spite of everything, we loved each other but our careers were thousands of miles apart and now promised to stay that way for years. How could a marriage possibly go on like that? It wasn't fair to either one of us and I wasn't willing to be the one who had to again sacrifice everything for him to do what was important to him.

I put off doing anything about this dilemma as long as I could and then made the painful decision we had no choice but to get a divorce. So I flew up to Seattle, not telling my parents what I was going to do, and asked my friend Georgia to drive me to the ferry to Oak Harbor.

When I saw Rob, my heart broke. We had both made mistakes which had negatively affected our relationship; neither of us was perfect; but we had been through so much in our short, young lives and if everything had gone according to plan, we would both be in California, living a wonderful life together. But here I was, at his secluded house on the sound, a freezing cold wind blowing, waves crashing on the beach and storm clouds overhead. I wanted to wave a magic wand and make it all better, and then for a few seconds thought maybe I *could* come back up here and avoid a divorce. What an ugly word. I never thought it would happen to me. But the prospect of sitting in that house, staring out at the water day in and day out while Rob was out on a carrier for months on end, seemed just as bad. Of course, there would have been other things to do in Oak Harbor, like whatever it was that Navy wives do up there. But I knew it wasn't for me. Oak Harbor was just as depressing as I thought it would be. I got up my courage and told Rob I thought it would be best if we ended it here and now. Even though we had been living apart for a long time, it took him by surprise. He was very upset and very, very sad. We both cried and mourned the end of our marriage, and I flew back to L.A.

On one of my trips to Seattle to visit my parents I had brought back a Siamese cat who I named Kitty. I can't remember who gave me this talkative, rambunctious little boy who, yes, became my closest and dearest friend. He became the substitute for Rob, and my parents, who hated what I was doing and constantly discouraged me. Kitty actually talked to me, practically non-stop. We had conversations back and forth all the time and understood what the other was saying, but never in front of other people lest they should think I was totally mad. The landlady had said no cats, but that didn't deter me. How could anyone live without a best friend? Kitty comforted me when I came back from Oak Harbor and life continued on as I went through the motions of getting an amicable divorce and dealt with my parents' shock and shame. My mother began her relentless campaign of begging me to come home, go back to the University of Washington and get my law degree. Law degree?! I don't know why she was so set on me becoming a lawyer. I never had the slightest inclination of going in that direction. But as nightmarish as it was to have a daughter who was an actress, to her, having a daughter who was a lawyer, for some reason, was the polar opposite. So that's what I heard for the next ten years: be a lawyer, be a lawyer, be a lawyer, until finally, after I remarried, she ended her hopeless but persistent campaign.

CHAPTER 8

Kevin, Kojak and Near Death

MAX'S MANAGER INTRODUCED ME TO Vince Conte who was one of the best photographers in L.A. and Vince took my first Hollywood headshots. He also became a very good friend. Beautiful actresses were always coming and going in and out of his house but it took me awhile to realize that some of them weren't exactly actresses. Vince was friends with a many famous actors and Las Vegas performers. Somehow a lot of Vince's actresses ended up with these celebrities; sometimes short term, sometimes longer. As for me, Vince always told me that if anyone ever tried to come on to me, I was to report it to him and he would put a stop to it. Vince had a houseboy named Tiger, a young man in his early twenties with brown stringy hair down to his shoulders. One day he came to me and asked, "Why are you hanging around Vince and coming to the house all the time, Britt? Why do you want to be a part of this?" I told him I didn't understand what he was talking about; Vince was my photographer and my friend. It took awhile for me to figure out who and what Vince really was.

Vince arranged for me to be invited to a party in Bel Air with one of the other actresses (a real one) who hung out at his house. When we arrived, the hostess was apologizing for the inadequacy of her big mansion. She insisted that they were just renting and would buy something much better soon. To me, owning that house would have been a dream come true. We met the other guests: Mama Cass, Cheryl Tiegs, Daryl Zanuck and his wife Linda Harrison, and many others. When we sat down to dinner, they started passing around a sugar bowl and putting what I assumed was sugar on a small spoon and holding it up to their noses to sniff. I wondered what the heck these people were doing! Weird! I decided rich and famous people had some strange habits. I let the sugar bowl pass me by.

A few weeks later I was introduced to an agent from William Morris who was the son of a famous agent who had represented Marilyn Monroe for many years. His Hollywood sophistication and supreme confidence intimidated me, but I went out with him anyway and we ended up at my apartment after dinner. He proudly talked about his father and his father's personal relationship with Marilyn and then took out a vial of white powder out of his pocket and a little spoon like I had seen at the party a few weeks before. He dipped the spoon into the vial and held it up to my nose and told me to breathe in. Afraid to appear naïve I hesitated and then pushed the spoon away. Annoyed, he sniffed the powder himself and I could see his interest in me headed downhill fast. Obviously coming to the conclusion I had just ridden into town on a turnip truck, he didn't even coax me into changing my mind, which was a good thing since I suddenly had a very strong aversion to him and whatever was in that vial. After I ushered him to the door, we parted company with an unspoken agreement never to see each other again.

Vince told me that he had arranged for his niece, Charmian, and I to visit the set of a movie his long-time friend, Telly Savalas, was doing with Martin Sheen and Sally Fields. Dick Donner was directing, and when he saw Vince's cute little niece, who had recently moved to L.A. from back east and looked like she was about 16, he was instantly attracted. But Vince had asked me to take Charmian under my wing and let her stay with me for awhile until she found her own apartment. No way was any Hollywood director coming near her. What I remember most about being on the set was the way Martin Sheen would put his raincoat on. He would grab it with both hands, fly it around over his head like a kite and somehow ended up with his arms in the sleeves and then would shrug it on his shoulders. He did it exactly the same bizarre way every take. Amazing.

One day, when I was at Vince's house, he told me he had arranged for a limo to take me to Bob Evan's house in Palm Springs and I would stay the weekend. Bob was producing a television pilot and Vince wanted me to be considered for a part in the show. I was hurt and offended that after telling me he was my protector that he now was sending me down to Bob Evans in a blatant attempt to get an acting role by sleeping with a producer. I told him I couldn't possibly go down and have sex with a man I didn't even know, let alone have a relationship with him. He tried to persuade me to change my mind but after awhile backed off. He already had his number-two choice in mind and I had seen pictures of her. She reminded me of a young Ali McGraw and would appeal to Bob a lot more than I would have. She went down to Palm Springs and she got the part.

At UCLA, as I was half-heartedly going through the motions to earn my four-year degree until I was discovered by Hollywood, I met Reid Smith. With his long blond hair and perfectly sculpted face, he looked like a Norse God. Unfortunately, he was in love with an actress almost as beautiful as he was. His advice to me was, forget college acting classes, they suck. Charles Conrad's studio is the place to learn how to act for TV and film. So I signed up for classes and, after one session, wondered if I hadn't been too hasty in taking Reid's advice. Meanwhile, Reid ended up under contract to Universal, starring in a TV series and *Granny Goose* commercials. He must know something.

Charles believed that theater was dead as a doornail. No one was going to buy that phony stage acting anymore. His teaching method involved us sitting across from our partner at a table, staring at each other and reacting no more or no less to the other actor's lines using scenes taken from popular novels. The problem was, since Charles didn't believe in us creating ahead of time any subtext or emotional reality that the scene called for, we would sit and stare at each other for several minutes at a time waiting for the other actor to say his or her lines so we could react to them. Eventually, one of us had to say something even if we didn't feel anything or we'd still be sitting there. We didn't want to over-act, God forbid, so every scene was devoid of emotion, even if it involved your entire family being slaughtered by a mass murderer.

My friend Chuck, who I met my first day in class, pointed out a lady in class to me and said, "That's Judy Lewis, Loretta Young's daughter with Clark Gable." That was news to me. I didn't know they had a daughter together. "She doesn't know he's her father or that Loretta is her birth mother. She thinks she's adopted." Now that seemed awfully far-fetched to me. How could Chuck know who she really was and Judy not know. That was just plain crazy. Although Judy did look a bit like both of them.

Years later, when I read Judy's autobiography, I found out that Clark Gable had visited her when she was a child and that, yes, Loretta had told her she was adopted and that is what she had believed all her life. It was eventually revealed to her that Gable was her father and that the woman she believed to be her adopted mother was actually her real mother. Loretta's Roman Catholic faith would not allow her to admit she had become pregnant while working with Gable on location while filming the movie *The Call of the Wild*. It was a devastating discovery for Judy. When I looked at the dates when the truth had been revealed to her, I realized it was *after* Chuck had told me. How could that be?! How could he, of all people, know these things before Judy knew? I don't know where Chuck is now but how he knew the truth as early as he did is a mystery I would love to solve.

It was while I was trying to undo, with the help of Charles Conrad, all the "damage" I had done to myself as a stage actress, that I met my new very best friend, (after Kitty) brilliant actor and director, John Lombardo. We ran into each other at Goldwyn Studios and immediately hit it off. He was about to direct a play called *Mary, Mary* and brought me in to audition. He cast me in one of the leads and I found out what it was like to be directed by a really talented comedy director. I played the role of "Tiffany," and my natural ditzy self was perfect for the role.

After the run of the play, a principal role opened up on the soap opera, *Days of Our Lives* and since John was good friends with the director, he got me an audition. I decided I was going to do this the Charles Conrad way. I barely worked on my lines and went in to the producers' office confident that this was my first chance to show off what I had learned in an authentic, Hollywood acting class. It was a very emotional scene and I waited for the casting director to begin. He spoke in a quiet monotone, giving me nothing. I panicked. I was supposed to cry and carry on hysterically and this man was sitting there with a dead-pan expression on his face, not even looking at me. The producers waited. The casting director waited. I waited...nothing came. Sweat ran down from my armpits in rivulets. I felt empty and devoid of direction or purpose. Eventually, I said some lines and made a quick exit. It was an unmitigated disaster. I ran to my car, raced home and hid under the covers, knowing it would get back to John, he would be humiliated and never cast me in any play ever again. He did call and didn't hate me. He said when I walked in the room they agreed I was exactly what they were looking for, except for the acting part. And he couldn't figure out what happened, seeing as he had seen me be spunky and funny and give it my all on stage every night. He didn't know that I had found out from Charles Conrad that stage acting will never be accepted in Hollywood and that in TV we have to learn to do NOTHING! Nevertheless, after this disaster, I was ready to dump Charles Conrad and his wack-job acting theories.

Besides Chuck, I had also met an actor named Kevin Dobson in Charles' class. I first saw him as I started to cross Cahuenga from the park near Charles' studio and we met in the middle of the street at the center line. All traffic seemed to stop as he gave me a look as if I were the Virgin Mary and Marilyn Monroe rolled into one. It truly was as if he were looking at me, seeing a vision of perfection, and embracing me and surrounding me with overwhelming adoration. Years later, I found out this is the look he gives to every good-looking woman he meets. Since I didn't know this was his standard opening salvo and knowing I was fairly attractive, I thought to myself, this must be love at first sight for this guy, and I found myself drawn into his seductive aura. Chuck introduced me to Kevin and needless to say, after talking to each other for about one minute we hit it off. The next day we took a trip to the beach with the top down in my green MG and Kevin waved his arms above his head and yelled at the top of his lungs at other cars on the San Diego Freeway, "We're going to make it in this town! We're going to make it big! Whoo-oo!" From his mouth to God's ears I thought. And where was God in my life at this point? I had put him on the back burner. I was so busy fighting for my parents' approval and not getting it, feeling badly having to block them out of my life, and pushing down guilt about Rob and everything that happened with him, trying to find my way as an actress, let alone get work and get through UCLA, I forgot I could call on God for help and for comfort. I was focused on my goal and couldn't see that decisions must be made and plans carefully laid out, and that taking time to meditate and pray and slow down in order make the right moves was all important. I was racing full speed ahead, things were falling into place. I had no need to slow down and contemplate my actions. Charles Conrad, of all people, had given me a book, *Key to Yourself*, which has the exact same philosophy and advice as *The Secret*, but was written decades earlier. If I had read it then, and paid attention to what it said, how different my life might have turned out. But there is no going back. It was destined that I had to make many drastic mistakes and learn everything the hard way. And depression doggedly followed me everywhere I went.

At the beach, Kevin and I talked for hours. It felt like we were soul mates. Acting was everything and we couldn't imagine going through life having to do anything else to earn a living. He worked on the railroad and had been for awhile. He was going through a divorce and said his soon-to-be ex-wife Susan thought he was crazy for leaving New York for L.A. There had been some sort of big upheaval in their marriage that couldn't be overlooked or mended and he, even being a very strong Catholic, couldn't put it behind him, so he filed for divorce. Since I had recently divorced, I commiserated and it made us feel even closer. We stayed out all night, just talking, then I took him home to where he was staying with the ex-wife of a famous television star. She was also in our acting class, and I was too dense then to figure out that they were in a relationship that ended as soon as he met me. She didn't appreciate my intrusion into his life, so he moved in with his agent in Beverly Hills and vowed it wouldn't be long before he had even a better house of his own.

One night in the middle of the night, Kevin called me from Pink's on La Cienega and told me he had fallen off his motorcycle and needed a ride to the railroad yard where he worked. So I hustled myself over the hill and picked him up. He had obviously been drinking and was in no shape to either ride a motorcycle or go to work. But I drove him down to the railroad yards where he was working and he asked me to come back and pick him up when he was through or sleep in my car until morning and drive him home. Wanting only to make him happy and reassure him that I cared, I agreed. I parked in the dark, scary, deserted railway yard and settled down to go to sleep. Soon a flashlight was shining in my face. It was the cops. "What are you doing here?!" they demanded. I told them I was waiting for my boyfriend who would be finished working in a few hours. They immediately put the kibosh on that great idea and told me it was dangerous waiting there and I had to leave for my own safety. Any of the lowlife crazies that hung around there could slash through that convertible top and rape and kill me. They looked at me like I was a complete fool. I had to agree and started my car and left them there shaking their heads. I drove all the way home to spend the night but was back in the morning to pick up Kevin.

Sometimes Kevin would spend an evening with his friends, drink too much and demand that they take him to my apartment. I would let him in, put him in my bed and sleep on the cot in the living room. I never gave a second thought to the fact that he might be in the beginning stages of alcoholism. I had never known an alcoholic before. I thought drinking to excess was something young guys did to blow off steam. And he was so lovable and fun when he wasn't drinking I didn't think anything more of it. He constantly talked of his wife and how she had cheated on him and lamented the fact that he couldn't stay married to her. He was a strict Catholic and to him divorce was a sin and I'm sure he went to mass and confession and felt a great deal of guilt for leaving her. I assumed he would get over his guilt as the divorce proceeded on schedule, but as time went on I wasn't so sure.

Vince announced that Telly was about to star in a series from a TV movie he had made the year before and the name of the series would be *Kojak*. Vince said for sure I could get a part on it once the show got going. I told Kevin about the show, and he already knew about it. He was clearly uncomfortable when he approached me to ask me to do him a big favor; there was a regular role on the show that he wanted to audition for, would I ask Telly to have him brought in? "I hate asking for favors and I'm not exactly right for the role, but I know I can get them to cast me if I just get a chance," he pleaded. They wanted a short "banty rooster" type guy for the role of "Crocker" and Kevin was over six feet tall, but I started lobbying for Kevin to get in to audition and for him to get this role. I bugged Telly and his brother George to the point where they both said, "Why do you keep asking for a role for Kevin? Why aren't you asking for yourself?" Good question. But it's always been easier for me to ask for a favor for other people than it is to ask for myself.

Kevin was called in, wowed everybody in the audition and got the role. The first time I went on the set I was visiting Telly in his trailer for awhile and then left to find Kevin. He was livid when he saw where I was coming from. "What are you doing in there? Why are you in his trailer instead of mine? I'll remember this," he said savagely and repeated it, "I'll remember this." I was shocked. I wasn't allowed to say hello to Telly, the man who I had begged for Kevin to get this job? I was shaken and sat down and talked to another actor working on that show who impressed me with his humility and friendliness. But I remember thinking, "The makeup on that actor sure is orange." But Harvey Keitel looked great when the show aired and not orange at all. I had a lot to learn about acting, make-up and Kevin.

I still remember when Kevin and I saw the first episode of *Kojak* and his credit came on. We were at his agent's house where he was still living and in the excitement of the moment, we both stared intently at the TV as the credits came on. Everything that he had been working for had come true and I thought, "I'm next. It's my turn now." Years later, when we met up after not seeing each other for awhile, he said, "You know, my agent said he was the one who got me that part, not you or Telly. My agent had a relationship with the head of casting." I thought to myself, "He really believes that a casting director had more power than Telly and George?" But regardless of who did what for whom, Kevin never realized what it took for me to speak repeatedly to Telly about him. And a few years later when I was down and out and homeless with a child and five cats to provide for, he turned his back on me. By that time, his on-again, off-again wife ruled the roost with an iron hand and he didn't dare to even acknowledge that I existed.

One day, I went to Charles Conrad's class intending to make it my last. I knew I needed a lot more guidance to become a good actor than what he was offering. Kevin had studied with Sandy Meisner in New York so he already had grounding in some sort of "method" and coming up with subtext and emotion. He could deal with Conrad. I couldn't. I walked up the steps to the class, looked around and said to no one in particular, "Chuck said Kevin might be here today." One of the girls there who didn't like me for whatever reason, said, knowing full well the impact it would have on me, "Oh, Kevin is down in the parking lot with his wife." His wife? Kevin didn't have a wife...or maybe he did.

Confused, I walked downstairs and out into the parking lot and there he was, surrounded by other students and, sure enough, his wife Susan was there. He glanced over and saw me and a look came over his face as if to say, "I'm sorry!" but he didn't move. He just stayed there with his friends and his wife and I walked away feeling totally betrayed.

Apparently, Kevin with his strict Catholic upbringing, couldn't bring himself to go through with the divorce, so he had been vacillating between Susan and me for months but I didn't know it. One time Chuck asked Kevin's agent where he was and his agent joked, "Oh, Britt and Kevin went to the airport to pick up Susan." Big laugh. When I found out the hard way exactly what had been going on, I walked away from Kevin and that was that. I thought.

My friend, Alena, came to L.A. to stay with me, not wanting to lick her wounds in Carmel anymore. She had been married to Tony Coogan, whose father, Jackie Coogan, had been famous as a child actor and had had all his money stolen by his mother resulting in the passage of a new law protecting child actors. Tony tried to win Alena back for a long time but finally gave up and I ended up becoming friends with him. Tony was also a great photographer and took headshots of me. He was a gentle, soft-spoken, good-looking guy and I never understood why Alena wouldn't give him another chance. At one point, Alena married a man I didn't meet until months later. It was obvious to me that Tony was still deeply in love with her and liked being around me so he could talk about her and what had gone wrong in their marriage.

After Kevin had chosen to go back to Susan, Chuck introduced me to Michael Walker, an actor friend of his, maybe thinking since his friend was very nice and was the kind of person who would never hurt me, it might work out between him and me. Michael was working as an usher at a movie theater in Hollywood at the time and Chuck said, "Wait until you see him, he looks *exactly* like his father, even more than his brother does." I asked Chuck who his father was and he said, "Robert Walker, the actor who was married to Jennifer Jones." Chuck was right. We went to the theater where Michael was working and when I saw him I had to agree he was the spitting image of his father, even more than his brother Robert Walker, Jr., and, like his father, soft spoken and very sweet. We dated for awhile and he took me to his tiny apartment and I wondered why he would be living in circumstances even worse than mine. He told me that his mother Jennifer, who was married at the time to Norton Simon, a billionaire, expected him to make it on his own and he was determined to do that. It was difficult for me to understand why his parents wouldn't at least help him out enough to allow him to live in a decent apartment. He came to care for me too much and I had to tell him I didn't reciprocate his feelings. It put me off that he had been obsessed with the same girl in Conrad's class who didn't like me. She had treated him very badly, and the worse she treated him the crazier about her he became. A man who likes mean women would never be satisfied with me so I assured him it would be better for us to be friends. I regret that as the years went by we lost touch and that I didn't even know until recently that he had died.

One day Alena brought home a date who ended up becoming my life-long friend. He was model-handsome with long blond hair and looked very young so Alena nicknamed him "the boy." His name was Tony Eldridge and much later I found out he had been in that same movie *The Strawberry Statement*, in which I had made my auspicious debut. Alena soon moved on from him to start dating my friend Chuck, but Tony and I stayed friends and had many long rides through the Santa Monica Mountains on his motorcycle. I still remember being at the apartment he shared with actor Wendell Burton (*The Sterile Cuckoo*) and said offhand, as we were going through record albums, stopping at one of Bette Midler's, "I love you Bette. Too bad you're just a passing fad." Lucky for her, he was as wrong about her as I was about Dustin Hoffman.

After wallowing in self-pity over the fact that my acting career was not taking off and wondering if I would ever get a job, I finally got a featured role in a show about paramedics, after my extremely forceful agent just about browbeat the producers into casting me. I had to audition three times for *Emergency* before I was finally cast, and agonized over every one of them. When I got the call that I was cast, I was so wrung out from anxiety I felt more relief than joy. I was to play "Daisy" in an episode called "Daisy's Pick". It filmed at Universal where *Kojak* was shot and I ran into Kevin one day during lunchtime. He made it clear he still didn't want to give up on me even though his "ex" wife kept flying in and out of town. He told me how great I looked with all that stage make-up on, said I should look like that all the time. I was not flattered.

I was friends with another actor in Conrad's class, Randy Carver, who was cast in a sitcom called *Taxi* as one of the regulars. I hadn't known that he was on the show until it came on and I saw him playing the role of a quiet-talking cowboy, which fit him to a tee since he was from Texas. After the first season, he was dropped from the cast and I commiserated with him. I thought his character was interesting and had a lot of appeal and couldn't understand why they wouldn't want him to continue to be on the show. So much goes on behind the scenes with producers and networks that have nothing to do with an actor's talent or lack of it. It's just one more thing that is beyond an actor's ability to control.

Max Baer was getting ready to go into production on a new movie and he hired me to type his script as he dictated it to me. I had attended his screening for investors of *Macon County Line* starring Alan and Jesse Vint and thought it was a pretty good movie. For a low-budget feature it was doing very well and now he was ready to produce another one. We started out working at his new house in the flats of the valley and when we came closer to filming I ended up working in his office. One day, unbeknownst to me, a man who had his office in the same building saw me walking down the stairs and out to my car and he told Max he would like to meet me. So Max called me and said a friend of his would like permission to call and ask me out to dinner. I quizzed Max on who the guy was but he didn't tell me much; just that he was an acquaintance of his and a nice guy. Reluctantly I told Max he could give the man my number and I would go out with him one time and then take it from there. Max's friend called almost immediately and we arranged to meet for dinner that night. He told me his name (let's call him "Sonny") and I thought it sounded like a name out of *The Godfather*. I wondered what I was getting myself into. That night there was a knock on the door and a young man, dark hair, not bad looking was standing there smiling. On the landing stood another man who looked as if he did come straight out of *The Godfather*; six feet tall, no neck, and muscles rippling underneath a dark suit. His eyes never stopped moving and he looked as deadly serious as the President's own Secret Service men. Oh boy. We walked downstairs to where a black limousine with tinted windows was waiting and Sonny's bodyguard opened the door. There was another burly guy seated behind the wheel, and I suspected the dark windows were bullet proof glass. I was terrified, and if I survived this date had every intention of killing Max when I saw him again. I barely remember the evening but we went to an Italian restaurant and ate in the back room with about 20 other people. It was a raucous evening, everyone having a great time, eating and drinking and me wishing it was all over. My date took me home and was a gentleman all the way and deposited me on my doorstep unscathed. He said he hoped he could see me again and I nodded, smiled, shut my door, leaned against it and breathed out. Oh my God! If Sonny isn't Mafia, Al Pacino is Swedish. Never again, I vowed.

A few days later, my own Al Pacino called again. I tried to make excuses for why I couldn't go out to dinner with him and used Charmian as a reason why; "A friend is in town and staying with me and I don't want to leave her at home alone." He told me to bring her along and informed me what time he would be by. I was afraid to argue. Again, he showed up with his bodyguards, and Charmian, Vince's Italian niece, acted like it was all very normal. The three of us sat in the back seat and Sonny made his move on me. I backed up against Charmian and started chattering about nothing. Thankfully, the car phone buzzed and Sonny picked it up and as he listened his expectant expression turned into a scowl. He hung up and looked at me, "I have to go to a recording session and have a few words with Glen Campbell. I'm sorry, but we won't be able to have dinner." He handed me a hundred dollars. "This is for dinner and a cab home." With that he dropped us off at a restaurant on Ventura Boulevard and I breathed a huge sigh of relief. I had been granted a reprieve.

Charmian and I may not have had much money but we ate well. Vince was good friends with Nicky Blair, who owned a restaurant on Sunset. Whenever we wanted a nice dinner, Charmian and I would head "over the hill" into Beverly Hills and get fed by Nicky. Not only did we eat, it was hugely entertaining for us to gawk at all the celebrities who came in to see and be seen. It didn't take long for us to realize that Nicky's was one of the *in* places in town.

I told Max I had started having nightmares about Sonny wanting to kill me because I offended him in my dreams by refusing to go out with him and Max thought that was hilarious. Sonny called and asked me out one more time but I managed to beg off and I didn't hear from him again. About a year later I read in the papers that he had been shot while eating dinner in a restaurant. I wondered if it was the same one he took me to.

About this time, I met a friend of my neighbor's, an actor by the name of Siegfried. I had only known him for a short time when I went into the hospital with appendicitis. When I came home, the incision opened up and I could see all the way down to where I didn't want to think about what I was seeing. I called the doctor in a panic. He told me to stop being such a baby and just pour hydrogen peroxide over it and cover it with gauze. I couldn't possibly do this for myself and enlisted Chuck to come over and do it for me. I was lying in bed and had, for some insane reason, left my door unlocked. Suddenly a black woman was looming over me with a heavy pot in her hands and proceeded to smash it over my head. I was knocked to the floor and blood was streaming down my face and my arms and all over my nightgown when I saw her come toward me, holding a pair of scissors. I was barely conscious as she raised the scissors above her head and, as if in slow motion, as I lay on the floor unable to move, I saw the downward motion of the blades coming toward me. I was certain I would die. The tips of the scissors were inches away from my chest when a hand came down and grabbed the woman's wrist and pulled her away from me. It was Siegfried. He wrestled the crazed lunatic all over my apartment and eventually wrestled her out of my apartment. After a few minutes, he came back and lifted me off the floor onto the bed where I lay completely dazed and disoriented. He drove me to the same doctor who didn't give a damn about my open appendectomy incision, and this completely bored and uninterested doctor cleaned up my wounds, bandaged them and said I was fine without doing any further tests or finding out if I had a concussion.

I found out the woman who had tried to kill me was Siegfried's former girlfriend who thought I had stolen him away from her. Trying to kill me was not enough for her. While we were at the hospital she had painted the inside of my little MG yellow with oil paint and I didn't find that out until I discovered Siegfried trying to clean up the mess. When I went to the police in Van Nuys to report the crime, they said not to bother them, that they didn't get involved in family disputes. I became very angry and frustrated, "I don't even know the woman! She's not my family and she tried to kill me!" The more I insisted they do something the more they ignored me. I gave up and went home to nurse my wounds and called Chuck to ask him to come over and deal with the re-opened gaping hole where my appendix used to be. A few weeks later Kevin called to say he had heard what happened and saw Siegfried talking and laughing on the Universal lot with my would-be killer who worked there as a film editor. He told me he wanted to walk over and knock the crap out of both of them. He would have had my blessing.

My apartment became a convenient place to stay for friends who needed room and board while finding something permanent. Alena came and went a few times between trips to San Francisco and Mexico, Charmian stayed until she found her own apartment a few blocks away, Rosemaria came down to make a fortune in real estate so she'd be free to follow an acting career, but by the time she made her fortune, she no longer wanted to be an actress and decided to study opera instead. After divorcing her second husband, Alena came to stay with me again.

Kevin Casselman, Alena's agent, set it up for her to go to the Golden Globes with Maximillian Schell, a very distinguished, famous actor whose work I was very familiar with. Alena wasn't home when he came to pick her up and he took a liking to me. We talked for a few minutes with him showing little interest in anything I said when suddenly he lunged at me across the coffee table and I ducked and ran into the bedroom. He chased after me and I hopped on top of the bed to the other side of the room as he tried to grab me. I was laughing like crazy the whole time, thinking this was the most ridiculous scene I ever could have imagined – Max Schell, award winning actor, was acting like a crazed teenager. He was determined to get to me and I was just as determined that he wouldn't and in the middle of all this juvenile high jinx, Alena came home, thank God, because I had a very small apartment. Later that evening, Alena brought Maximillian over and he acted like nothing had happened. They had had a great time at the Golden Globes, especially since he won for best actor. But, for whatever reason, a future for the two of them together was not to be.

Alena had not been in town long when she was "discovered" eating dinner in a restaurant. Because she was so stunning, for her, "getting discovered" was inevitable. A director, Terence Young, wanted her to come to Italy and test for a new movie he was about to start production on, *The Amazons*. He was interested in Alena for the leading role of "Queen of the Amazons." She was still dating Chuck when she left for Europe where she met actor Bo Hopkins in Spain and wrote to Chuck and told him their relationship was over. Of course she won the leading role in the movie and before she even started filming, fell in love with her leading man Angelo Infanti, who had been one of Al Pacino's bodyguards in Italy in *The Godfather*.

It was difficult for me to witness how easy it was for Alena to attract work. With her beauty, all she had to do was *be*. I, on the other hand, was always reaching out to people, trying to meet casting directors, doing plays, writing letters and postcards to producers hoping something would pay off. It seemed to me as if everything were roses for her. But, of course it wasn't. She was having relationship problems with the people she was working with and was dealing with her own demons. She wrote me beautiful letters and poems from Italy and we consoled each other through our letters.

Kevin Casselman, Alena's agent, allowed us to have a huge party to celebrate Alena's homecoming and imminent stardom at his mansion in Beverly Glen. The kitchen was three times as big as my entire apartment. The rest of the house was immense and outside were tennis courts and a pool. Gloria Swanson was a regular visitor and stayed in Kevin's guest house when she was in town. The first time I met her, I thought I was looking at a woman who was in her forties. She reached out her hand to shake mine and said with gusto and warmth, "Hi, I'm Swanson, who are you?!" She believed in natural health and healing and was far ahead of me in the knowledge and practice of healthy eating and shunning sugar and other toxins. It would be years before I caught up with her.

We invited everybody we knew to the party and it ended up a massive affair, with one of Alena's boyfriends catering the party for free. Two actors I had been dating were vying for my affections and Kevin Dobson had brought his sister so she could be a part of this huge Hollywood scene. After more than a few drinks, Kevin brought me over to where his sister was sitting on the couch next to Alena and, with the two of them as witnesses, asked me to marry him. I was stunned. I assumed it was only the alcohol speaking and I brushed it aside. The next day we talked about it seriously when he was sober and we both agreed that the two of us getting married wasn't the best idea since he still didn't seem to be through with Susan.

Meanwhile, at another party, I met an actor I had seen on television many times and we started going out. He more than filled the bill as the quintessential dark, handsome Italian New York actor type that set my heart beating. He said he was separated from his wife, but later I learned he was only separated because he came out from New York to work on a television series. We double-dated with his co-star on the series, Don Meredith, and his gracious, beautiful wife. Don, like Max Baer, was the life of the party. But one time, when the four of us were in the car driving, Don lit up a joint and started smoking. I was horrified. To me, anybody who smoked marijuana was a dope fiend. I said to my friend, "I can't be in the car with this. We have to get out." They all looked at me like I was a visitor from another planet, but Don put out the joint and dropped us off at a movie theater. During the movie, I had to sneak out to the ladies' room and vomit. I had been doing that a lot lately and would soon find out it wasn't just something I ate.

After Alena came back from Italy she spent time in Palm Springs with one of her many admirers who didn't have a chance in heck of ever winning her love. So she would have a place to live in Los Angeles, her Palm Springs admirer had rented a suite for her at the Sunset Marquis, which was where many out of town New York actors stayed when they were working in Hollywood. With her earnings from *The Amazons*, she was planning on buying a house and possibly having me move in with her, which would help her out with house payments and help me out by having to pay a lower rent.

It didn't take long for Rosemaria to find the perfect house for Alena, and I was offered a pretty decent role on *Kojak*. But fate intervened. One night the pain in my abdomen which had been bothering me for a year and which the all-knowing doctors had told me was my overactive imagination, became unbearable. I knew it wasn't another kidney stone because it wasn't that kind of localized piercing pain. It felt like it was all over my lower abdomen. I called Chuck and told him what was happening and begged him to take me to the hospital. Both he and Kevin came over and drove me to one emergency room after another. Every E.R. we went to turned me away without helping me. I had no insurance and, as the E.R. personnel coldly observed me crying and begging for pain medication, they assumed I must be a drug addict. Finally, when I was barely conscious, an ambulance took me from yet another E.R. that had rejected me and sped me off to USC County Hospital. By this time, I was out of my mind with pain and in and out of consciousness. I remember the doctor who examined me saying he thought I might have cysts on my ovaries and inserted something sharp up my vagina. He did puncture some cysts and told me I should be fine soon. But I wasn't. I prayed for an end to the pain.

That was the last thing I remember until I saw a black tunnel up above me and then someone was slapping my face and yelling, "She's going into shock!" Apparently, I did pass away on the operating table but obviously, they managed to bring me back. They took out a chunk of my intestines that had become clogged and was spreading peritonitis all over my abdomen. They sewed me back up, put all kinds of tubes into more than one orifice and wheeled me into a ward with about five other people. I remember none of this. My friends, and I still don't know who all was there, were in the waiting room waiting for me to wake up and when I finally did, my first words were, "Kitty, where's Kitty?" The nurse frantically ran out into the waiting room and told my friends, "I think she's regaining consciousness and she's asking for her friend Kitty. Are any of you here Kitty?!" My friends had to tell her, no, none of them were Kitty. Kitty was my cat.

My memory of my time in the hospital is hazy. The first thing I saw when I woke up was a huge flower arrangement with a card that said, "Who loves ya, baby?" It was from Telly. I remember Rob coming to visit, having flown all the way from Oak Harbor. I don't know how he got away but the fact that he came to make sure I was okay made me fall in love with him all over again. My agent and two other friends visited, but Alena had taken off for Palm Springs before I even fully woke up. I never knew why the person who was supposed to be such a good friend was a no show when I was in the hospital and never called to check up on me. But my mother and Georgia called often, worried sick about me, and I assured them I would be out of the hospital in no time. Chuck and Kevin didn't come by, but they had saved my life so I was eternally grateful to them for that. I was told my intestines had rotted away because of a blockage and peritonitis had set in. By weird coincidence, one of our Navy friends was now a doctor at USC County Hospital, and he told me in confidence that the botched appendectomy probably created the blockage. Apparently, the doctor who performed the surgery was going through a rough divorce and his work had become sloppy. I had already figured out that much. If the ambulance hadn't taken me to USC when it did, I would have died.

Kitty was foremost on my mind. As it turned out, a man I didn't even know, a friend of a friend, ended up taking Kitty to his house, where Kitty lived in the bathroom until I got out. It was my strong desire to see Kitty again and making sure he was all right that really motivated me to get better. I trudged up and down the hallways hanging on to my IV pole as many hours a day as they would let me. Then, because it was a teaching hospital and I had no family to say no, some student doctors decided to do a spinal tap on me. I objected strenuously, said I couldn't go through any more pain and I didn't want them to do it. They ignored me and I endured the excruciating pain of a spinal tap for no reason at all. They wanted to learn how to do a spinal tap, I was a welfare case and I could be of use to them. Two days later I told them I was leaving.

Kitty's new friend was the one who came to pick me up at the hospital and took me by his house to pick up Kitty. I wept with joy to see that he was safe and gave him lots of pets and hugged him. I had given notice that I was moving out of my apartment just before I ended up in the hospital and how, when and who moved my things and stored them for me is a blur. I was so weak by the time I got out of the hospital (I weighed around 95 pounds), I felt like a little bit of a breeze could knock me over. It would be awhile before I got my strength and my faculties back.

When my new friend dropped Kitty and me off at the Sunset Marquis where I would stay with Alena until we moved into her house, I desperately wanted to take a bath and wash the big orange spot off my back which was still there from the spinal tap. But Alena's new boyfriend, Dirk Benedict, arrived straight off the set of his TV series and said he wanted to shower to get his makeup off. I asked Alena if he please couldn't wait because I was close to collapsing and really needed to shower and get into bed but Alena told me to sit and wait while Dirk showered. I was too weak to argue.

After Dirk finished in the bathroom I was finally able to shower and get into bed. I was on the verge of falling asleep when Kevin appeared by my bed and lay down beside me. He started saying crazy things about getting back with me and how hard it had been for him to decide between Susan and me. I hardly knew how to respond. I was so dead tired and weak all I could do was listen until I fell asleep.

I went by the *Kojak* set as soon as I was able and saw Telly and thanked him for the flowers. My agent had informed me a small role was coming up before the end of the season and I would be doing it. I was grateful for any good news. Until then, all I wanted to do was rest and be with Kitty and make him feel loved after the ordeal he had been through.

I had two scenes in my *Kojak* episode. In the first scene with Dabney Coleman and Jane Elliott, I actually had a few lines, and in the second scene I walked to my car and as soon as I sat inside and turned the key, an explosive blew it to smithereens. But it was a credit and I was happy to be on the set. I took loads of pictures of my car being blown up and all the cast and crew. I envied Kevin for being on the show as a regular and never having to say goodbye to everyone, until whenever the show was cancelled. Meanwhile, it was back to temping for me. My office skills weren't the best but I had high hopes of working as an actress and soon, never having to work in an office again.

One night I had dinner with Reid Smith and his girlfriend and met a man named Bill Stark who produced several shows at Universal, and the two of us hit it off. A few nights later, I went to dinner with him and Jack Webb and his girlfriend at a restaurant called Dominick's. Apparently, it was *the* place to go for the A-listers even though we entered through the kitchen and we were all seated together at crowded tables in the dining room with barely enough space for any of us to move. But anybody who was anybody was there, including Mary Tyler Moore, who entered through the kitchen ahead of us, and I couldn't fathom why people with all the money in the world who could go to the finest restaurants in town would want to eat in a cramped little restaurant like Dominick's.

Kevin still wasn't through with me. He invited me to go to the affiliates' banquet with him and I, excited about meeting all the movers and shakers in the television business, said yes. My mother made a dress for me and I anticipated a fun evening, even if I still wasn't sure of Kevin's intentions toward me. A week before the big night, Kevin came to me, apologized, and gave me some inane reason why he had to take Susan to the banquet. I packed away the dress where it stayed until I gave it away to Goodwill.

That disappointment didn't stop me from responding whenever he called. One day we drove out to Will Rogers Park and found ourselves all alone on the polo field. We threw a Frisbee back and forth, and Kevin paced and shouted out all his great plans for forming his own production company and creating a series that would star George Savalas. There was no doubt in my mind that, with his drive and determination, he would accomplish whatever he set his mind to.

Through the years, even after Kevin and Susan were living together and had a daughter, he would call me and want to get together. Sometimes I met him at a restaurant and we talked about what could have been, which was entirely pointless because now he was committed to Susan.

One time, after my second marriage was on shaky ground, he suggested that we take our daughters to the zoo together. I told him that was crazy since both our daughters would tell our spouses – and then what?

I had one last interval with him when he was going through yet another "divorce" from Susan and I was once again single. He took me up to Santa Barbara so he could show me his mansion in Montecito and his beach house on a cliff overlooking the ocean. Then I never heard from him again. Maybe this was his final moment of revenge to get back at me for sitting in Telly's trailer instead of his all those years ago. He had said he'd never forget.

CHAPTER 9

Winning the West with Bruce Boxleitner

ALENA AND I SETTLED COMFORTABLY into the new home Rosemaria had found for her in the Valley and I waited for the acting jobs to come rolling in. They didn't. So like all young girls, I focused on dating the various guys who came my way. One of them was Jesse Vint, who had starred in Max Baer's movie *Mason County Line* with his brother Alan. One night, Alena and I and some others were swimming in Jesse's pool and it became obvious that Alena and Jesse hit it off. That was fine with me. I had already met someone who interested me more.

When Max's movie, *The McCullochs*, was about to go into production, I worked in his office, mostly retyping the same script. One day Max's new production manager, Alan Godfrey, walked through the door. He was several years older than me, had salt-and-pepper hair and a congenial, outgoing personality and we hit it off right away.

Everybody on the production staff started hanging out after work and in no time at all, Alan and I became good friends and I eventually found out about our near-misses on *The Strawberry Statement* and *Then Came Bronson*. My green MG had broken down in just about every intersection in L.A. It was hard to find a street where I hadn't been stranded because of that poor old car. Every time I called Alan, he would come rescue me, help me get the car towed and drive me to where I needed to go.

By this time, John Lombardo had cast me in another play so I was coming home late at night. One night, I arrived home to an empty house and went straight to bed. I had been asleep for a few minutes when Alan, Alena and some other people came tromping into the house and woke me up.

"Why didn't you join us?" Alan asked. I responded, barely awake," I didn't know you were all out together. Why didn't you call?" Alan seemed confused. "I was going to leave a note for you but Alena said she would." Alena seemed nonplussed as she said, "Oh sorry, I forgot." No, she didn't. She wanted to have my friends for herself. But I didn't know that then.

That was only one of many times when Alena tried to shut me out of, not only her life, but my own as well. Her startling beauty won the attention of anyone who saw her but she wanted me nowhere near any of the rich and famous people who came into her life because she was so incredibly insecure. She would go out of her way to make sure I never met them. I had welcomed her into my life with open arms and shared everything and everybody with her and now I was living in her home, contributing to her house payments but, as she later explained when I questioned her about why she wanted me to stay away from her friends, she was afraid they would end up liking me more than her.

I had set her up on a date with Reid Smith and had warned her about him. I said that he was a good friend to me but that he dated a lot of women and she shouldn't take anything he says about a relationship seriously. He said those things to everybody. I firmly believe close female friends should keep those kinds of confidences between each other. Not Alena. Reid called me the next day and said "Alena is no friend of yours. The first words out of her mouth when I picked her up were, 'Britt told me I shouldn't believe anything you say to me.'"

Living with her was definitely a factor in my willingness to escape to Malibu on weekends to stay with Alan and his best friend and roommate Paul Krasny. During my years with Alena, both our lives were so focused on her

I had become a co-star of my own life. If my life were a movie, she would have been the star and the marquee would have read; *The Story of Britt Lind Starring Alena Johnston*. Wherever I went and whoever I talked to the greeting was the same; "Oh hi, Britt, how's Alena?" This couldn't go on.

The play I was doing for John Lombardo was called *Susan Slept Here* and I loved my role. Bill Ewing was my leading man and Dick DeCoit the second lead. We worked very well together, even though I was supposed to be a lot younger than Bill and he was actually in real life younger than me. In the middle of the run, Bill was cast in a series and Frank Bonner was brought in to replace him. The whole time I worked with him, I kept trying to get him to look at me during our scenes together and he just wouldn't do it. That didn't stop him from being funny. I guess the people who cast *WKRP In Cincinnati* must have thought so too because he ended up being cast as a regular on the show.

When I stayed with Alan and Paul in Malibu, Alan's son and daughter by his ex-wife would come to visit as well. He did not get along well with his ex-wife and there was tension all around for years to come with him, his kids, his ex-wife and me. She threatened once to drive the kids and herself off a cliff if he didn't send her more money. And after my daughter Erika was born she called me and said that she was going to burn down our house with Erika and me in it. I had no doubt that she was deadly serious and she scared the living daylights out of me. To this day, I regret I wasn't a better stepmother and closer to Alan's children but I was young and lived in my own selfish world and wanted nothing to do with a woman who I considered dangerous. I had already been through that once before.

We found a house to rent on Valley Vista in Sherman Oaks and I hoped that after moving away from Alena I could finally become the focus of my own life with Alan. Kitty seemed content there and that mattered a lot. Even after he had to spend time imprisoned in a bathroom the whole time I was in the hospital and even as I moved him from place to place, he was my main comfort and accepted me unconditionally with all my flaws, which were many. I was obsessed with finding acting work and when the jobs did not materialize, I became desperate and depressed. Even though Alan loved me, he was as obsessed with his career as I was with mine. Kitty was the only living thing that gave me real comfort.

Besides being a talented director, John Lombardo was an accomplished comedy actor and was cast in a play called *Norman is That You?* as Milton Berle's son. They toured all over the country and one night about one o'clock in the morning the phone rang. A call in the middle of the night is always a worrisome thing. "Is somebody we know dead?" is always my first thought. Alan picked up and I could hear the voice on the other end of the line from my side of the bed, "Hello, this is Miltie! How the hell are ya?!" It was Milton Berle and John calling us after a performance and they were oblivious to the time. "It's two o'clock in the morning and we were sound asleep. Other than that, we're fine." Alan replied. I clamored to say hi to Milton which I did and then John came on and we chatted a bit about their show. I would have loved to see him play Miltie's son but unfortunately the play didn't come to L.A. I had seen him in *The Boys in the Band*, a play that he effortlessly stole from all the other actors. He deserved to be a big Broadway star. I wished that for him so much.

Alan and I both wanted to get married and decided, why wait? Paul Krasny and a girl he was dating volunteered to stand up for us and we planned our wedding trip to Las Vegas. As we were going out the door, the phone rang and Alan ran back in to answer. It was MGM. Gene Kelly was going to direct a TV movie with Rene Taylor and Joe Bologna and they wanted Alan as production manager. Of course, he'd be happy to! But could he get married first? Sure, get married then come back on Monday and get started. We cheered our good luck and headed off to Vegas to tie the knot.

With Alan busy working, I was thrilled to land a role on *The Rookies* as a teenage runaway. I had always admired George Sanford Brown as an actor and my last scene that day was with him, as I died in his arms after being hit by a car. I thought I was finished for the day, when one of the other regulars on the show sat me down on the curb and offered me a drink out of his thermos. I drank in relief that I had done a pretty good job and hadn't gotten fired yet. After one swallow, I realized there was booze in the drink and said, no more thanks, I don't drink alcohol. But he insisted and to be a good sport, I took another gulp and immediately became woozy. Just then they called me for my close up. "Oh no, I thought I was through! George will smell booze on my breath and think I'm totally unprofessional!" But I made it through my dying scene again and all went well.

The next time I saw George I was a dead body on a slab in the morgue, and his wife Tyne Daley walked on to the set. She was absolutely gorgeous in a short yellow dress with a great figure and friendly to everybody. I thought they were a perfect couple. Years later I saw her at Hughes Market in the Valley followed by a huge group of children and I wondered if they were all hers and how she had fit them all in while having a busy acting career.

I was called in to 20th Century Fox to audition for a new series called *Dog and Cat*. I thought I read well, but Kim Basinger ended up getting the part. I will never forget sitting in the outer office going over my lines and seeing Tom Selleck walk in and approach the casting director. He was not a known actor then but I had seen him on a soap opera and in ads for something I couldn't recall. He was extremely handsome. I died a thousand deaths when, in front of everyone in the waiting room, the casting director chastised him, "Tom, there isn't anything in this show for you! I told you I'd let you know when something comes up!" I was so embarrassed for him I wanted to slide under my chair, but Tom took it well, smiled and left. Needless to say, his dogged determination paid off big time.

I was reunited with Jessica Walter when I was cast in her series, *Amy Prentiss*. She played the first female Chief of Detectives in San Francisco. I never would have dreamed that the stalker/murderer in *Misty* would have that infectious sense of humor she had. All the way on the flight up to San Francisco, between her and another actor on the show, Art Metrano, I laughed almost non-stop until our plane landed. She remembered me from *Misty* and was happy to see me again. I didn't have much dialogue, but I had scenes all through the show as I played a benign stalker of her handsome partner, Steve Sandor. Oh well, the last time I was in a movie in San Francisco I didn't have any dialogue at all.

John Lombardo continued to be my savior and cast me in another play. Alan, being very proud of me, forced all his friends to come watch me perform: Bruce Geller, creator and executive producer of *Mission Impossible*, Emmy-award-winning editor and director and his best friend, Paul Krasny, director and producer Bernie Kowalski, casting director Gary Shaffer, and several others. Unlike almost everybody else in the business, Alan was afraid of being accused of nepotism but he figured if his friends thought I was a good actress and wanted to hire me that was up to them.

Alan was asked to work on another show at MGM called *Super Cops* and he had me attend a screening where they were looking at possible stars for the show. I still clearly remember watching footage of a young Nick Nolte, thin and pale, in a small part in a TV movie with Andy Griffith. As he absolutely did not fit my image of the dark, Italian New Yorker, I emphatically voted no on casting him. Even though his acting was okay he didn't appeal to me at all. After my bad call regarding Dustin Hoffman I don't know why I thought anybody should listen to my opinion, but they did. I preferred Alan Feinstein, a tall, sexy, good-looking New York actor who I had had a crush on when I had watched him on a soap opera *Love of Life*. Steven Keats, who had blown me up in my Volkswagen on *Kojak* and still slightly scared me, was cast opposite Alan. They were a great team but the show didn't last long. A few years later, *Starsky and Hutch* picked up the mantle on that same cop buddy theme.

Bruce Geller created and was executive producing *Bronk*, a show starring Jack Palance, and he hired Alan as co-producer. After the show had filmed a few episodes, Bruce asked Alan if he wanted to do a rewrite on one of the scripts involving a brother and a sister who were on a murder spree. Somewhere along the line, between Bruce and Alan, they decided the episode should be a vehicle for me; the brother was written out and the episode became all about Jack Palance and me. I was fully aware of his track record as an actor and was afraid I would get thrown acting opposite someone of his caliber. But, like most veteran actors, he was warm and friendly and easy to work with. I was hesitant to ask him to run lines but he came to me and asked if I would like to and we ran lines again and again until I was completely secure. This was my first guest-starring role and I wanted to do well. Dick De Coit and Frank Bonner visited me on the set when I was preparing to do my big emotional scene with Jack and I was so nervous I could hardly talk to them. But thanks to Jack, it went well and I was happy with what I had done.

After hearing me sing in a nightclub one night with a friend's band, Bruce Geller became my chief supporter and mentor. His dream was to write and produce a Broadway show, and he was determined that that was where I should be headed as well. He bought me all the albums of famous Broadway shows and I went ahead and learned a lot of the songs, even though Broadway was a much bigger goal than I could ever visualize for myself. Working in television shows was all I expected and would make me very happy. I took singing lessons because I loved it and because my teachers, Lee and Sally Sweetland, kept telling me I was a singer who acted, not the other way around. Going to my singing lessons was better than going to a psychiatrist and I treasure every moment that I had with them. One day I was sitting in their kitchen drinking tea when Jane Russell walked through the door for her lesson. She may have been a legend but she was also a nice lady and could really sing. Other famous people studied with the Sweetlands, but Jane is the one who made the most lasting impression on me. I'm glad I didn't ask her about Marilyn. I guess Marilyn must have been to her what Alena had been to me; "Oh, hi Jane, what was Marilyn Monroe really like?" Jane was more than enough of a talent in her own right.

At some point in time, Lee and Sally must have put in a good word for me with the Music Center people. I was shocked when my agent called and said that I had an audition for the musical *Gigi* at the Dorothy Chandler

Pavilion. Katharine Hepburn was the star. I was to audition for the role of "Gigi." At the Music Center, I walked into a huge rehearsal hall and faced a group of people at the far end of the room behind a table. I handed the accompanist my music and launched into "I Could Have Danced All Night." When I was finished, there was total silence and I froze. Was I *that* bad? No one said a word for what seemed like minutes. Then someone behind the table said, "Go with him." The piano player stood up, taking my sheet music, and waved at me to follow him. I almost had to run to keep up as we wandered through one corridor after another. Finally, I found myself on a stage in the biggest, most gorgeous theater I had ever seen. There was one man seated in the audience in the middle of the orchestra section. The piano player sat himself on a stool at the grand piano and gestured at the lone audience member and said, "Britt Lind, Alan Lerner." I smiled, heard my intro and began to sing. I was throwing myself into the song whole-heartedly when I realized in the middle of the song, "Oh my God, that's Alan J. Lerner! He wrote this song!" Somehow, I managed to remember the lyrics and finish on a perfect high note. Mr. Lerner said a few words to me of which I have no memory and I followed the piano player out.

I waited and waited, and finally heard from my agent, "Lerner likes you but Hepburn wants her protégé to do the part. Lerner doesn't want the protégé and so there's no decision yet." Lerner and Hepburn were fighting over who would play the role and I had a feeling I would come out the loser. And I did. Hepburn won, the protégé got the part and my career as a musical stage actress failed to launch. I vowed never to go through the agony of another musical audition again but, as always, fate intervened.

Lee and Sally must have put in another good word for me because I was called in again to audition at the Music Center. Debbie Reynolds was going to star in *Gypsy* and I was auditioning for the role of "Gypsy Rose Lee." *My* Debbie who had talked to me when I was a kid and waved at me as she drove by my house! I had a good feeling about this even though I didn't know any of the songs and had to learn one fast. They wanted to hear "Little Lamb" so I took the sheet music in to Lee and Sally and the song, which was about lying about your age for show business reasons and talking to stuffed animals, felt so personal to me I had no trouble learning it. Again, I went in and faced the long table of people in the rehearsal hall. I sang the song, which was placed perfectly for my range and I left on an optimistic high. I was right to feel that way. They called me back to sing "Let Me Entertain You," and I asked my friend Katy, who was a professional dancer and actress, to help me prepare a dance routine. It went well, and again I waited for the agent to call, and he did – "The Music Center people liked you but Debbie wants her daughter Carrie to play the part. If they won't let Carrie do the show then Debbie won't do it either." I couldn't believe that. The subscription booklets had already been mailed out. She couldn't back out now. I was told Carrie had no interest in singing and didn't want to accept the role. I stayed hopeful. Maybe there were other actresses in contention for the part, I wasn't told. As far as I was concerned, it was between Carrie and me. None of us won the role because Debbie dropped out and I was crushed. This time I really meant it; never again would I go through this terrible stress and uncertainty.

At the same time these auditions were happening, I had been called in to play a Norwegian lady in a Western. My accent was right on, I was the perfect age and had the perfect look and I *was* Norwegian. I had dreamed of being in a western since I was a little girl playing cowboys and Indians and pretending I was Annie Oakley, and that dream was about to come true. The producers called my agent to make the deal and then fate once more intervened; either the Writers Guild or Screen Actors Guild (I don't remember which) went on strike and the movie was put on hold. I never heard from the producers again or know if the movie was ever made.

After several stints as production manager and co-producer, Alan started actually producing shows. We were now friends with an extremely talented song-writer named Porter Jordan, who we met through my friend Chuck and who had written a brilliant Broadway musical. The problem was, every time a backer agreed to put up the money to produce it, that person would die. Porter seemed cursed but he still wrote great songs.

He decided to teach me how to sing in a recording studio voice, so he began the task of trying to bury my Broadway belt and operatic soprano and resurrect me as Olivia Newton John. By this time, for some reason, Alan, Kitty and I were living in an apartment on Tower Road off Sunset. Porter would come over to rehearse, mix a little vodka with Crangrape to loosen me up and attempt to turn me into Olivia. One day, while waiting for Porter to arrive, I looked out the window and saw that a car was on fire several yards down the hill. Suddenly, I was afraid it might be Porter's car. I ran downstairs and slowly approached the burning car and saw Porter standing a few feet away as the fireman put out the fire. Porter will never let me forget that the first thing I said to him was, "Did you get your guitar out?" He contends that all I cared about was rehearsing even though his car was in ashes. I insist I cared deeply that he didn't lose his guitar as well as his car.

I was making headway on this journey toward sounding like Olivia when the opportunity came up for me to record a song as source music for the show Alan was producing. Porter would write the lyrics and Tom Scott, the legendary saxophone player, would write the music. This was my first time in a recording studio and he told me Olivia had recorded there as well. I don't know if I believed him. Anyway, there I was at Universal Studios recording a song that would be played on a hit TV show. Porter guided me through the process every step of the way. Then I left Porter and the music producers to their editing chores. A few days later I was called in to Universal to hear the result. As soon as I walked into the editorial building I heard my voice coming over speakers from every direction. It was echoing throughout the whole building. After all the post production had been done, I couldn't believe it was me sounding so incredibly professional. Porter had managed to turn me into Olivia Newton John and I liked it. The feeling was so satisfying I had to finally admit that maybe at heart I was a singer who acted.

Porter ended up writing another source song that I sang on the same show, and thinking I was ready for a proper recording career, he arranged for us to have dinner with a music producer. He says I tanked the interview because the man ordered veal and I made a big stink about it. I don't remember that but it sounds like me. However, other things in life were taking precedence and my recording career was never to be.

After living in our first small house and our apartment on Tower Road, Paul Krasny gave us the opportunity to rent a house he owned up in the hills on Beverly Ridge. When my mother came to visit, she called it a movie star house. And it was. It was an L-shaped house built around a swimming pool with a view of the whole San Fernando Valley, and music from outdoor stereo speakers serenaded you as you floated in the pool under the stars looking at the world below. It was while living there that my favorite role came along.

Like I said, ever since I was a little girl, I had dreamed of acting in a western movie: cowboys, Indians, shoot-em-ups, the whole nine yards. John Mantley who had produced *Gunsmoke* for many years was going to produce a mini-series called *How the West Was Won* for MGM. It was to star James Arness and a new young actor named Bruce Boxleitner and feature a host of veteran cowboy actors. When I went in to read, even though the role of "Erika Hanks" seemed perfect for me, I didn't think I had much of a shot at getting the role. I was competing with many other actresses, some of them "names." I wore a high collar white blouse and tried to look as pristine and untouched as the character I was playing and, having prepared for days, read well. (Thank God, I had abandoned Charles Conrad long ago and went back to my own "method" of getting into mood and character.)

I waited to hear and, after an eternity, my agent called and said the executive producer John Mantley wanted to meet me at a restaurant on Ventura Boulevard. I thought, "Oh no, doesn't he know I'm married? What is this?" But I drove down the hill to meet him and he explained why he wanted to talk to me in private. One of the studio execs overseeing the movie hated Bruce Geller and since Alan worked for Bruce and was his close friend he didn't want me in the series. This exec also said I was too old to play a teenager and wouldn't look right next to Bruce Boxleitner. In *Bronk*, which had also been filmed at MGM, I had played a dual role of a young girl and an older, murderous woman, so that was his reason for rejecting me.

John and I discussed all this for awhile and he reassured me that no one else they had read was more perfect for the role than I was; Arness wanted me, John wanted me and that was all that mattered. Later I found out Eva Marie Saint, one of the regulars, tried to keep me off the show as well because I was a blond like her. Even though I was playing the love interest of her son in the show, she considered me competition and made her thoughts known to the studio through her husband, who was one of the producers. But Mantley and Arness prevailed and I was cast. Once I was on location, however, the hairdresser told me she was going to take some of the blond streaks out of my hair and then went ahead and dyed my hair brown.

Bruce and I met for the first time on the plane and for some reason his girlfriend, who played his sister, wasn't coming to the location yet. They had met and fallen in love during the filming of the pilot, but she wasn't there when most of my scenes with Bruce were shot. The van that was taking us from the airport to our hotel had to go by the set on the way and I still remember that awesome moment when we pulled up to park by a hillside and suddenly a large contingent of cavalry came riding over the hill and passed by us as the cameras rolled. The bright colors of the uniforms, the powerful horses kicking up dust as their hooves pounded into the dirt made my heart stop. It was everything I had ever dreamed of and better. Later on, when we'd been filming for awhile and the villains who had tried to rape me rode into to town looking for Bruce, my rescuer, the affect was chilling. The townspeople were all in hiding and I was behind the camera watching the bad guys slowly ride toward us with their rifles slung over their saddles in front of them. It was like being a kid again, but this time everything was for real. I didn't know how I could be so lucky as to be able to experience this, but I thanked God I was. The cast read like a who's-who of character actors I had been watching since childhood and it seemed like some of them could drink all night and get up early the next morning none the worse for wear. Jack Elam was my next-door neighbor on my floor and he would prowl around at night and bang on my door wanting to be let in. I don't think he remembered a thing in the morning.

If Bruce and I didn't have an early call, we'd have breakfast together in town. I was always too excited to eat very much so Bruce would finish my breakfast. Soon word came back from MGM after they had seen the dailies – I was getting skinnier and Bruce was gaining weight, time to do the reverse. In the restaurant and the hotel there were pictures on the walls of famous actors who had worked in westerns in Kanab. We were filming in one of the most famous western movie towns in the world. When Bruce and I and one of the bad guys in the film hiked through Zion National Park we rested in a small cabin that had been part of a set in a Clint Eastwood movie. After dreaming and hoping for this all my life it was almost unreal how surrounded and immersed I was in the culture of western movie making.

Filming ended in Utah and it was a letdown but I looked forward to working at Warner Brothers and Lake Sherwood when we got home. When I was a kid watching *Surfside 6, Bronco, Cheyenne, Maverick* and all the other Warner Brothers shows on television I would thrill as the logo and voice-over came on before every show, "FROM THE ENTERTAINMENT CAPITAL OF THE WORLD!" and over that announcement would be an aerial shot of the Warner Brothers lot. It seemed like the end of the rainbow to me, paradise on earth. And that is where we would film our interiors; in the very same place where one of my childhood idols, Diane McBain, used to shoot *Surfside 6*.

When I came home to Beverly Ridge I found out that there had been a lot of partying going on at the house in my absence. My friend, Georgia, had visited, John Lombardo had come up with his long-time friend, Isabel Sanford, who had a series, *The Jeffersons*, and Porter and his friends had been there, of course. I don't think I was missed by anyone except Kitty, who had to sleep on top of me every night to make sure I wasn't going anywhere any time soon. Alan was happy to be working and so was I. Both our identities were so wrapped up in acting and producing we thought of little else. He was at Universal by now and I was going to continue working on *How the West Was Won* in a few weeks. I was finally too busy to think about being despondent.

I decided Kitty needed a friend and somehow Mabel, another Siamese kitten, came into our lives. She was quiet and very sweet, not demanding and talkative like Kitty, but the two of them became inseparable. They both slept with me and were not allowed outside. One day, I could not find Mabel. I searched for her inside and outside, talked to all the neighbors, but no one had seen her. Somehow, she had sneaked outside and become lost. I was determined to find her. I looked in the shelters and kept talking to the neighbors. Finally, someone explained the facts of life to me; there were coyotes who came into the neighborhood at night; Mabel had probably been killed. I refused to accept what they told me and kept looking for her until even I knew it was hopeless. Another terrible loss during what should have been a happy time.

On the set in Burbank Studios, I finally met Bruce's girlfriend, Katherine Holcomb, who he would soon marry. Then we shot added exteriors and close-ups at Lake Sherwood which were directed by John Mantley. He was the executive producer, but the first real screen director I had worked with since Clint Eastwood. In the scene where Bruce tells me he is leaving and asks me to go with him and I tell him I can't, John talked to me with such sensitivity the tears flowed effortlessly down my face and with more genuine emotion than was the case in Utah where the director had merely yelled at me, "Lots of tears! Lots of tears!"

Knowing that my six hours of the series was forever over was painful. Bruce, Katherine and the others would continue shooting as long as the show got ratings but I had to leave my new family and adjusting to normal life was difficult. I hadn't worked enough to realize this was the unending cycle of an actor's life: getting a job, becoming close to the other actors and then moving on, often never seeing those people again. I had always felt that loss after a play closed and even when we vowed to get together soon, lasting friendships were rare. I haven't seen Bruce since our last scene at Lake Sherwood, but I'm happy he's done so well.

Years later, I worked with James Arness again in his own series, *McClain's Law*, playing a prostitute who, at one point, gets badly beaten up. When Jim saw me he made a sad face and said, "Oh little Erika, what's happened to you? You used to be such a sweet little girl." He always had a great sense of humor, and at Warner Brothers, when we shot interiors, made me laugh so hard I could hardly pull myself together for my very serious scenes. Why is it that so many veteran actors spend half their time joking just before we have to do a dramatic scene? It always loosened me up, that's for sure.

After I read for that part in *McClain's Law*, I found out I must have been convincing because I was cast before I even made it home. Then, a few days later, when I was in the wardrobe department picking out my clothes with the wardrobe lady, the director and producer walked in. I was being my usual perky self, which came out in spades every time I landed an acting job because I was so happy. They looked at me from afar, very concerned, and approached me cautiously and asked, "You won't lose what you had in the reading will you?" And the perverse side of me chirped in an even perkier voice, "No, don't worry about it. I'll be fine!" I think I did such a good job convincing them in the reading that I was a sullen, jaded prostitute, they forgot I was acting.

After I finished filming *How the West Was Won*, I convinced Alan that it was time for him to get a reversal of his vasectomy. I wanted a baby sometime in the future and since the doctor had said it would take awhile to get the sperm flowing healthy and strong, I figured in a year or two the timing would be perfect. But after auditioning for two pilots, one at Universal and one at Columbia, I was shocked to find out I was already pregnant. I was offered both shows, but the producer of the one I had my heart set on doing at Columbia was told by one of my agents that I was pregnant. I could easily have finished the pilot before I started showing but the agent betrayed my confidence and told them before I had a chance to explain. I lost that role, which Cheryl Ladd and I both had been up for, and they offered it to her. But she wasn't available by then and actress number three happily accepted the role in the Columbia pilot. So instead of the action/ adventure/ spy movie, I ended up in a show about a fireman, played by Kent McCord, who lived and worked in a wooded rural area, whose girlfriend, me, was a school teacher. We shot the show completely on the lot near the "shark lake" and tour buses would drive by regularly and cause us to stop filming until they passed. Sometimes Alan would visit the set with Robert Blake who would constantly ask me when I was going to work on *Baretta*. Alan would always tell him I was busy since Blake was known to be hard on guest stars.

The pilot turned out well and for about a minute we were excited to hear that it sold and was to become a regular series. Then another hit show, that had been on the air a few years, changed networks and knocked us out of the box. Because of getting cast in that show at Universal, my agent arranged for me to go under contract to the studio. That wouldn't last long after my pregnancy became very obvious.

About this time, Farrah Fawcett decided to leave *Charlie's Angels* and a replacement was needed. The producers of the show, Ron Austin and Jim Buchanan, were good friends who we socialized with several times a month. They asked Alan if I would be interested in joining the cast as Farrah's sister. Alan said, "Absolutely not!" What a thankless role that would be!" I wasn't told until much later that Ron and Jim had asked for me. It was a terrible blow to find out Alan rejected the chance for me to be on the show without even talking to me about it.

I was quite large when my agent called and told me I had an interview with Sylvester Stallone for a movie he was about to star in. I asked her if he knew I was big as a house and she said she had told him that. He still wanted to see me. So I went in and met with Sylvester, knowing that getting the part was hopeless. He was much shorter and better looking in person than I had expected and very considerate of my condition. He told me the start of the movie was months away and my pregnancy would be no problem. I think Anne Archer got that part and deserved it. She is one of the most underrated actresses in Hollywood.

It was while I was pregnant that Alan's drinking became a big problem. I had turned a blind eye to it because I still didn't understand what alcoholism was except for having seen *Lost Weekend*, an old movie with Ray Milland, and Alan was certainly not in that kind of bad shape. All of Alan's producer friends drank at lunch and after work and when we went out to dinner on weekends. Even Bruce Geller drank so what's the big deal? Bruce was incredibly successful and Alan wanted nothing more than to follow in Bruce's footsteps. I didn't know it then, but Alan was doing more than drinking.

When I came to Hollywood, I barely knew what cocaine was. When we invited Alan's friends for parties at our house, I couldn't figure out why people would go into the bathroom three or four at a time. How weird. I guess Alan had told them not to snort cocaine in front of his goody-two-shoes wife.

So Alan was drinking, doing drugs, not coming home until late at night and I insisted on telling myself, after he staggered in the door, that he was working late and just had a quick one before coming home. But after awhile, the cocaine changed his easygoing personality. His temper flared easily and he hit me while I was pregnant. Now I was afraid for both myself and my baby. I left that night and stayed with friends until Alan begged my forgiveness and talked me into coming back. Worrying about how the baby, Kitty and I would survive on our own, and wondering where we would live made me weak and indecisive.

We named our baby, Erika, and she truly was beautiful. My mother came down to help out for a week or so and then Susan Dobson, of all people, convinced me that I must have a live-in maid to help take care of Erika. I had run into her at a supermarket in Studio City, where she and Kevin had moved after it was decided she was in and I was definitely out when she became pregnant. She knew she had won and I had lost. It must have put her in a magnanimous mood. My mother loved Alan, who could be as charming as ever when he was sober, and she was very happy for me. I dreaded ever having to disappoint her again. And when she reluctantly left her little Erika to go back to Marysville, our new housekeeper Vilma took over and life went on. Even as I worked and enjoyed my time with Erika, I battled depression, wondering what would happen in the future, bailing Alan out of jail for drunk driving, pretending everything was fine.

Then one night, in a cocaine-driven rage, he hit me again. I called Porter telling him what happened and that I had to leave immediately. He made a few calls and found Erika, Kitty and me a house to live in temporarily. I placed little baby Erika on the bed beside me that night surrounded by pillows to keep her safe and tried to go to sleep. I was frightened of what the future held for us but determined never to go back to Alan. My resolve faded as Alan relentlessly begged for me to come back. Two strikes so far. Would there be a strike three and then what would I do? Obviously, I was a coward and I hated myself for being so weak and dependent.

In the middle of all this upheaval, my friend, Rosemaria, found us a house to buy in the hills of Encino with a pool and a panoramic view of the valley all the way from the blue skies of Woodland Hills to the black smog where Pasadena was supposed to be. On the outside, it looked as if we had everything, but I wondered what I would do if Alan kept drinking. How could he possibly hold a job? A friend whose husband was also an alcoholic came over and suggested she and I go to Al-Anon. Me, go talk about my life in front of strangers? Never. Saying no to her suggestion was one of the worst mistakes I ever made. I still wonder what would have happened if I had gone with her and learned how to deal with Alan's addiction problems.

Instead, I chose to stick my head in the sand and pretend everything was okay. It was so lovely on the outside. Why ruin everything?

One thing about Alan that I very much appreciated was that he loved animals. One day he decided we needed another cat and that we should rescue one from the downtown shelter. The L.A. shelter then was in a dark, depressing building that discouraged anyone from going there to adopt animals. We walked past the cages and saw all the animals who desperately needed homes, and felt overwhelmed with helplessness and pity. We stopped by a group of cages that held one or more cats and we could tell by the tags that they were going to be put to death the next day. One black cat sat and stared at us from the back of her cage and stared at us, as if to say, "Well, what are you waiting for? Take me home." I immediately knew I had to have her. But there was also a gray cat, a striped gray cat, a small, skinny black cat and a brown-and-white cat in adjacent cages all facing death the next day. Alan said, "Let's take them all." I wasn't sure I heard right. "All of them?" He was adamant. "All of them." I wasn't about to question him and rushed off to find someone who worked at the shelter. They all came home with us: Maude, the arrogant black kitty; Gilbert, the Russian Blue; Tilly, the skinny little black kitty; Sullivan, the striped gray kitty; and Millie, the slightly cross-eyed, brown-and-white kitty. We had the handyman make a cat door for them that led out from one of the bathrooms into the garbage can room where I put their litter box and they had the run of the house. Kitty decided to take charge of Maude, made her his best friend and taught her how to talk as incessantly as he did. They both slept on my pillow every night and the rest were scattered all over the bed with barely enough space for Alan and I to move. Every time I looked at them I felt such incredible relief that we had saved them and that now they were alive and happy. I vowed that no matter what happened, I would take care of them and they would stay that way.

But the family was still not complete. A few months later, Alan came back from picking up one of our cats from the vet and, along with our cat, brought home yet another member of the clan. Scooter had been hit by a car and his back legs didn't work quite right; hence the name. It didn't take him long to fit in. I still love Alan's willingness to open our home to so many cats. Not many men would have been so generous.

Alan left Universal and took a job producing *Vega$* for Aaron Spelling. I landed a job on *Starsky and Hutch*. Casting director Joe D'Agosta brought me in and I was halfway through the audition when the director stopped me and said I had the part. I love when it's that easy and I don't have to agonize waiting for word. David Soul, one of the leads, was a congenial guy, sipping on a can of beer throughout the shoot. Paul Michael Glaser was a little more temperamental and in the middle of a scene one day announced that, according to his contract, it was time for him to leave. I ended up doing my close-up with the script supervisor instead of Paul, but I didn't care. To me, the worst day of shooting on a set was better than any good day doing anything else.

I visited Alan on location when he was shooting the movie, *The Man with the Power*, later changed to *The Power Within*, and as soon as I entered the star's mobile home I sensed I didn't belong. I didn't know why at the time. I thought maybe it was because all the actors and crew who were in the mobile home had bonded by now and I was an outsider. All I knew is that everything seemed to be put on hold for the few minutes I visited, leaving me to feel completely out of place. I didn't stay long and felt that they all, including Alan, were happy to see me leave. Much later I found out that like Alan, certain members of the cast were drug users, probably cocaine, and, having been warned by Alan that I was oblivious to the drug use all around me, hid it from me and waited until I was gone to resume their snorting. One of the actors became so addicted, it destroyed his career.

Because of personality clashes with some execs on the show, Alan wanted off *Vega$*. As producer of the show, he had to move to Las Vegas and live at the Desert Inn, but I couldn't leave all our cats and I didn't want Erika living in the atmosphere of Las Vegas. I flew over at least every two weeks and enjoyed being treated like royalty whenever we went to watch famous performers in the big showrooms. Even Johnny Carson asked us to wait after his show so he could have drinks with us. I was impressed. Alan insisted to Aaron that I do a certain starring role on the next show and Aaron, the nicest man in the world, said, of course, but wouldn't Britt want to wait for something better? But Alan insisted this was the one. It was as though he were daring Aaron to fire him.

The set had a carnival-like atmosphere. When I was getting ready for my big crying scene with Caesar Romero, Bob Urich, the star of the show, was tickling my back and making me feel totally discombobulated. I faked my way through the scene. I had to remain in my bathing suit for the entirety of the episode, challenging my personal acting "method" when I had to shoot Moses Gunn dead and react. After seeing the show, the head of casting for Aaron told me I was brilliant which I found to be an inexplicable reaction because I was not especially proud of my performance.

The most exciting thing about doing *Vega$* was actually meeting and working with Tony Curtis. He had a great sense of humor, as did Caesar Romero, and the moments with him went by so quickly I never had a chance to talk to him about his career. After reading his book years later I was glad I hadn't asked him what it was like working with Marilyn Monroe. It was obvious from what he wrote that he hated her for keeping him and the rest of the cast and crew waiting for hours while she did whatever she had to do to prepare to come out and do her scenes.

Kim Basinger came up to star on *Vega$* as well. When she arrived in Las Vegas, everyone was shocked at how much weight she had gained and the wardrobe people scrambled to disguise it. She also made outrageous demands that Aaron himself had to deal with and put a stop to. After she saw herself on television in the role, our friend and casting director Gary Shaffer said she called him and said she was such a terrible actress she never wanted to act again. Several years later she won an Oscar for *L.A. Confidential.*

CHAPTER 10

Finally, My Life's Purpose?

ALAN HAD NOW BECOME AN executive producer of a Universal show called *Quincy, M.E.* and I was mainly focused on Erika and making the house look great. My parents came down and my father put in floor-to-ceiling windows in the master bedroom and French doors leading out to the pool, while my mother and I painted and wallpapered. I was extremely grateful to my parents for working so hard to make improvements on our house and wanted to tell my father how much I appreciated all his hard work. But trying to talk to him was, as always, awkward. He never wanted to have any kind of intimate conversation with me and unspoken resentments on both sides lingered on and made it impossible for me to have a close relationship with him.

I had a fence put around the pool to keep Erika from accidently falling in. But she was also getting baby swimming lessons from the best teacher we could find to make sure she'd always be safe around pools. All the construction and painting my father, mother and I were doing didn't hinder my continuous efforts to get acting work and worry about money. I had read the feature script, *Count to Five*, which Alan had written, thought it was very commercial, and was determined it should be produced. I gave it to my agent and he tried to find possible producers, which he did. But Alan thought he could get a better deal elsewhere and the movie was never made.

My spiritual life at this point was still on hold. You'd think that with all the chaos I was going through I would have finally figured out I needed some direction. Like a lot of people, I would pray for help when things were bad, then as soon as things got back on track I would go back to putting the blinders on, pretending all was well, making bad decisions based on how I *wanted* my life to be and how others perceived it. Erika had filled the empty hole in my heart and Alan would bring his son and daughter home to play with their new little sister. I was still wary of their mother and worried that she would follow through on her threats, but Erika loved her brother and sister and they needed to spend time together.

I was convinced that there was a purpose for me being on this planet. Not only had my life been saved twice, instinctively I knew I wanted to help animals in some way. I had always thought that someday I would become rich and famous and lend my name and donate lots of money to an animal cause. As for the present, the demands of getting in the trenches and being an actual activist was something I didn't have time for, considering that I was a wife, mother, actress and mistress of many cats. That's what I told myself – how convenient.

One day, reading one of many animal magazines I constantly perused, I saw an article about a man who lived in Vancouver, B.C. and had founded an organization called The Sea Shepherd Conservation Society. Paul Watson had co-founded Greenpeace but had broken off with them when he became dissatisfied with the direction they were going. He had risked his life to protect a whale by piloting the tiny Zodiac he was in between the whale and a whaling ship. The article also described how he had been arrested while attempting to protect the lives of baby seals who are still being slaughtered and skinned alive on a yearly basis in Newfoundland. Reading the article, I immediately grasped that Paul was dedicated, sincere, intelligent and didn't get paid one penny. I shared Paul's story with Alan and insisted that we must try to get a television movie made about this man. The next day he went to the executives at CBS and pitched his story about Paul and the Sea Shepherd. They agreed it would make a great movie and told Alan to have Paul flown down for a meeting. This we did, and when Paul arrived, after talking to him for a few minutes, it became obvious that he was the genuine article.

Paul and Alan had their meeting at CBS, but meanwhile, another producer, Tony Bill, had heard of Paul as well and asked to meet with him. Paul was offered a lot of money from Tony for the rights to Paul's story for a feature and, with our blessing, he accepted. It enabled Paul, along with donations from Cleveland Amory, to buy a new ship to replace one that had been destroyed. I was disappointed that we wouldn't be the ones who would get to tell his story but at least now the world would see it via a major motion picture. As it turned out, Tony Bill never did film Paul's story but Paul made other connections in Hollywood, including director, Dick Donner, who eventually led him to many more high profile show business supporters, and fame, via *The Whale Wars* on television.

It was because of Paul I first learned of the baby seal slaughter in Newfoundland. Bridget Bardot and other celebrities and animal welfare groups had been fighting this barbaric "tradition" for many years but I knew nothing about it until I read the article about Paul. The sheer horror of the baby seals being clubbed and skinned alive appalled me and I was inspired to begin writing letters to Canadian officials and getting petitions signed to help in the efforts to end the slaughter. I decided that I would sign over all my acting residuals to the Sea Shepherd from then on and did that for years. I may not have been rich and famous but I had now become an activist. Having spent a lot of time in Canada on vacations with my parents and then, years later, working there, I found Canadians to be kind, compassionate people, and it is shocking and amazing that they still have not been able to convince their government to stop the seal slaughter.

One late afternoon, Kitty was crying to go outside but I was not about to let him out because it was too late and soon the coyotes would come down from the hills. But Kitty kept crying and Alan pressured me to allow him to go out for a few minutes and, against my better instincts, I did. A few minutes later I went outside and called him but he didn't come. I walked up and down the street calling his name but there was no answer. Alan, not at all worried, said, "Come inside. He'll show up before dark." But he didn't come home and I went outside again with a terrible feeling of dread, searching for Kitty for hours. I finally gave up and hoped against hope that he was trapped in someone's garage, which had happened to Gilbert when I couldn't find him. I couldn't sleep a wink all night and got up at dawn and knocked on the door of my neighbor who lived across the street and asked if he would open his garage because Kitty was probably trapped inside. My neighbor hesitated as he spoke to me with downcast eyes and told me he had seen Kitty last night being attacked and killed by coyotes. My neighbor had yelled and run as close to them as he dared but it had all happened so fast he couldn't stop them. My heart stopped and I stumbled backwards and felt like I was going to collapse. My beautiful, cross-eyed, talkative, loving Siamese cat was gone. I was overcome with guilt. I should have stayed outside all night if necessary and not left him to the mercy of coyotes. Being ripped apart by coyotes is a painful, terrifying death and I had let it happen to my best friend who had been with me through every happy and miserable moment of my life in L.A. Even though I had lost many animals through the years, the pain I felt over Kitty was especially agonizing. Only people who feel as connected to animals as my friends and I do can understand how devastating it is when an animal you are so very close to dies a terrible death. Alan tried to comfort me but I was inconsolable. It shouldn't have happened. It was my fault. And the loss was profound. As I sat and gazed out over the Valley, wishing I had never listened to Alan but knowing I shared the blame, my other cats, Maude, Gilbert, Hughes, Millie, Sully, Scooter and Tillie jumped on my bed and lay down beside me. Animals always seem to know when you need them. Years before, Siegfried had taken pictures of Kitty when we lived on Moorpark and he had enlarged and framed one. I still put it up in my bedroom every place I live, his eyes so crossed you'd think it was a wonder he could see anything at all. And he probably never saw those coyotes coming.

Not long after, my little yellow striped Scooter became sick. At first I didn't think anything of it; figured it was just indigestion. When he became weaker and very listless I took him in to the veterinarian but it was too late. The vet told me his system was failing and that Scooter was in a great deal of pain. The kind thing to do would be to put him to sleep so he wouldn't suffer. I loved this little cat whose twisted hind feet hopped and skipped as he moved along in his own funny way and I couldn't bear the thought of letting him go. But I knew I had to. I held Scooter as his sweet, gentle soul left this earth and went to heaven. Even as I cried again over another bitter loss, I was grateful that Alan had brought him home and that Scooter had had a good life with us even though it was for much too short a time.

My agent called with an audition for a feature! It turned out the director was Paul Krasny, which was definitely in my favor, but the producers wanted "names." Paul got his way and I was cast. Then I was off to Miami to film an independent feature called *Joe Panther*. I always loved working with actors I had seen in black-and-white movies when I snuck over to Lorna and Nancy's house to watch TV, and on this set I got to meet another veteran, Ricardo Montalban. Needless to say, he was as handsome and charming as he had been in the MGM movies he made in his heyday. Our good friend, Alan Feinstein, also was working in the movie but we had no scenes together. I played Brian Keith's daughter and had a nice scene with him and A Martinez in the hospital. Brian, like a lot of the old timers, could really put it away all night and somehow appear on the set in the morning ready to go.

I still was not used to leaving fellow actors who I became close to while working together. That was always a wrenching experience for me, but soon shooting was over and I was back home. The good thing now was I had Erika to come back to and, like a friend had said after Erika was born, being with her was like having Christmas every day. Nevertheless, the acting obsession was never far underneath the surface. As an actor, you always wonder if you'll ever work again. Journeyman actors, not under contract like big movie stars to do one movie after another, always feel that dread. Even Henry Fonda admitted he felt that way after every job was finished. But I bided my time, played with Erika and took care of all my kitties while Alan was gone all day at the studio.

With all this free time, I decided I would work as a volunteer at the Motion Picture Home. I thought I might enjoy working with the aging and forgotten people in the home, especially those in the hospital, most of them never receiving any visitors and who needed someone to keep them company, fix their hair, read to them, talk and joke with them and make what was left of their lives worth living. For the healthy seniors, we had many activities like the wheel chair parade, costume parties, and arts and crafts in the occupational therapy room. Dennis Weaver's wife Gerry was especially good at bringing people out of their shell and making them laugh.

One day, Gerry pointed to a beautiful lady who had an ethereal look about her. She asked me, "Do you know who that is?" I immediately recognized Norma Shearer. I remembered seeing her on forbidden TV at Lorna and Nancy's in M.G.M.'s *Romeo and Juliet* when I was young and thought then that she was exquisite. Amazingly, it seemed that she had hardly changed. But Norma always had a strange, far-off look in her eyes. One of the other volunteers told me she was almost blind because of the harsh lighting that had been used on set early in her career. When I or anyone talked to Norma she had a habit of suddenly grabbing our arm and not wanting to let go. She seemed desperate to cling to us and keep us close. After every visit by her husband, who was younger than she by 12 years, she seemed especially depressed. I didn't know what passed between them but gossip had it that he had a younger girlfriend whom Norma was aware of. I thought of how

Norma and her former, then deceased, husband, Irving Thalberg, back in their day, were at the very top of the Hollywood "A" list, living lives of wealth and glamour with all of Hollywood at their feet. Now, here she was, alone and sad, dependent on strangers for companionship and comfort.

Another patient I saw on a regular basis was Lincoln Perry. He mostly laid on his bed and stared at the ceiling, looking extremely despondent. Sometimes he would come out into the hallway and sit, and Gerry and I would try to talk to him but even she, who had been known to make stroke victims smile, couldn't coax a word out of him. She asked me one day if I knew who he really was and I told her I didn't have a clue. "That's Stepin Fetchit," she said. And I was shocked that he was still alive and still looked so young. He was one of the most successful black actors who had worked in the 30s and 40s. He always played a stereotypically lazy character and slowly drawled out his words. I had seen him many times on TV as a child. I had no idea he was still alive and I would have loved to hear his stories. But there was never any response to our questions and eventually we gave up trying to crack open up his self-imposed cocoon. Later I read his biography about the many ups and downs of his career. No one now who hasn't studied the history of movies can fully understand how difficult it was to find employment as a black actor in those days and in order to work he latched onto a character that enabled him to earn a living acting in movies. He did what he had to do within the limited parameters in which society and movie goers found it acceptable for a black actor to function. Later, some people, including a few African Americans, came to look upon him as an object of scorn. I believe that is patently unfair and wish someone would make a movie of his turbulent life and give him the respect due him. I'll never know what made him stare at the ceiling so sadly day after day, but for him or anyone else, it is never easy to be at the top of the world for years then find yourself alone and disrespected at the end of your life.

One day my neighbor called and told me a gray cat was lying dead in her driveway and she thought it was one of mine. I ran up the hill and down her driveway and saw that it was Sully. I knelt down and touched him and he was still and cold. He had no wounds and I assumed he had eaten something poisonous and laid down and died. Again, my heart was broken as I picked him up and took him home and buried him in our back yard. When you choose to adopt animals, because they live much shorter lives than humans, you have to accept that you will experience many deaths as one by one they pass. That never makes it any easier when one of them dies. But I comfort myself by knowing they were loved and taken care of and enjoyed their lives to the fullest. Many people think cats should never be allowed outside and some of mine did prefer to be indoors all the time. I made a choice to let the cats who implored me to be let outside during the day be outside and then locked them up safely inside in the afternoon. Sully had proven it wasn't even safe to be outside during the day, and from then on, while living up in the hills, I wouldn't let my cats out at all. When an animal dies of old age or long illness it is not quite as painful as when they are suddenly taken away from you by tragic accident or events that could have been prevented. Now, my three former feral kitties are prisoners of the house no matter how much they beg and plead to be let out.

I had read a book called *No Acting Please* by Eric Morris, and it both frightened and intrigued me. He had created his own acting method after working in New York with Lee Strasberg, and discovered that Strasberg's method didn't meet all the needs actors had to fulfill in order to create a compelling performance. First of all, his picture on the back of the book made him look extremely intimidating. I remember seeing him play villains on TV and I didn't think that I could ever hold up to his scrutiny in an acting class. His acting method seemed very personal and invasive and I didn't know if I had it in me to expose my inner demons and all my hideous flaws to a room full of strangers. Eventually, somehow, I found the courage to attend a class and it was just as scary as I thought it would be. Eric was relentless in getting actors to open up and allow their emotions to flow unimpeded by using various exercises he had created. I knew I would never have the guts to do what they were doing and gave up the thought of ever coming back. On the other hand, the scenes those actors did were so *real*; nothing like most of the acting I had seen either on TV or in the theater. After thinking about it for a day or two, I knew that this is the kind of acting I wanted to do. Faking emotion wasn't good enough. I wanted to *feel* it.

That was the beginning of the creation of an actual craft in my acting and a friendship with Eric that has lasted for decades. I am forever grateful. Eric has eased up and become a kinder, gentler teacher than when I started with him but I still prefer the intimidating character he presented when I first began taking classes. I don't think anyone could have cracked open the protective shell of Miss Goody-Two-Shoes and made her shout, scream, cry and show anger the way he was able to do. He showed me that all the emotions that I believed were "negative" were actually the colors we use as actors, that we all have them and everyone in Eric's classes accepts those perceived ugly emotions in everyone else. There is no shame in showing them, only admiration for the willingness to expose our souls to achieve reality in our acting. If we're not willing to do that, we're faking it. And I don't care what Laurence Olivier supposedly told Dustin Hoffman when Hoffman came in disheveled and out of breath to play a scene in Marathon Man. Legend has it (maybe not true) that Olivier told Hoffman, "Why not try acting, dear boy." Actually, I believe they both did everything they could to make a performance *real*. And that is exactly what Eric Morris strives to have his students accomplish.

Alan was tapped to produce *Of Mice and Men* starring Robert Blake and Randy Quaid. I wanted badly to be in this movie and thought I had a shot since I had worked for the director, Reza Badiyi, twice before but Cassie Yates won the role I wanted and was actually more right for the part than me. The writer, E. Nick Alexander, would go on to win a Writers Guild award for the script adaption and everyone I knew told me later it was the best version they had seen. Alan was good friends with Nick and they worked together on several shows. We visited Nick and his wife, Maggie Mason, who starred on the soap opera *Days of Our Lives* for many years, but I never got to know either one of them very well. I could never have guessed that decades later Nick would once again enter my life in an unexpected way.

As Alan's addictions drove us further apart and my denial of it all became harder and harder to justify, I came to dread dinners out with our friends. I knew that he would become rip-roaring drunk and I would have to drive home, pour him out of the car and get him into bed. One day a phone call came with catastrophic news. Alan, white as a sheet, walked into the bedroom where I was dressing and told me that Bruce Geller and Steve Gentry, a network executive and friend, had been killed in a plane crash. It was a devastating personal blow to us both. No one had been more supportive of Alan's career. Bruce gave Alan his first co-producing and writing jobs and Alan dreamed of following in Bruce's footsteps and eventually creating his own television show. Bruce had been a friend and mentor to both of us. After that, Alan began to drink even more and having to deal with a man who was constantly drunk made me more and more depressed.

Totally out of character, one day Alan told me I had to be careful of our spending. I had repeatedly asked to be allowed to check on our finances but he kept all the records at the office and had his secretary handle everything. He always told me not to worry about it; everything was fine. Since I didn't want to deal with our finances anyway I didn't press very hard to find out if that was true. The "Cinderella" girl still wanted to be taken care of, even by an addict and alcoholic.

As it became more and more obvious that Alan was losing the battle with booze and drugs, I, refusing to expose our ugly secrets at Al-Anon where I could get help and support, became so despondent I had to see a therapist so I could function. He prescribed a drug, Elavil, which I later found out has many harmful side effects. The drug left my emotions completely flat. I felt nothing. For awhile, that seemed so much better than being depressed all the time that I didn't care that I didn't feel any joy or excitement about anything either. But when I went out on an important audition where I was supposed to cry and in the middle of the scene, for the life of me couldn't figure out why I should be sad, I knew I had to stop taking Elavil or never be able to act again. Coming off the drug gave me chills and fever and friends helped me through the hours-long ordeal. What would it take to make me realize I couldn't do this alone?

Our favorite person to go out to dinner with was our neighbor, Freddy Travalena, a comic and genius impersonator. We would be sitting in a restaurant with Freddy and his wife Lois, and Freddy would do an imitation of a famous person like Ted Kennedy and everyone would look around for Ted, fully expecting him to be there. His voices were so authentic and people in the restaurant who heard him were so incredibly baffled I would laugh hysterically. It was like enjoying our own personal nightclub act. The Travalenas had a little boy, Freddy Jr., about Erika's age, who would come over to our house and spend time with her and other little kids their age in the neighborhood. Freddy Jr. used to bite the other toddlers, including Erika, and Lois said the best way of curing him of this terrible habit was to bite him back. Which she did. Forever after we called him "Freddy the biter."

Happy moments became few and far between. My friend, Rosemaria, always listened patiently as I poured out my heart about Alan, my money worries, my lack of work, etc., etc., ad nauseum. How she remained my friend through this endless outpouring of grief is further proof that she is an angel. I felt paralyzed, afraid of what I would face as a single person who had to take care of a child and five cats by myself. Then a fateful moment changed everything.

One night we drove down to a club in Orange County where musician friends were performing. During a break, I went to the ladies' room and as I passed by the men's room, the door opened up and I saw Alan taking a deep snort of cocaine and saying, "I really needed that!" I stood and gaped at him and he at me and we both knew it was over. I couldn't bury my head in the sand denying the obvious anymore. During the long ride home, neither one of us said a word. I didn't know how I would make it on my own. I only knew I had to get out.

For weeks, I agonized over the end of another marriage. Having to tell my parents was the worst part. I knew my friends would understand and accept it. I procrastinated until New Year's Eve. We were supposed to go to Robert Blake's house for a party and I knew I couldn't face a house full of people and pretend nothing was wrong. That day, while Alan was taking a bath – maybe I thought I was safer if he had no clothes on – I went into the bathroom and told him I was filing for divorce. He became so enraged he jumped out of the tub and slapped me to kingdom come. I fell backwards and tried to fight him off but he was very strong and all I could do was try and protect myself against the blows. Erika had been in the bedroom and when she heard me screaming she ran into the bathroom and hid behind the toilet. I don't know if the neighbors heard the commotion coming from our house or how the police ended up at our house but soon they were pounding on the front door. I went into the bathroom to comfort Erika and when I came out into the living room, Alan was chatting and laughing with the cops as if nothing had happened. I described to them how he had attacked me but Alan pooh-poohed what I was saying and declared with a straight face that *I* was attacking *him*. I was shocked that the cops preferred to believe him instead of me. After they left, I demanded that he move out or I would call my friends and get help moving him out. Apparently, he had no more energy left to argue and he packed up, went out the door and drove away without saying a word.

Alan was scheduled to leave for a location scouting trip to Dallas, Texas in preparation for shooting a television movie, but first he called and begged me for another chance before I filed for divorce. He said he would go to therapy, stop drinking and doing drugs; anything to stop me from divorcing him. As far as I was concerned, it was three strikes and he was out, but

I told him that if he didn't immediately get into therapy as soon as he came back, I was heading straight for a lawyer. He was supposed to be gone for a week, but two weeks went by, three weeks, then production on the movie started and I knew he wouldn't be returning to L.A. until the end of the shoot. I remember walking down the hallway in our house, and being overwhelmed by a terrible, empty feeling. It was really over. Time to face the music and get it done. I filed for divorce.

CHAPTER 11

Into the Abyss with Dustin Hoffman

ALAN CHOSE TO AVOID BEING served with divorce papers, which is easy to do when you're out of state. So the process dragged on endlessly while I desperately wanted to get it over with as soon as possible. I would sit in my bedroom, look out over the valley, as I loved to do and had done so many times before; knowing that very soon all that I had worked for would be gone. I had finally checked out our finances and found out we were in catastrophic shape. House payments weren't being paid, tax bills had been ignored and we needed to sell the house before Erika and I were evicted. Acting jobs were too few and far between to count on those supporting us and the only office skills I had were typing and answering the phone. We were going to lose everything and I felt powerless to stop it.

Three months later, when Alan finally came back from Dallas, bringing with him a new girlfriend, we were finally able to finalize the divorce. He told the court he was now out of a job and was able to get the judge to agree to minimal child support payments. But he didn't pay them anyway. I went to court again and again, but it was all to no avail. Eventually I went to the prosecutor's office to try and get them to force him to pay up but they told me the list of fathers who were avoiding child support was a mile long and it could be years before they got around to him. My mother paid for Erika to go to pre-school at a Lutheran church near our house and I signed with a temp agency. Because the owners were friends with John Lombardo, they immediately found me a job typing checks at a downtown Bank of America. The one thing I clearly remember on the way to my first day of work is sitting on the freeway in bumper to bumper traffic and listening to the song, "I Can Take Care of Myself," and thinking, that sounds like he's singing about my friend Wendy, an actress who I had become friends with after we worked together on *Vega$*. I didn't know who sang it or that soon I would meet the man who wrote and recorded the song, Billy Vera, and that we would become friends.

During the months that the house was on the market, I kept looking for acting jobs and going to acting classes. Working in class with Eric Morris kept me sane, going on auditions gave me hope, and Erika gave me a reason to keep on living. It was tricky juggling temp jobs and auditions, but I had to make it work to maximize my chances of making money. One of those auditions was for a movie called *Once Upon a Time in America*, produced by Arnon Milchan. I drove to the Chateau Marmont, off Sunset Boulevard, early in the morning and parked my car on the street next to one of the bungalows. I remember thinking as I walked by that they were nothing special to look at and I didn't understand why celebrities would want to stay there when they could afford something so much nicer. I barely remember the audition (Elizabeth McGovern got the part), only that the hotel felt old and strange and I wondered why the auditions were being held there. I didn't have a good feeling as I walked back to my car, happy to drive away from there. The next day I read in the paper that John Belushi had been dying of an overdose in Bungalow Number Three as I unknowingly walked by. An incredibly talented man had destroyed himself with drugs a few feet away from me while I passed by oblivious. But I wasn't the one who failed him. I couldn't have possibly known what was going on inside the bungalow. But his friends knew, especially the ones who had visited him the night before. They knew what he was doing to himself and did nothing. Be that as it may, *Once Upon a Time in America* and Arnon would still play a role in my future.

About this time came the opportunity of a lifetime for me. My agent called and told me Dustin Hoffman wanted to interview me regarding a new movie he was doing called *Tootsie*. Hal Ashby, who had directed *Coming Home*, would be directing. I was to meet Dustin in Beverly Hills at his agency, CAA. I was both excited and relieved that I wouldn't have to audition the first time I met him because I would be much too nervous. And I definitely would not say anything to him about predicting some years ago that he would never make it as an actor. So I went in to meet him enveloped in euphoria just at the thought that Dustin Hoffman wanted to interview me for a role in his movie. We talked for an hour, chit-chatting about the business and a little bit about the movie. I asked him what it was like being super famous and having everyone stare at him every time he was out in public. And his answer? He smiled that familiar smile I had seen so many times on the movie screen and said, "It's like being you." Quite a compliment I thought but not the same as being famous.

At the end of our conversation he walked me over to a full-length mirror and we looked at ourselves standing together, then at each other, thinking it was a pretty good match. My hopes soared when he said he wanted to see film on me. "Lots of colors," he said, "Lots of colors." I promised him he would see colors. I sailed out of there on a cloud and immediately called my agent to tell her we had to send film over to CAA for Dustin to look at. Then came the inevitable wait for word. It didn't come. Hal Ashby died and the project was put on hold. But still I kept hoping that Dustin would call, and when I read in the trades that Sydney Pollock was signed to direct and the project was to go forward again, I figured it would be a matter of time before we heard something. After waiting patiently for what seemed forever, I called my agent and said I didn't understand why we hadn't heard *something* one way or the other, and as I listened in disbelief, my agent said, "Oh, Dustin called from New York and wanted your home number and I told him I couldn't give it to him. You know how some of these people are with actresses. He probably wanted you to come to New York to take advantage of you." I almost fainted dead away. I could not fathom that she would ruin this chance for me. She sounded more like somebody's Aunt Nellie from Kansas rather than a Hollywood agent. I don't know how many actresses Dustin had seen, or if I was at the top of his list, or one of a handful, but he had seen my acting and was still interested in me. *I had a shot.* And now it was gone forever. Jessica Lange ended up being cast in the part of the nurse and she was perfect and I loved her in it. And *Tootsie* is still my number one favorite movie. That agent was history.

Jan Natarno was the go-to guy when it came to making acting reels. They were long in those days; some as long as twenty minutes. You'd never get a casting director to look at a reel that long now. Sixty seconds and out would be the perfect length, but few actors can bring themselves to limit their scenes to that short a time. At one point, while sitting in Jan Natarno's waiting room with a motley collection of actors like myself, apparently, I caught the eye of one of them, even though I was pretty much oblivious to anything around me at that point in time. I wanted to get in and get out and pick up Erika at school. Men were the last thing on my mind. But surprisingly, there were a steady stream of them very interested in taking care of Erika and me and relieving us of all our cares. And some were very nice, as well as being good-looking and successful. But it was too soon to even consider being with anyone else. I was barely getting over my divorce from Alan and all the pain and humiliation that entailed. I had my temp work, Alan sent money every now and then, and we got by. The house was still for sale and we hadn't been evicted yet.

I had run into someone who was taking acting lessons with Darryl Hickman and he persuaded me to give him a try. I loved Eric and would always use what I had learned from him, but apparently, Darryl didn't just teach acting; he believed in giving his students chances to work in the business and had producers and directors observe his classes from time to time, and I needed to work more than I needed to be in class. I had had a crush on Darryl since I was a little girl, having seen him on *The Many Loves of Dobie Gillis* as Dobie's older brother, and in real life he *was* Dwayne's (Dobie's) older brother. Darryl accepted me as a student and I became friends with two actors in class, Bill Zipp and Michael Simms, who would end up giving me a place to stay later, and with Loren Koslow who I worked with on scenes that Darryl made us do over and over again until they were perfect. Loren was a receptionist in the Sherman Oaks Galleria and had access to the Breakdowns. Every other day I would go over to her office and we would look through the Breakdowns hoping to find something we could submit ourselves for since neither one of us had an agent at that point. She would jab at the switchboard as it buzzed, "I hate this job, I hate this job, I hate this job!" she would hiss. I knew the feeling.

The best scene I have ever done in class or anywhere else was in Darryl's class with Michael Simms. It was from the play *The Detective* and Michael, brilliant actor that he is, became so enraged, and frightened me so much, I forgot we were acting and everything became startlingly real. When we were finished, Darryl told us this was one of the few times when he forgot that he was watching an acting scene and believed that what we were doing was so absolutely real he was worried for my safety. I had used some of Eric Morris and some of Darryl and I don't know what Michael used. I think he was just born a good actor.

Bill Zipp was also a very good actor and he and I ended up doing a scene where two actors were addicted to cocaine and fighting over it. It was supposed to be a comedy but considering what I was going through, I had a hard time finding the humor in it.

Bill, knowing how much I loved animals and always listened to me talk about Paul and the Sea Shepherd, told me I ought to get in touch with Chris De Rose. Chris had just formed a new group, Last Chance for Animals, and its focus was getting animals out of research laboratories. I was not interested. I couldn't possibly get involved with something like that. Having to look at pictures of baby seals was all the horror I could deal with. Ending vivisection was a hopeless cause and the suffering of lab animals was so brutal I didn't want to think about it. I didn't know then that that was just God's first push in the direction he wanted me to go, but in those days, I wasn't listening.

CHAPTER 12

The Young and the Restless and New York

ONE DAY THE TELEPHONE RANG and it was my agent calling with what I hoped would be an audition. Instead, she told me an actor who had seen me at Jan Natarno's wanted her to give me his telephone number so I could call him if I so chose. Disappointed, I wrote down the number and thought, "No way am I calling. This is the last thing I need." I couldn't even remember which one he was. Then, as I sat on my bed looking out over the pool and view, I remember thinking as clearly as if it were yesterday, "Why not call? It's not as if it's going to change my life." Wrong again.

His name was Steve Hirsch and we arranged to meet. I don't remember where we met the first time but when I saw him I had a vague memory of seeing him in Jan's waiting room. He was tall with dark hair and was from New York, just the type I was staying away from these days. But I was needy and desperate and, since no offers had been made yet on the house, was facing eviction, and Steve made it clear he was very much interested. Best of all, Erika liked him and we had fun together. Steve was an actor who also drove a limo but he had big dreams and was certain he would achieve great success in the business. One day he drove me to the top of a hill near Bel Air and pointed to a mansion across the valley. "I'm going to live in a house like that one day" he said with total conviction. And like I had with Kevin, I believed him.

Other men I had dated had made their intentions clear in the past few months; they wanted to marry me and take care of us, and it was always *so* tempting to say yes and let somebody take over my life and relieve me of all my worries. But even though I had that "C" complex down pat, I needed to be attracted to a man to be with him and have at least the beginnings of what could turn into love. With Steve, I finally felt that possibility.

One day Steve told me we had been invited to a brunch at his friend, Stephen Macht's house. They had just worked in a movie together. So we accepted and drove into Beverly Hills where Stephen lived with his family, including young son, Gabriel, who would grow up to star in the television show *Suits*. The Machts had a beautiful house in Beverly Hills south of Wilshire and the party was outside in the garden. I was seated by myself, quietly watching everyone eating and talking when I saw a man come walking up the driveway with a woman who was extremely plain and had teeth missing. My first – admittedly shallow – reaction was, "Why on earth is he with her?" Then I concluded that he must be a really nice guy for being willing to escort this woman to a Hollywood party and not worry at all about what people thought. Sensing that he and I were like-minded people, we drifted together and spent at least an hour talking to each other. It turned out that he was a musician and sang with a band, Billy and the Beaters, and his name was Billy Vera. I could not *imagine* this gentle, quiet man singing with a rock band. When he told me he was play-ing at a club and invited me to come see them perform I figured that would be a disappointment that I'd rather avoid. Stephen, however, overheard and told me I had to come with him and his friends when they went to see the Beaters in a couple weeks and I would be shocked at how good Billy was. I had my doubts about that but said I would and went into the house to go to the bathroom. Steve followed me, angry and consumed with jeal-ousy, and started hissing at me in an angry whisper because I was spending so much time with Billy. I was so embarrassed, I grabbed my things and headed for the car. I knew at that moment I would never see Steve again. I had a million things to worry about and I didn't need this kind of ugliness in my life. All I wanted was to get home and get away from him. But paying attention to red flags has never been my long suit.

Eventually, Steve apologized and actually offered to take me to see Billy play. I admit I was curious to hear his band even though I had my doubts that Billy's singing would come up to my high Sonics standards or even be as good as Dobie Gray and Pollution but I said yes. When we walked into the huge, packed night club in Santa Monica, The Beaters were playing full blast. Billy was on stage singing and I just stood there listening to him for a few seconds, open-mouthed, not moving. He was fabulous! His quiet persona had morphed into a full-blown rock star and he held that entire club in the palm of his hand. I ran over to where Stephen and his friends were seated and yelled over the music, "He's good! He's really good!" And Stephen yelled back, "Well, yeah, that's what I told you!" Steve and I sat down at a table and I was totally engrossed listening to Billy. And blues? My God, blues? I had never heard blues sung the way Billy and his band sang and played them. As I watched and listened to the Beaters, Steve ignored the band and stared at me, still jealous of my obvious admiration for Billy. But nothing was going to stop me from enjoying this moment, and luckily for him, Steve controlled himself.

"At This Moment" had not turned into a mega-hit yet. That was still a few years away, so when I heard it, I liked it but what really impressed me was when Billy sang "I Can Take Care of Myself" and I realized he was the one I had heard on the radio on my way to work months ago. I didn't tell him that, though. I was too embarrassed to tell any of these people I wasn't really an actress. I was just an office temp.

It was inevitable that Billy and I became friends. He was kind and gentle and a great listener. He had just broken up with one soap opera star and was involved with another. He was a soap opera addict and especially loved *The Young and the Restless*. It is ironic that that is the same show that offered me a chance to rescue myself from my dire situation.

My agent called and told me I had a reading for a principal role on *The Young and the Restless.* I would be replacing an actress who was leaving the show. When I read over the scenes for my audition I knew I was perfect for the role. The audition went well and I was called back for a screen test. When I finished, there was not a doubt in my mind that I had nailed the test, and afterwards the casting director was all smiles and complimented me on my performance and my appearance. I had known her for years and knew she was sincere and wouldn't lead me on. I waited for the call and it came; my agent told me I didn't get it. The disappointment was overwhelming and not only that, I didn't understand why I wasn't cast. I was exactly what they had been looking for. This had been my chance to keep the house and support Erika and me with no more worries. And I had failed. A couple of years later I found out my agent had lied to me. I was at CBS for a small role on *The Young and the Restless* and I ran into John Conboy, the producer. He walked up to me and said, "Oh Britt, I was so sorry that you were unavailable to be on the show." What?! It took a few moments for what he had said to sink in. I was unavailable? No way. He disappeared behind a closed door and I didn't have a chance to respond. By that time, I had another agent and didn't know where the agent who had betrayed me had gone. By sheer coincidence, years later, my literary agent set me up on a blind date with the ex-husband of the actress I was supposed to replace. He told me my agent sabotaged me for his own selfish reasons; he had also represented this man's ex-wife, had represented her longer than me and wanted her to stay on the soap instead of allowing me to have the chance I had earned, but she left the show anyway because of illness. That role could have changed the lives of Erika and me. For us it was a catastrophic betrayal.

Twice, Steve worked as an actor on shows with Kevin Dobson and, twice, he never mentioned my name to him, and that was fine with me. In the depths of my despair when Erika and I were homeless, I had written to Kevin and asked for his help but received no response. I thought he owed me something for helping him move from a job in the railroad yards to a successful career as an actor, but then again, if not for him and Chuck,

I would surely have died of peritonitis so I didn't allow myself to dwell on bitterness. They had literally saved my life. Steve was being very nice at this point and there was no avoiding Erika and me getting evicted. I sold or stored everything I had, watched tearfully as the new owner of my little red Mercedes SL drove out of the driveway and said goodbye to my home in the hills. I temporarily placed my cats, except for Maude, in the Kitty Motel in Glendale and visited them every day to make sure they were safe and happy and knew I hadn't forgotten them. Eventually, after house-sitting, sleeping on my friend Wendy's couch and living out of my car, Erika and I and the kitties ended up in a rented house in the valley with Steve, and I stopped worrying quite so much. I worked temp, took care of Erika, went on auditions and took singing lessons with Lee and Sally for the sake of my sanity. I didn't foresee that I would ever again get called in to audition at the Music Center, but well... you never knew and I might as well be ready. I briefly met Steve's son and daughter, who both lived back east with their mother. His son was very friendly, but the daughter wanted nothing to do with me. She had been very close to Steve's former girlfriend, who had left him for someone else, and I guess I couldn't fill her shoes.

Steve was showing signs of being over-controlling but he also had great charm and most of the time he was fun to be with. He also had immense confidence in his talent and never doubted for one second that he would become very successful. But even then, I knew in the deepest recesses of my heart, this was not someone I wanted to spend the rest of my life with. We lived in a nice neighborhood in a cute little house, Erika was happy and at that point in time, I couldn't think any further than that. I just wanted to spend a little time not stressed about what was going to happen to the two of us. Even though I now had an agent, I still looked at Loren's Breakdowns for possible roles for me and, at some point, introduced her to Steve. She used to come over to the house and the two of them would go into the garage and he would help her with her acting. I hope that's what was going on. Like my mother said, I'm trusting.

We were put in a total quandary when Steve was offered a position working for Arnon Milchan in New York. Arnon was one of the biggest producers in Hollywood, but based in Manhattan, and he wanted Steve to move there and function as vice president of Regency Films. Steve's brother-in-law was president of Fox and had worked with Arnon and introduced him to Steve a few months earlier. From actor to producer? Steve had been brilliant in the play *Chapter Two*, directed by my pal John Lombardo, and he was also finding acting work on network shows. Was this the right move? And what about Erika and me? Did we want to be uprooted from L.A. to New York after everything we had been through? It seemed we were just beginning to feel we had a little security again. It was an exciting thought, but was it the right thing for all of us? And what about my cats? They were my family and now had a good, safe home far away from coyotes. In spite of all the reasons not to move, after we weighed the pros and cons, we decided it was an opportunity he couldn't pass up. I had always wanted to live in New York but never thought it would actually happen. Steve would fly there first and choose a place for the three of us to live. Arnon would foot the bill.

We had to sublet our little house first and we found a great young couple to take over our lease. He played keyboard for Rick Springfield but they needed a base in L.A. when they weren't touring. Friends offered to take care of my cats at their house in Hancock Park until we returned to L.A., which I hoped would be soon. Even though leaving them was the hardest part of moving to New York, I knew they would be in good hands until I came back. And not coming back to them was not an option. Each and every one of them was special to me. Maude, my best friend, would come with us. So Steve flew off to New York and we would join him when he found a place for us all to live. I wanted Erika to stay with my parents until Steve and I were settled in our new home so again, she flew up to Seattle and Maude and I flew to New York.

When the plane landed, I had high expectations for all the possibilities which were opening up for us and was incredibly excited about living in

Manhattan. Steve picked me up in a limo, and instead of a warm greeting, he gave me the full force of his foul temper. We had an inconsequential disagreement over something and he went off on me. I considered then and there leaving and going back to Los Angeles. I was afraid his anger foreshadowed unpleasant things to come, but my parents already thought I was insane for living in New York with a man I wasn't married to and if I turned tail and ran, I would once again feel like a failure in their eyes. I had to stick this out and make it work.

We stayed at the Drake Hotel for a few days then moved into an apartment on the Upper West Side near Lincoln Center. I called my mother and told her to put Erika on a plane right away, but she and my father felt it would be best for her to finish out the school year in a church school they had placed her in. It was agony waiting for her to finish up and come to New York. Finally, when I met her at the airport I wrapped my arms around her and felt incredible relief that we were together again; the two musketeers, no matter what happened with Steve or anybody else. I enrolled her in a neighborhood school and hoped and prayed that she would adjust well. I signed with a temp agency and started getting hired. I had an acting agent already who was bicoastal between New York and Los Angeles and every now and then I went out on auditions.

Waiting outside of Equity one morning for a cattle call, I saw a class-mate from Erik Morris' class, Billy Hayes. It was hard to miss him with his white curly hair. Billy had written a book, *Midnight Express*, about his nightmare experiences in a Turkish prison, and it had been made into a movie. But he was also an excellent actor and I was happy to see he was in New York pursuing his career. Later, we had lunch and caught up. As always, I made everything seem rosy, which already it definitely wasn't. We made plans to get together for dinner.

I was ironing clothes one day watching *The Young and the Restless* when I saw my friend Loren on it and was so shocked I almost dropped my iron. Darryl, who had executive-produced the soap *Love of Life* in New York years before, must have had one of his soap producer friends come to his class to check out Daryl's students. Loren was very beautiful and with her flawless complexion was perfect for the soaps. How could they resist her? I tried to reach out to Loren in various ways for a long time to tell her how happy I was to see she had been cast on the show but never heard from her again.

Steve would pass scripts and books on to me to analyze, because that was the job he had been hired to do by Arnon, and considering the amount of scripts that came in, he wanted to get an idea from me of which ones were worth reading and producing. Eventually I singled out the book *Man on Fire* and the script of *War of the Roses* as projects I strongly recommended. Arnon decided to produce both of them.

After reading a lot of scripts, many of them submitted by top agencies and most of them badly written, I decided I could do better, and attended a screenwriting class at NYU. I had written dialogue for Alan when he was writing TV shows, but I knew nothing about structuring a script correctly. A few years earlier, a friend of mine had showed me a magazine article about a charismatic preacher named Jim Jones who had a church up in San Francisco. He was considered more of a cult leader than a man of God and was sending some of his followers to live in Guyana. After reading the article, my imagination took flight. I envisioned that he was brainwashing these poor, desperate people and that they were actually imprisoned in Guyana and weren't able to leave and wanted to escape and come back home. I came up with an ingenious way to make that happen, wrote out the script and asked Alan to help me but we weren't able to get anyone interested. A short while later, almost everything I wrote about Jim Jones turned out to be true. But I never envisioned the tragic mass suicide. My story had had a happy ending.

At New York University, Michelle Cousins was a supportive, insightful teacher and I looked forward to every class with her, learning about story and character arcs, crises points and climaxes, all of which I had never heard of before and made me realize writing scripts was a lot more complicated than I had thought. I realized that my favorite movie of all time, *Tootsie*, followed the rules exactly as she laid them out for us. Amazing. You couldn't argue with success. I started writing and was soon deep into my first real script.

Arnon was still editing *Once Upon a Time in America*, which was now back in my life as I was one of several people asked to watch the various different cuts of the movie. As I watched Elizabeth McGovern in the role I read for, I kept being reminded of John Belushi dying next door as I was reading my lines. The movie, even the extra-long version, was excellent, as was Robert DeNiro. He was a good friend of Arnon's and came to the office now and then. I saw him there and didn't recognize him at first. He seemed shy and unassuming and shorter than I thought he'd be. But he introduced himself and we briefly made small talk. I think he is the one actor all other actors dream of working with and I was no different. I didn't get that chance but Steve gave me the hat De Niro wore in the movie as a souvenir. Not quite the same.

Every day I would pick up Erika from school and we would walk home and often times grab a slice of real New York pizza. Sometimes Erika and I would be alone in the evening and, from her room, listen to a choir that sang in the park outside of Lincoln Center. I knew she missed our house, Encino and her school but she was trying to adjust to her new life, did well in her classes and always was an affectionate, loving little girl. But here I was again, depending and leaning on a man to make sure our needs were met. My goal was to get on a soap, preferably in Los Angeles, and stay on it for the rest of my life and never be dependent on a man ever again.

Steve had several issues with women. The main one was fear of abandonment, and both his wife and his last girlfriend had left him. Now he was determined that that wouldn't happen with us and the result was he had an overwhelming need to control me and be hypercritical of my every move. This began to grate on me as he began to find fault with me 24/7.

As time went on Steve grew more and more possessive and difficult to live with. He went regularly to his therapist to try and understand his insecurities, and sometimes I was asked to come to the sessions with him. One time I asked one of his therapists in private if Steve would ever change, and the man gave me a flat out, no. That was not very encouraging and did not bode well for me. I knew we couldn't go on like this much longer. Erika was becoming unhappy in New York and needed to go back to living in the more suburban atmosphere that she was used to. I worried about the cats I had left behind and missed them very much. This wasn't supposed to be a permanent move and I wished Arnon would allow Steven to be based in Los Angeles. Maybe back there in familiar territory he could lose some of his insecurities. That's what I told myself.

Then an audition for *One Life to Live* came along and I was excited and again, like with *The Young and the Restless*, saw it as my escape; we could leave Steve, buy a house outside the city, send for the kitties, and go back to being the two musketeers. My hopes exploded like beautiful fireworks. This could happen! The role I was auditioning for was "Karen," who had been played by Judith Light some years before, and now they were going to bring the character back. I had watched the show when she was on it and knew every tic and mannerism Judith had displayed on that show. When I went in I decided to be "Karen" to the nth degree. After I was finished, I had no doubt that I had done well. My agent reported back that they had liked me and my chances of being cast were very good. Then he called a few days later and said the executives on the show had been replaced and the new people decided they wouldn't be bringing "Karen" back. *One Life to Live* was not going to rescue me after all.

One day I was walking down Central Park South and as always, it was impossible not to notice the carriage horses and agonize as I always did over their appalling work and living conditions. As I was watching the horses I glanced away and saw a group of paparazzi outside of a hotel taking pictures of someone. As he walked away down the street I realized it was my friendly tormentor from *Vega$*, Bob Urich. I came up behind him and yelled, "Hey, Bob!" He turned around, his face broke out into a smile and we hugged. We continued walking and he asked me what I was doing in New York and I told him I had moved here with Steve and pretended I was having a wonderful time; Steve was great guy, didn't miss L.A. He wished me luck and joked that now that all those photographers had pictures of us hugging we'd end up in *The Enquirer* and Heather would think he was cheating on her. And I thought, fat chance, not with the kind of marriage they have. But I just laughed and wished him well and walked away. That was the last time I saw him before he died of cancer at age 55.

There were good times in New York as well as the bad. Sometimes Erika, Steve and I would take long drives out to Long Island in Arnon's red Porche, and there were walks in the park, Sunday brunches with friends, visits to the museum, shopping, and dinners with his sister and brother-in-law when they came into town. And my favorite memories are of being bundled up in my warmest clothes, walking with Arnon in the snow as he and Steve discussed upcoming projects and scripts to consider. Feeling so intimately involved in the movie-making process was one of the things that kept me hoping that Steve and I could make it together.

One day, and I don't know what brought it on, Steve became so viciously verbally abusive and threatening, he actually had me cowering in the corner of the living room. When he was finally finished berating me, I was thoroughly disgusted with myself and knew that I could no longer go on acting as a willing victim. The next day I made plane reservations for Erika and me to fly to Seattle. As long as the two of us were together that was all that mattered. We were the two musketeers plus Maude and we would survive and get everything back we had lost. Even sleeping on friends' couches would be better than this.

Erika at Work

Maude

Favorite Head Shot

With Paul Watson

How the West Was Won

Britt Lind

On Joe Panther

Starsky and Hutch

148

With Tony on Vega$

With Robert on Vega$

Wonderful Peter Falk

Chris De Rose and Me

Erika and Chewy

Me, Mama and Peter

E. Nick Alexander

Georgia, My BFF

Squeeky

CHAPTER 13

Finally...Chris De Rose

$\sim\!\!\!\!\sim$

ERIKA, MAUDE AND I CAME back to my parents' house in Marysville, Washington and my mother was thrilled to have us. Erika was grandpa's special girl and they spent hours together with her helping him in the garden and with his carpentry work. Meanwhile, my heart felt so heavy it was as if I had a rock in my chest that made it hard to breathe. I didn't think that the heartache over leaving Steve would be so severe but it was. I set about planning what our next move would be. Michael and Bill, my two friends from Darryl's acting class, were willing to put me up until I could find work and a place for Erika and me to stay. At the same time, unbeknownst to me, Steve had had a heart attack the day we left from the shock of seeing that Erika and I had gone and it was so serious he had ended up having heart surgery as well. I had written to him while I was at my parents' house, pouring out my feelings, but hadn't heard back. I thought he was just angry and never wanted anything to do with me again, but he was in the hospital recuperating. I felt a little guilty about that until a few years later I ran into him and found out he was still smoking. So his heart attack wasn't *all* my fault.

After a brief stay with my friends, I found a house in the valley in Encino that Alan was willing to help us pay the rent on. My friend, Tony Eldridge, loaned me the money to ship my furniture and clothes back to L.A., and fortunately, I was able to pay him back in a few months. The little house was close to a grade school that was just a few blocks away, and Erika and

I and the cats settled into a new life in the "flats." Then my friend, Kevin Krasny, Paul's son, bought a house two doors down from where we were living and offered to share it with us. This was even better. Now we would have some financial breathing room, a place where Erika and I could be happy and a yard where the cats would never have to worry about coyotes ever again.

Rosemaria had been my friend and confidant through all my crazy moves from place to place but never judged and always encouraged me to look for solutions instead of feeling sorry for myself. She called one day and told me that Steve wanted his fiancé to come over and look at her house, which she had up for rent. How Steve heard about that I'll never know. Apparently, he had moved back to Los Angeles, left Arnon to form his own company, and became engaged to be married. When Rosemaria saw Steve's fiancé walking up the street she had thought at first it was me, we were that similar. Rosemaria showed her the house, but they decided not to rent it after all. I'm sure he wanted me to know that he was moving on and getting married and couldn't care less about me anymore. Eventually, his new wife moved on as well and I saw him again years later, still good-looking, charming and as successful as he had predicted he would be.

Kevin Krasny was editing *Miami Vice* and was good friends with the associate producer Danny Sackheim, brother of Andy, who I had met years before on *The Harness*, and the two of them hired me to do voice-overs on the show. I loved doing voice-overs and was good at it because I had had a lot of practice on Alan's shows. I would do police calls, replace actresses' voices and do walla as well. Walla is as much fun as you get in post-production. A group of actors stand around in the recording studio and talk as if they're at a social gathering, reporters yelling questions, or part of an angry mob. It's like getting paid for being at a party. With the help of residuals, some child support from Alan, and temp pay, we were making it.

You never know when working temp if the people you work for will treat you kindly or like what you are, the lowest person on the totem pole. Somehow, I landed a job as a receptionist for a company in Hollywood where the phone hardly ever rang and very few people came in. Loved it! My boss, Diane Dolphin, blond, beautiful, a fellow Norwegian, and, as I found out later, an incredible singer and dancer, told me to bring a book to read and showed me where, right around the corner from my station, there was a kitchenette with coffee and English muffins every morning, so feel free to indulge. At first I was a little nervous getting paid for doing almost nothing, but then I settled in and enjoyed my leisurely day of reading, eating and answering the phone once in awhile. Even if the job hadn't been so easy, I can say without reservation that Diane was the kindest, most considerate boss I ever had, and became a dear friend for life.

Around this time, two friends who knew I loved animals and that I was a member of The Sea Shepherd Conservation Society told me I had to meet Chris De Rose. No! Animals being tortured in laboratories was not something I would ever want to deal with. Absolutely not! Just thinking about it tears my heart out. Chris De Rose, who everybody I knew seemed to know, wouldn't leave me alone! One friend was very insistent and I had to keep reiterating there was no way that I was getting involved with the anti-vivisection movement. Gruesome experiments on animals were something I had avoided thinking about my entire life. But I was having no luck convincing him that I meant what I said. So after more of his badgering, I caved in, and figured I might as well meet Chris and get this over with once and for all. I called and set up an appointment to meet him at his apartment, where he had his office. On the way there, I steeled myself against the pictures I knew he would show me and took a deep breath as I knocked on his door.

Chris turned out to be a very handsome, dark-haired New Yorker with the distinct accent to go along with it. But I was in no mood to admire his looks and he wasted no time in expressing his passion to liberate animals in laboratories. Speaking with a deep loathing for vivisectors, he showed me pictures of tortured animals and asked how people could be capable of such cruelty. I couldn't help cringing at the heartbreaking photos but kept looking even though I wanted to scream and cry and escape back to my car. Chris was more outwardly passionate and vocal than Paul Watson in describing his plans for achieving his goals but both were equally dedicated and focused.

Chris also showed me the logo he intended to use for his group, Last Chance for Animals; a man's strong arms protectively holding an invisible small animal. Considering Chris' well-built body and soft heart, I thought it a fitting symbol for his group.

As I was leaving, he expressed hope that I would join Last Chance and help him in his efforts to expose the barbaric treatment of animals in laboratories. I told him I'd think about it and left him my phone number and said he should call me when their next event was scheduled. Of course, I knew I wouldn't be joining, but it would be so much easier to say no on the phone. I hoped no one from his organization would call me. But it wasn't long before someone did. A girl called and informed me that they were planning a big demo at USC in a couple of weeks and they needed me to come to a training session. I thought, "training session? Who needs training to go to a protest? You go, hold signs, maybe yell a few slogans, go home, whatever it is changes or it doesn't and that's it. Who needs training for something like that?" I did ask the girl why and she insisted it was necessary and protesters needed to know the rules and differences in protesting and actually getting arrested. Arrested? I told the girl I thought I would be busy the day of the training so thank you but no thank you. I thought that would be the end of it.

But it wasn't. She called again. Why not just come to the training, see what it's all about and then decide if I want to go to the protest? I replied that I would think about it and hung up knowing I wouldn't think about it for one more minute. So of course I did. I thought, what can it hurt to go to the training? And if I attend, maybe they'll stop calling me. I need to get Chris De Rose off my back once and for all.

A week later I found myself in a small theater at a packed training session for a protest at USC. Chris led the meeting along with his lieutenants, Jack Carone, and Mary McDonald Lewis. All of them were incredibly knowledgeable about vivisection and how to organize a protest. They made it clear that a police officer must warn us if he is going to arrest us and if he does, do what he says and we'll be fine. If we are going to get arrested on purpose by practicing passive resistance, that is something that is planned ahead of time. So no worries, we were not there this time to get arrested. Whew! That was a load of my mind. Wait a minute! I wasn't going to go anyway, was I?

The three of them also went on and on about something I did not understand; no signs about animal cruelty, blood, animal Auschwitz or anything of that nature. There would be large photos of animals in laboratories but the signs all had to be about scientific fraud, greed and grants. And if we couldn't speak knowledgeably to reporters regarding the issue of scientific fraud, send the reporter to Jack who was the spokesperson. Gladly. I couldn't imagine having a reporter and cameraman interviewing me about something I had avoided all my life and obviously knew less about than I thought I knew. What am I thinking? Am I going to the protest? I guess I am.

I asked Mary if Chris was a vegetarian and she told me he was vegan. Like most people at the time, I had no idea of what that was and becoming a vegan myself was a few years down the road.

Besides animal suffering, other things were weighing heavily on my mind. Considering the drastic mistakes I had made in my life with terrible consequences for Erika and me, I was yearning for some spiritual guidance and relief from daily depression. I had done my best making sure Erika was always surrounded by love and well taken care of through years of upheaval and never failed in my responsibility to all my cats, but instead of praying for guidance at every step I had blundered blindly forward clinging to the hope that *this* was the right move, *this* was the right man, desperate to win back everything I had lost. And here I was; in the flats of Encino light years away from the home in the hills I had loved. One day I sat on the front steps of Kevin's little house and thought, "Well, this is it for me. Unless a miracle happens, this is where I will be living for the rest of my life. But Erika is happy here. She can walk to school and we have a yard for her and her friends to play in and we still have that closeness between her and I and that's all that's important to me." I overheard one of the other moms comment one day after school, "They're so clingy at this age. I can't wait for her to grow out of it." And I thought, "They'll grow out of it soon enough. Now is the time to enjoy it." Erika still asked me to hold her on my lap and would say to me, "Hold me like a baby, mommy, hold me like a baby!" And I would rock her and sing to her like I did when she was little. Yes, I was very grateful to Kevin for giving us a place to live but there still resided somewhere in the depth of my heart a kernel of hope that I would act again. It's that dreaded disease that just will not disappear no matter how buried it might be under years of rejection and disappointment.

I decided I had to find myself a church home and do some communicating with God again.

My mother loved watching Pastor Lloyd Ogilvie of Hollywood Presbyterian Church on television and had often encouraged (nagged) me to watch him as well. I decided it was time for me to tune in and listen to him. He wasn't your typical television evangelical preacher, yelling and carrying on like a mad man, pacing back and forth, warning of dire consequences if people didn't do exactly as he said. And most of these mean, hysterical, threatening, exhibitionists had southern accents and sounded very much like the racists I had clashed with in Mississippi. It never surprised me when some of them ended up being convicted of crimes and going to jail. I'll never forget watching Jimmy Swaggart preaching on television, going absolutely berserk about women wearing shorts. I thought he was going to break down and cry just thinking about it. As I remember it, to him, women who wore shorts inflamed men's minds and bodies and rendered them helpless to resist temptation. Wearing shorts was an unparalleled sin and something decent women should shun like the devil and hell itself. As I listened I thought, "This man has some serious issues with his sexuality." And sure enough, a short time afterwards it came out that Jimmy Swaggart had been visiting prostitutes to fulfill his needs. Didn't surprise me one bit.

I decided it was time for me to visit Lloyd's church (and he insisted we all call him Lloyd even though he was really *Dr.* Ogilvie) and found the church to be not only beautiful architecturally, but filled with friendly people who reflected the warmth of their pastor. I started attending and loved the choir, the packed house for every service, and, above all, Lloyd's gentle guidance and words of support and encouragement, which he put into every sermon. I became a member soon after the first time I visited and decided it was time to listen to what God had to say to me. I prayed about every move I was going to make, including the upcoming protest at USC. I also prayed that I would find just one person, just one new friend who was at a protest for the first time, who I could commiserate with.

I drove to USC and parked, a little late, to make sure I wasn't the first person there, and saw at least 100 people with signs outside the laboratory buildings. I wasn't sure where to go or what to do but I spotted a pile of signs and headed for it and grabbed one that said ANIMAL RESEARCH SCIENTIFIC FRAUD. Chris DeRose was busy talking to a short, thin, dark-haired man dressed in a suit and an attractive young woman in a dark dress and high heels. The three of them obviously were in charge. Cameras and reporters were everywhere and focused on Jack Carone, who seemed extremely articulate and self-assured as he was being interviewed. At some point, the protesters started chanting various slogans and I tentatively and softly joined in. At one point a man came out of one of the laboratory buildings and walked up to Chris and the other man and woman. They spoke for awhile before he went back in. While all this was going on, I noticed another girl who seemed as lost as I was but had a great big smile on her face as if she were really enjoying the entire spectacle. I approached her and introduced myself. And that is how I met Debbie Widel, my future partner in crime.

Debbie told me the congenial man who came out to talk to Chris was in charge of all the vivisection going on at USC. Back then I found it amazing that such a nice, friendly man was actually a sociopath who oversaw the torture of animals. Now that I have seen them in their many disguises – distinguished "researcher," respected professor, Nobel Prize winner, veterinarian, pet owner – I'm never surprised at the seemingly "normal" men and women who find pleasure in bringing pain and death to helpless animals.

After the protest, we were told that there would be a screening of a documentary regarding vivisection in a few days. Several of us decided to go together. Debbie drove us to the screening and when we arrived, there were already 15 to 20 people there. We had no idea of what we would be seeing, only that we would finally understand the "scientific argument" against vivisection and why Chris kept insisting no signs about cruelty or blood. The documentary was over an hour in length but no one moved a muscle during the screening. We were too shocked, horrified and repelled by what we were seeing: human beings perpetrating horrible acts on animals, the narrator explaining why those terrible experiments could not be extrapolated to humans because of physiological differences, that vivisection is a multibillion-dollar industry, and why it continues even though it is a fraud and harms everyone. When they showed the footage of the head injury lab at the University of Pennsylvania and in graphic detail showed vivisector Generelli and his cohorts slamming chimpanzees' heads ninety miles an hour into a steel plate and joking about it, I wanted to go to go to their homes and choke the life out of those sadists and not give a damn about the consequences. I swore to Debbie if Generelli had walked into the room I would have gone for his throat and no one would have been able to pry my hands off.

On the drive home, Debbie and I felt like we had been hit by a train locomotive. The horror of what we had seen overwhelmed us. We had learned a lot but we couldn't think because our brains were overloaded with ugly images and a multitude of facts we still had not processed. But the next day we both knew our lives had been changed and we had found our purpose in life. And what a relief it was to me. The next day I stood in my back yard and looked up at the blue sky and said, "Okay, God, I give up. I know what I have to do even though I don't want to do it, never did want to do it, and am not happy with what you have chosen to be my life's purpose." Then I breathed a sigh of relief and went back in the house.

CHAPTER 14

Debbie and I Prepare to Change the World

As I was slowly morphing into a full-fledged anti-vivisectionist, Kevin Krasny and I were becoming close friends. He was caring, hardworking and considerate, everything a woman could want in a man. I wished he weren't so much younger than I and that he and I could have a future together. One time we went to a Rams game with his father and stepmother and it felt very strange. For years, Alan and I had gone to Rams games with Paul, and, now, here I was with Paul's son, Kevin, who I had met when he was a teenager. I tried to explain to Paul, "This isn't what it seems...I know it must feel strange me being with..." I hemmed and hawed. Paul just laughed and said, "Go for it! Doesn't bother me a bit!" Yes, it would have been nice to actually be with someone who wasn't cruel, didn't have psychological issues, didn't do drugs or drink and treated me well, but we both knew he had a lot of living to do before he settled down with anyone and he was just too young for me. He had found a house to rent up in the Hollywood Hills overlooking the whole world and allowed Erika and I to keep living in his house. The only person I had met in my age range as nice as Kevin was Tony Eldridge, and he was always married when I wasn't and vice versa. Tony finally met someone who became his best friend, fell in love and married her. A part of me wanted to meet and marry my soul mate as Tony had done, but another part of me just wanted to become successful on my own and depend on no one but myself.

It took weeks for Debbie and me to recover from what we had seen in the documentary. Seeing it had been that traumatic. But we both began reading Hans Ruesch's *Slaughter of the Innocent* which tells the history of vivisection from its inception and explains why it has no relation to human beings; the book has even more horrific descriptions of vivisection than the documentary. We read the book a few pages at a time and persevered until we made it through. Then Debbie insisted we go to the UCLA medical library and read the protocols of animal experiments; I reluctantly agreed. We were not surprised when we read that after every experiment the vivisectors would write, "Of course these are only experiments on cats (or dogs, mice, rats, goats, etc.), so we have no idea of what the result will be in human beings." Every single protocol we read had that same disclaimer. Why do them is the logical question? By then Debbie and I knew the answer to that; money.

Alena came back from wherever she had been, which turned out to be Virginia, the Philippines, Arizona, and Del Mar. She didn't say much about what had happened but I vaguely remember being told she had married a Navy Seal and now it was over. Her agent, Kevin Casselman, was still enthralled with her and vowed again to make her a big star. He just needed Alena to stay in town long enough to make that happen. But she was a free spirit who couldn't stay in one place for very long.

Paul Krasny was directing a television show that was to shoot in San Francisco, and I was called in to audition. Being as Paul was one of my dearest friends, I was cast and flew up to San Francisco for the shoot. My big scene was opposite veteran character actor, Jack Warden. I thought I was underplaying the part of a grieving widow perfectly when Jack complained to Paul in front of the whole cast and crew, "I'm not getting anything from her!" I was so horrified and hurt by his criticism I immediately threw out the last vestiges of Charles Conrad and upped my grieving several notches.

Debbie and I prepared our three-ring binders with all of our anti-vivisection material and decided to start changing the world at Venice Beach. We assumed that once people understood that vivisection is a fraud we could end vivisection in five years. We didn't understand why animal rights groups were not jumping on the bandwagon with Last Chance for Animals and a few other organizations attacking vivisection with the scientific argument and instead kept fighting a losing battle talking to the public only about cruelty, morality and philosophy. After writing and calling the large, well-funded animal groups and encouraging them to change their hopeless tactics that had failed for over a hundred years, and getting stone-walled, we gave up on them and decided to do what needed to be done ourselves.

We set up a table on Venice Beach with our sign ANIMAL RESEARCH SCIENTIFIC FRAUD hung up in the front of the table, started hand-ing out our leaflets and waited for people to thank us for educating them. We didn't have to wait long for reactions; "You stupid b---ches, how do think they'll find cures?!" "I hope your mother gets cancer and dies!" "People are more important than animals!" "You're both full of crap!" and so it went. We actually heard much worse. Every once in awhile, someone would glance at our handouts and ask questions and seem interested in what we had to say, but that was very unusual. Debbie had no fear of taking on the worst verbal offenders; some guy could yell at her, "Your mother is scum for ever letting you be born you piece of sh-t!" and Debbie would smile and follow him and respond, "Okay, why don't we talk about that? You don't have to leave. Let's have a friendly conversation here. You could learn something helpful." And somehow, she managed to convince some of those maniacs to talk to her. As for me? If they came at me with foul language and insulted my heritage I told them where they could shove their two-digit IQ that they undoubt-edly inherited from their idiot parents who were probably first cousins, or words to that effect. How we managed not to come to blows, ever, was a miracle.

Eventually I calmed down and learned to take the abuse almost as well as Debbie, and we became better at talking to people and convincing them we cared about people as well as animals and hurting one was not going to help the other. This was in the 1980s and the scientific argument against vivisection was new. We had to take the brunt of the attacks from both the public and animal groups who wanted nothing to do with standing up to the scientific community using science, preferring instead to fight vivisection with guilt, philosopher's quotes and animal rights arguments. Unfortunately, animals do not have the rights of humans; they can't go to court, they can't sue those that do them harm, and how many times have you seen yellow police tape surrounding the body of a raccoon who has been hit and killed by a car? Animals only have the rights that people like us demand that they have, and those rights usually involve animals in entertainment or animal testing of cosmetics or household products, but if it comes to a choice between letting beloved Fifi the poodle go to a vivisection lab or letting Aunt Martha die of cancer, nine times out of ten, Fifi's owner will say, "Well if experimenting on Fifi means Aunt Martha will live, then go ahead and take my precious Fifi." It is our job as anti-vivisectionists to make it clear that cutting up Fifi will not save Aunt Martha.

After a short time, Debbie and I were forced to admit that changing the world might take a little longer than a couple of years, but we both knew that however long it took, we would stay the course. Educating people was the key to making them demand changes. Besides taking abuse at tables at Venice and outside the zoo, we went to protests and now knew that we were capable of being interviewed by the press, even though we rarely had the chance to talk to them. But we did our part, yelling and chanting outside vivisection labs at UCLA, USC, Loma Linda and other places. We came to know Sandra Bell, who was the attractive lady who had been one of the leaders of the demo at USC. She was co-director of another group and I envied her knowledge and ability to debate vivisectors. Vivisectors were perfectly willing to debate animal rights people regarding cruelty (humans are more important than animals) but were increasingly wary of debating anti-vivisectionist who would say, "The moral issue is self-evident. Let's talk about science." For them, that debate was lost before they began. Vivisectors know better than anyone that what they do is useless.

In the midst of my new-found passion and anti-vivisection activity, I still ached from the bottom of my soul to work as an actress, and fought depression every day, afraid that would never happen again and that I would end up a miserable failure. At Hollywood Presbyterian Church, there was a small group of professional actors, all members of one or more of the acting unions, who met once a week in the missions building and practiced cold readings, shared "praise reports" on good things happening for them in the business, and supported and prayed for each other. I decided that this was a group I would love to join. David Schall was the founder and leader of The Actors Co-op. He was a kind, jovial white-haired man who welcomed me and made me feel like I had found a real home with other actors. He had visions of us founding a theater on the church campus and producing plays and musicals that would be recognized in Hollywood as worthwhile of recognition and reviewed in the trades. We all dreamed of the day that would happen, while David made plans to bring it to reality.

While I was concentrating on Erika, work and acting, Debbie and Sandra had become close friends and decided to form a new group to make sure that dedicated activists would have an organization that not only would continue the work of Hans Ruesch and keep fighting vivisection on scientific grounds, but would connect the dots between vivisection, our failing health and the destruction of the environment. They didn't have a name for the organization so I spent a few hours with my legal pad and came up with the name People for Reason in Science and Medicine.

The new group, PRISM, networked with Heal the Bay and other environmental organizations. It became more important than ever for activists to educate themselves on the scientific argument in order to effectively debate people who were pro-vivisection or simply did not understand the issue. And since understanding that argument only involves common sense – all species are physiologically different from each other, therefore experiments on one cannot be extrapolated to another – it's easy to learn and easy to deflect any pro-vivisection arguments.

David moved forward with plans to renovate the children's puppet theater on the church campus to include a venue for The Actors Co-op at the church. Everyone helped out with the easy stuff and let the experts who knew carpentry do the rest. In no time, we had a workable theater and David started planning productions. But being a part of a theater group was not earning me money and after one temp job ended I was in need of a more permanent solution. I had to pay bills and rent on our little cottage. I had to make sure that our home was secure even though I knew Kevin would never kick us out. One of the actors in the theater group was working as a telemarketer for the Hollywood Bowl selling tickets to the Los Angeles Philharmonic. Even though I thought telemarketing was almost as repugnant as being a hooker on Hollywood and Vine, he convinced me I would get used to it in no time, after I developed a tough skin. I was desperate for work so I took the job.

We all sat around a table in a small room in a building near the Hollywood Bowl with our computer printouts of former subscribers and everybody started calling people early in the morning. Some of the telemarketers were quiet and polite and others loud and insistent. It seemed like the loud ones had the most luck. My spiel went something like this: (very quiet) "Hello I'm calling from the Hollywood Bowl to ask if you want to renew your subscription probably not I'm so sorry to bother you goodbye." Not much of a saleswoman, I didn't have much success. I dreaded going in to work every day. I kept hoping I would get hit by a truck so I'd have an excuse not to go in, but every once in awhile, I'd get a positive response and it kept me going.

I didn't have an agent at that time and so again, would submit myself for acting jobs from Breakdowns someone shared with me. One day I sent in my headshot and resume to *General Hospital* for a role I knew I could do, and waited for a call. A week went by and I heard nothing. Christmas was coming up and my mother arranged for Erika and me to fly up to Seattle for a short holiday break. What a relief to not have to go in to that job I hated for a few days. The family all doted on Erika and my parents and sister and my two nephews did everything to make her feel special. My parents, of course, showered Erika with presents and had to give us extra suitcases to carry it all back to L.A. How I hated the thought of going back to that miserable call center with the dreaded phones and printouts. If it weren't for Erika, I would have considered throwing myself off the roof of the Bowl or at least, playing hooky for a day or two. But bills must be paid and I persevered. I was so bad at that job, why I didn't get fired is a mystery.

When I heard from the *General Hospital* casting office, I almost didn't know why they were calling me. It had been weeks since I submitted myself; since before Christmas. But I pulled myself together long enough to realize they wanted me to come in for an audition, which meant taking time off from getting rejected one hundred times a day, and I figured one more rejection would be child's play by this time. But that was not to be. I had barely finished reading my lines when they ushered me into producer Wes Kenney's office, the very same producer for whom I had read so abysmally for *Days of Our Lives*. I hoped to God he didn't remember. He asked me if I had a pair of glasses I could wear for the role, I said yes and he instructed me to go back to the casting office and sign papers because I had been cast. So that is how I ended up with a principal role on *General Hospital* that was going to reoccur for a few months which meant I had been rescued from the loathsome telemarketing chamber of hell.

I only worked one or two days a week on *General Hospital* which meant I had plenty of time to work for PRISM and be involved in protests at anti-vivisection labs. I still remember so clearly one protest involving over 100 protesters at the Cedars Sinai vivisection lab where Debbie and I were seated on the sidewalk blocking a side door to Cedars' vivarium. As well-dressed Beverly Hills residents walked by us and cast disparaging glances our way, I had never felt so absolutely at home there on the sidewalk and so absolutely sure of my purpose on this earth. Even though I was only a few feet away from where animals were being tortured and I would have liked nothing more than to turn into Superwoman, break through the door, and rescue every last one of them, I had a feeling of calmness and rightness that might have been happiness if not for the heartache this cause of mine would always bring me.

We used to visit vivisectors' mansions in Beverly Hills and Westwood and walk up and down the block letting everyone know who their neighbor was and what he or she did. One man in particular, I remember, had been doing gruesome experiments on dogs at UCLA, cutting them up and removing their hearts and other various experiments he delighted in perpetrating. For decades, this pathetic excuse for a human being had been doing these gory experiments just for the fun of it while his grants were renewed year after year. Vivisectors don't have to show the government that what they do is useful in any way, just write down a bunch of pseudo-scientific gobbledy-gook and the money comes rolling in. One day at his house, we were loudly enumerating his crimes loud enough for the neighbors to hear when a hysterical woman came out of the house and demanded we stop because the vivisector was not feeling well and we were upsetting him. Needless to say, that was all the inspiration we needed to yell even louder. When it was announced a month later that the vivisector had died, we rejoiced. To us, it seemed like karma that he died of an extremely painful heart condition.

One of our anti-vivisection protests was outside a fur store where vivisectors were having a fundraiser for a disease organization; a double whammy – fur and vivisection. We were all dressed in black and were not to speak a word, instead, we were to be deadly quiet and serious as if we were at a funeral. It was a huge demo and was proceeding as planned when I saw Kevin and Susan Dobson walking toward the entrance. Without reservation or a second thought I ran down the sidewalk and accosted him, "Kevin! What are you doing here?! Do you know what you're raising money for?!" He looked startled and his face turned red from embarrassment as he backed away from me towards the entrance to the fur store. "You're raising money for vivisection! At a *fur* store!" A none-too-pleased Jack Carone rushed over to me and hissed, "No talking!" But I kept following Kevin, staring at him, demanding that he answer me. He whispered, "I'll come back out and talk to you." A very annoyed Susan pulled him toward the door and I doubted very much if he would have the nerve to defy the woman who ruled his life and face me again, and I was right.

Medical students at UCLA had been calling the Last Chance for Animals office begging Chris to try to do something to stop the school from forcing them to vivisect on animals in their classes. The most compassionate, caring medical students did not want to torture animals while learning how to care for people. They would rather drop out of medical school. Other students had parents who had paid an astronomical sum for their education and these students did not want to torture animals either but were forcing themselves to do it rather than risk their parents' wrath. In response to their pleas, Chris planned a sit-in in the office of the dean of the medical school and asked for volunteers. I was one of several people who were willing to do it. There was a huge demonstration of at least 900 people going on outside while those of us who were planning on getting arrested sat in the library and waited for word from Chris when we were to enter the glass-enclosed office of the dean. Heart beating (never having been arrested) and a little scared, I followed instructions and we headed for the dean's office and locked ourselves inside. We put up a huge banner that said ANIMAL RESEARCH SCIENTIFIC FRAUD, which could be seen through the window of the dean's office, and waited for the media. And they came. Every news station was there aiming their cameras right at the scientific fraud sign. For whatever reason, security was unable to unlock the doors for quite awhile, giving our spokes-people time to be interviewed by the news stations and explain why we were there. When the doors were finally unlocked, we practiced passive resistance and were carried out one by one to the waiting police van. Outside, a few of the protesters had figured out the police were taking us out the back door and were there, yelling encouragement to us.

After we were booked into jail, I started becoming very dizzy. I hadn't eaten or had anything to drink that morning because I always have to go to the bathroom and I wanted to avoid that, for obvious reasons. Now I was completely dehydrated and was just about to pass out when we received word we were to be released. I could barely stand and one of the other women practically picked me up saying, "You don't want them to put you in the infirmary. Then it could be days before you get out of here!" She hauled me out of that cell block single-handedly and she wasn't a very big woman either. Rod Grier picked me up outside the prison and drove me home. I fell asleep, exhausted, hoping we had done something to make a difference.

At our trial, we were represented by a brilliant attorney and charges were soon dismissed. Chris had assured us that would happen, but still it was a relief.

When we were demonstrating against forcing medical students to vivisect on animals, most universities in the country were involved in that fraudulent, unsavory practice. Now, thanks to the focused diligence of Last Chance for Animals, Physicians Committee for Responsible Medicine, PETA, PRISM, and thousands of activists, not one medical school, in the U.S. or Canada, require that medical students must vivisect on animals in order to earn their degree.

One day, as I was driving past Balboa Park in Encino, I saw a white dog with a red kerchief around his neck sitting on the sidewalk, with no human in sight. I stopped and got out of the car and looked around to see if the owner was anywhere in the vicinity. I didn't see anyone so I opened the passenger door; the dog jumped in and immediately settled down in the seat. I took him home and shut him up in my room, not knowing how he would be with cats and started making signs to put up near the park to try and find his owner. I drove back to the park and posted the signs and decided to place an ad in the paper as well. Since the dog had one brown eye and one blue, I named him Brue. It turned out that he loved cats and was willing to put up with being accidently scratched and clawed with only a whimper now and then. I found out what breed he was when I was out walking him on a leash and a neighbor said, "Oh, you have a Staffordshire Terrier!" I said, "A what?" He said, "A pit bull." I didn't know much about dog breeds, but I had heard that pit bulls had a bad reputation. Brue put a lie to that notion. No one answered my ads, and Brue became a part of the family. He loved Erika, the cats, and me and slept with his head on the pillow next to Maude's. Unfortunately, Brue could jump over our high fences and was constantly getting out. Fearful that he would be picked up one day by the dogcatcher, I found him a home out in Woodland Hills, where he could play with other pit bulls and stay safely inside a huge yard. I was so attached to him I could barely watch as he ran off with his new friends. I loved that dog.

After my role on *General Hospital* ran its course, I found a job that I truly enjoyed. I worked for a government project called "Options for Youth." I visited the homes of high school students who lived in the worst areas of the San Fernando Valley and tutored them in all subjects. Sometimes, arriving at my students' houses, I would find out that there had been gang shootings nearby the night before, and one student, to prove his point, showed me blood on the brick wall outside his house where someone had been shot. For various reasons, my students were not physically able to attend classes at school and this was their chance to earn their GEDs. Some had parents who were supportive, others had almost no supervision whatsoever. One girl, who moved from rundown apartment, to motel, to yet another temporary home with her mother, consistently did her homework and earned top grades. Students like her inspired me to work harder to help and encourage them. The program unfortunately was discontinued, to the detriment of the many kids who could have earned their GEDs and moved out of poverty to a better life.

Stray animals always seemed to know where I would cross their path and one night, on my way to attending casting director night at The Actors Co-op, I saw a medium-sized brown dog of indeterminate breed lying underneath an abandoned semi-trailer truck as I was parking my car in the parking lot next to the church. I walked over to him and saw that he looked sick and hungry and as abandoned as the rusty trailer that gave him shelter. He had no collar or tag so I went around to the apartment buildings in the area and asked if anyone knew who the brown dog belonged to. No one had ever even seen him. So I decided I would forgo the casting director night and take the dog, now named Brownie, home. Erika was happy to finally have another dog, and he was so meek and mild-mannered our cats barely took notice of him. I made a half-hearted attempt to find him a home. He fit into our family just fine.

While I was working at my various jobs, I was also writing scripts, most of them thrillers. Directors would read them and try to get them produced, actors would read them and try to find a film company or network that would produce them so they could star, and I would submit them to anyone important in the business who might be interested enough to read them. I always had great feedback, but no cigar. Even Bob Barker called me one day and said he would try to find a producer for one of my thrillers that dealt indirectly with vivisection. Having read many scripts submitted to Arnon when I lived in New York, I knew that mine were a level above most of those scripts, but I didn't have William Morris or CAA representing me as those writers did and representing yourself makes for an uphill battle in getting in to see producers.

Besides writing scripts, I was also writing a book, a sort of detective novel in which the two main characters were loosely based on my friends Porter and Alena and my cat Maude. I loved my story and had great faith that it could be a best seller, but convincing a publisher of that became a tough proposition as I submitted it to several publishers and received rejection slips in return. The only positive reaction I had was from a publisher who provided editing services, would publish the book, market and publicize it, but I had to pay $5000 for all of that to happen. Eric Morris said he would be more than willing to give me the money to do that but I couldn't bring myself to accept. I don't know why. If I had had more faith in my book and had been confident it would make money so I could pay him back maybe I would have. Now I wish I had.

After vivisectors, hunters are next on my list as sadists who I ardently loathe. Periodically, friends from Orange County would find out when and where pot-bellied, beer-drinking louts were planning hunting trips. That would open up an opportunity for us to spoil their "fun." I was introduced to "hunt sabs," as hunting interventions are called, by friends who did this on a regular basis. We made plans to intervene a hunting party led by a dentist from Sierra Madre who was looking forward to murdering long-horned sheep in the desert. We drove to the location and checked into nearby motel rooms then spread out into the hills with our air horns. Whenever we saw hunters nearing the sheep we would blow our horns and scare the animals away.

Needless to say, the louts were not happy and called the forest rangers for help, by land and by helicopter. Meanwhile, I was getting so disgusted with the louts I decided to go directly into their camp and confront some of them. "These animals are harmless! Why don't you leave them alone?! You're nothing but a bunch of spineless cowards!" They were too shocked to respond and after a few more choice words I got out while the getting was good because the rangers were on their way to save them from me.

None of us were caught and no animals killed that day. Later at the motel, one of my friends told me he heard one of the louts yelling at one of the rangers, "Get that blond b—tch! I want that blond b—tch!" and the helicopters scoured the hills for me after I was long gone. Why is what the sadists do legal and saving animals illegal? But it's the same with vivisection labs and fur farms; compassionate people go to jail and the psychopaths are protected.

One day, after taking Erika to school, I was surprised to get a call from my agent that the very same casting director who I was supposed to have done a cold reading for at The Actors Co-op the night I found Brownie was calling me in for a show called *Divorce Court*. She remembered me from another show I had done and thought I was perfect for the role of the divorcing wife of a no-good, cheating husband. On the show, actors do their utmost to convince the judge that they have a right to every penny and property they're asking for because the outcome of the show is not planned but entirely up to the judge. I did my best to state my case as did my husband and I was very pleased to win the monetary award I was seeking, which had never happened in real life. A few days later I had a call from Don, the man who played my husband, asking me for a date. As with Steve, I said to myself, "Why not, it's not going to change my life." The man was younger than me by a few years and who needed that kind of grief? I guess I did need it because another marriage was in my future.

I asked him to meet me in the patio of the church outside the Co-op. We talked for a long time and I found out he was a vegetarian, an environmentalist, and liked to cook vegetarian meals. He sounded too good to be true but I had no intention of jumping into anything. I was happy the way things were with just Erika and me; the two musketeers, together against the world. It couldn't hurt just to go out to dinner, could it? He was fun to talk to, very passionate about his beliefs, and was interested in PRISM and what we were trying to accomplish. Erika wasn't thrilled that I was dating him as she was very fond of Billy Vera, who she wanted me to marry. I had to explain to her Billy wasn't interested in me in that way so we had to settle for him being our friend and hearing him and the Beaters play. Nevertheless, when Billy married someone else, she was severely disappointed. Don, not Billy was in my future, for better or for worse.

One day, because my car was in the shop, a friend picked me up and drove us to El Torito in Encino to have lunch. After my friend had parked the car and we were walking toward the entrance, I heard a mewing sound coming from behind the Shell gas station next to the restaurant. I asked the parking lot attendant if they had heard the cat mewing for very long and they said they'd heard it all day. It sounded like it was coming from the bottom of the dumpster that was filled with old tires and other car parts. I told my friend that I was sorry I couldn't have lunch and asked her to take me home so I could change clothes and get a cat carrier. After I changed, my friend took me back to the Shell station and dropped me off and I started digging through the giant dumpster, listening to the pitiful mewing the whole time. It took me about half an hour to finally get everything out. I found a small shoebox wedged between some other boxes and lifted it out. Inside was a tiny gray-and-white kitten who looked scared to death. I lifted him out and put him in the carrier and headed for home. It took about an hour to walk back to my house and all along Ventura Boulevard people gave me strange looks and averted their eyes. I found out why when I got home and looked in the mirror and saw that my entire face was black with dirt. By now my new kitten was named Shell and I locked him in the bedroom with food and water and a litter box. He pretty much stayed under the bed for two weeks, coming out only to eat, drink and do his duty. After that, he was welcomed by the rest of the cat family and slowly realized he was in a safe place.

When Erika brought home a black kitten who she said needed a home or he would be taken to the shelter and put to death, I protested for all of five minutes. We named him Squeeky because that's what he did instead of meowing. He was a little more standoffish than the others and preferred to keep to himself. Not finished building our family, Erika brought home a little yellow-striped kitten that had big ears which made him look like a space alien. I couldn't say no and we named him Rocky. One day Rocky, who was not very bright, ran past me out of the house right in front of a car and had his back legs run over. I screamed and ran over to him and carefully picked him up and put him in my car. I sped him off to the veterinarian's office, not knowing if he would live or die. The vet gave him a pain shot, examined him and said it would cost $2,500 to transfer bones from his chest to his back legs. Rocky would walk again, just be a little wobbly. Not having a clue where the money would come from, I told him to do the surgery right away. Then I got in my car and prayed, "Dear God, you know I don't have the money to pay for this. Let it come to me somehow, some way." Before I had to pay the bill, John Lombardo called and said he wanted me to be in an infomercial he was directing. The salary would just cover Rocky's bill and he recovered fine, with just a little hitch in his step.

But the family was still not complete. One day Kevin brought me a small, dirty piece of fluff he had found on the Pen Mar golf course while he was playing. Naturally, he couldn't leave her there. So we washed little Penmar very carefully, getting a layer of grease off her, and wrapped her in a towel. She was a little yellow-and-white, long-haired kitten, sweet and loving and full of life. I always meant to look for homes for all of these wayward kittens, but somehow, I just never got around to it.

The very day Erika started junior high school, everything between us changed. She came home from that first day having decided she had no use for me and wanted nothing to do with my rules or doing chores. Overnight, she changed from the sweet little girl she had always been to a distant, sullen stranger. When I talked it over with friends, they assured me that this was the way all teenagers acted toward their parents and that she would eventually grow out of it. But for me it was unsettling because the change in her was so profound. Erika enjoyed her weekends with Alan where she was free to do as she pleased and come and go without being questioned. I figured it was only a matter of time before she decided that was where she wanted to live.

Jerry Lewis, on stage, crying and begging for money for his "kids" was a telethon tradition for years. One year, several anti-vivisection groups, together with former "kids" of Jerry Lewis, protested outside of a television station where the Muscular Dystrophy Association was having its annual telethon to raise money, purportedly for children with muscular dystrophy. In reality, it is actually a cynical vehicle to make people cry and give money so Jerry Lewis or whoever is hosting can haul in a few million dollars, and executives of Big Pharma can continue their cushy lifestyles. Meanwhile, many of Jerry's former "kids" were complaining to the press that they couldn't even get wheelchairs out of the Muscular Dystrophy Association, let alone any other kind of help. Jerry's response was to refer to the muscular dystrophy victims who were inside the studio in the front row of the telethon as "human waterbeds," and told security guards to remove them. In an interview with Vanity Fair, when asked for a reaction to the "kids'" complaints, Jerry said "F—em." The Vanity Fair reporter couldn't believe what he heard and Jerry repeated it, "F—em." Jerry has become a multi-millionaire off these kids after his career went down the tubes and this, in a nutshell, is what he really thinks of them.

With Jerry's "kids" and over a hundred anti-vivisectionist protesting, this was one of the biggest demonstrations ever against the fraudulent disease "charity." And it was at this event one of my fellow protesters told me that Billy Vera had gotten married. I was stunned. Even though we hadn't seen each other for awhile, he was one of my dearest friends and he hadn't even told me. I went to see him play at "At My Place" in Santa Monica shortly after I found out. I walked in early and saw him seated on a stool at his usual place. "You got married," I said. "Yeah, I got married," he responded and looked at me resigned with a little smile. Later his wife came in and I saw her going from table to table, very upbeat, smiling, talking, seeming to know everyone. I enjoyed the show as always and didn't see him for a long time after that.

After several months of dating, Don and I decided to get married. We wanted to be together so why put off the inevitable? He treated Erika very well and helped her with her homework and he loved all the animals. A vegetarian who I met for our first date at church, he was the answer to my prayers. It was meant to be. I was sure of it. We flew to Tahoe and married on the very day our *Divorce Court* episode aired. We joked that now that we already had our divorce, our marriage was secure. Back home he continued with his sales job and I with my usual routine of temping and looking for acting work. I saw nothing in my future that would take me off this path. My chances of becoming a working actor seemed pretty slim, but being an animal activist was a purpose I clung to because it gave meaning to my life. Unfortunately, I knew Erika would continue to grow away from me and there was nothing I could do about it. I had become the enemy and she let me know that every minute she was home.

CHAPTER 15

Peter Falk and the Beginning of the End, Again

WE WERE ONLY A MONTH into our marriage when Don betrayed me. I will never forget that night. He had gone to a bachelor party and I was at a book sale with Debbie and Sandra raising money for PRISM. Because of where Don was that night, Sandra and Debbie and I were having a discussion where they maintained that no matter how pretty, loving and sexy a wife may be, the husband is still capable of cheating. I completely disagreed and used my own brand new marriage as example. Don and I were in love with each other and nothing could possibly induce him to be with another woman.

After I came home that night I went to bed expecting Don home by midnight. When he wasn't home by two in the morning, my heart was racing; had he been in an accident? Why didn't he call? Then I wondered what else he might be doing? Finally, around three o'clock in the morning he came through the door with a guilty look on his face. I was livid. I demanded to know what he had been doing all that time, and after a half-hour of stonewalling me he finally admitted that after the bachelor party, the groom and a few others, including Don, decided to rent a room in the Hollywood Hotel and hire hookers to entertain them. I went ballistic. Only hours before I had been defending him and our unassailable marriage believing nothing could ever make him cheat on me. And here we were, only married one month and he had already broken his vows. I couldn't stand the sight of him. I ran out of the house and checked into a motel for the rest of the weekend. Thank God, Erika was with Alan. My long-awaited soul mate turned out to be just another man I couldn't trust. When I came back, he apologized profusely and asked me to forgive him, but I was not in a forgiving mood. In the time it took for him to tell me where he had been, I went from being madly love with the man of my dreams to feeling nothing but a smoldering, deep-seated hatred for the cheating S.O.B. The more you love someone, the more they can hurt you, and the more you loathe them for betraying you. Nevertheless, after a few weeks of uncomfortable, resentful silence on both sides, I did work at trying to forgive him and we tried to get past all the ugly words and recriminations. The marriage limped along with both of us pretending the relationship was not broken, but now I knew I could never trust him not to cheat on me again. In my heart, I also knew that sooner or later I was facing another divorce, another humiliation and setting another terrible example for Erika who, by this time, was completely lost to me.

She had decided to live with her father and do as she pleased, not attend school, and come and go without any supervision on his part. Erika, after two months of living with Alan, the truant officer called to inform me, had not been attending school, and I had better get her back to her classes or there would be consequences. What they were I don't know, I just remember being frantic to talk to her. Somehow, I tracked her down and told her she had to go back to school or come live with me again. I had no money for lawyers to try to get the courts to force her to stay with me while Alan could always charm someone to work for him for free. I allowed her to stay with Alan but warned them both that she had to stay in school or, forget about what I would do; the law would take care of it. Meanwhile, other mothers kept telling me that this was normal behavior for teenagers and that eventually she'll find her way back to me. That didn't make any of it less painful to deal with.

About this time, Sandra fell in love with the head of another animal group and decided to go back east to live and work with him, while

Debbie was going to concentrate on her studies to become a chiropractor. I was asked to run PRISM out of my house and I was only too happy to take on the job. I spent months organizing all the paperwork, paying bills, depositing checks, obtaining copyrights for our written material, corresponding with our members around the country, and organizing a huge Christmas fund raiser. I hosted the event and it was a big success, raising a lot of money for PRISM. After almost a year of running PRISM on my own with the help of several volunteers, Sandra came back to Los Angeles and wanted to take over again. I was reluctant but she had founded PRISM with Debbie, and I handed over the reins to the two of them again.

Don had a very rich grandfather who we used to visit. His caregiver was a mean, cranky old woman who we had heard from neighbors was abusing him. I didn't like her one bit and warned her we had heard negative reports from neighbors regarding her treatment of him and that she was on thin ice as far as her employment was concerned. Don and I both knew of the dangers of vaccines and how doctors were pushing for elderly people to be inundated with them. Vaccines were especially deadly for someone in his nineties like Don's grandfather and we told the caregiver that Don's grandfather was not to be allowed any flu shots. Shortly afterwards, the two of them went on a cruise and as soon as he came home, having enjoyed himself immensely, she took him to the doctor to be vaccinated and he promptly became deathly ill. He had been injected with a *pneumonia vaccine*, which is even more lethal than a flu vaccine. He died not long after that, and the caregiver disappeared. Don's grandfather had a multi-million-dollar estate that needed to be settled, and during that time we were asked by the family to be caretakers of his house in the Wilshire area until the will was out of probate. I was hesitant to leave the security of Kevin's little cottage, but the estate would pay me to take care of the property and I wouldn't have to worry about temping. Erika didn't care if I moved to Timbuktu so that wasn't an issue. I agreed to do it. Meanwhile, after the family went through the grandfather's things, they found out the caregiver had helped herself to his jewelry and other valuables and had managed to get him to leave her his car and buy her a condo in Las Vegas.

The cats took the move well and they were safe from coyotes here. I put their carriers in the garage and opened them up one by one. I had food bowls ready and figured they would eat and explore the yard and house. Since they were all walking around, slowly getting used to their surroundings, I felt safe in opening the carrier where my cat Shell seemed as calm as the others but as soon as I opened the cage door he took off like a rocket down the driveway, up the street, across Wilshire Boulevard and into the museum grounds with me running after him and screaming his name all the way. He slipped through the bars of the museum fence and I lost him. He had disappeared. I stared through the bars calling his name and crying hysterically while Don tried to comfort me. My Shell, who I had rescued from a dumpster and coaxed out from underneath the bed and who liked to ride on our shoulders, was gone and faced God-knows-what on his own.

Three times a week I visited every single shelter in the downtown area, having to look at hundreds of doomed animals every other day, breaking my heart into a million pieces. But I wanted to make sure Shell was not brought in and put to death because I wasn't there to save him. For months, I haunted every shelter, wanting to rescue every animal I saw, but no Shell. Then out of the blue, when I had almost given up hope, Kevin called. He had moved back into his own little cottage and I had asked him to keep the same phone number that was on Shell's tag in case someone found him. Kevin told me that someone from the Park La Brea apartments, which were right behind the museum, had called and left a message, not sure if they had the right phone number. They had managed to get part of Shell's telephone number before he ran away. They had fed him throughout the long, rainy winter and built a little shelter for him to keep him dry. I screamed, "Call them back! Tell them to call me!" I was out of my mind with joy and relief. In a few minutes a nice man called me and, after I gave him my most heartfelt thanks, he described the area where Shell usually hung out at night and where they left food for him. I jumped in my car to go to the feed store to rent an animal trap and drove to La Brea Park, set the trap and waited in my car for Shell to show up. It was only about an hour after dark before I saw a flash of white and heard the trap snap shut. I jumped out of my car, ran over to the trap and saw the most beautiful sight in the whole world – my Shell.

I took him home and, in the bedroom (he was never getting out again!), I let him out of his cage. I hugged him and talked to him and told him I would never lose him again. I was in heaven, relieved, happy, and couldn't care less about anything for days. He was home safe and all was right with the world. I wanted to thank Shell's rescuers in person and arranged to meet them at their apartment. They were a wonderful elderly couple and I tried to convey how grateful I was to them, but no words or actions could adequately thank them for what they had done.

Not long after finding my Shell again, I found out my cat Tilly had cancer, and selfishly I didn't want to let her go. She was in so much pain, but I couldn't face the prospect of losing her, so faithfully I would feed her intravenously and lay on the kitchen floor with her all night and pet her and quietly encourage her to get better. Finally, I had to admit I was doing it all for me and I needed to let Tilly go to heaven and join Kitty, Scooter and Sullivan who had gone on before her. Letting them go never got any easier and I mourned for her as I had all the others.

One of my favorite scripts that I had written was *Mother's Day*, and I sent it out relentlessly. One day I had a call from the vice president in charge of development of a major production company and he said he wanted to talk to me about the script. We met, we discussed the script and rewrites that he wanted and I worked tirelessly on the script for a few weeks and turned it back in. By now I was friends with the vice president and I thought we had a good working relationship. Unfortunately, in our next meeting he made it clear my project would go no further unless our relationship turned into something more personal. Even when it came to screenwriting I would have to deal with this? I tried to be tactful in rejecting him but nothing I said made any difference. My project was dead in the water.

My dog, Brownie, and I used to walk all around the neighborhood and looky-loo at all the beautiful homes. One time we wandered further afield into the famous Carthay area, which had been built in the 1920s. As we passed one house I spotted a green Mercedes in the driveway and could have sworn it was Billy Vera's. The next time we walked by he spotted us and we had a chance to talk, remarking on the coincidence we had ended up living in practically the same neighborhood. A long time ago he had told me his dream was to live in Hancock Park, so he was getting closer. But it seemed all was not well in his marriage and we commiserated a bit about it all. He was having fabulous success doing voice-overs and still was playing with the Beaters. He said he had fallen in love with his baby boy at first sight and even if his marriage wasn't everything he had hoped for, it was worth it to have Charley in his life. After we talked I knew I needed to take time to go hear the Beaters again. Listening to them play the blues always made me feel better about everything. Go figure.

My friend and fellow anti-vivisectionist, April, told me she was giving my picture and resume to the casting director on *Columbo* for a role I was perfect for. Peter Falk was doing another TV movie and April was his executive assistant, whom he depended on for everything having to do with the show. But she couldn't tell him that we were friends because that would work against me. If I got the audition I would have to get the job myself. I did get called in and auditioned for Peter himself in his office. April smiled but pretended she didn't know me as I walked past her. In the middle of my audition, reading with Peter, April's assistant came in with a food delivery and started talking to him. Peter shushed him and I just kept talking as if the assistant were part of the scene. When I finished, I wondered if that interruption had totally blown it for me. As always, I waited for the call. At the end of two weeks I had stopped thinking about it and assumed I didn't get it. When my agent called to tell me I was getting guest-starring credit but had to share a card, at first I didn't know what she was talking about. Guest starring on what? She had to remind me I had read for *Columbo* two weeks ago and told me I was cast. Yay! I was thrilled. I would get to work with Peter Falk for over a week on a series that had first aired on television before I even lived in L.A. I never dreamed that I would be lucky enough to be working on *Columbo* decades later. Who would have thought Peter would bring the show back as TV movies after all these years? I find Shell and I get to work with Peter. Yes! Two good things happened at the same time. Rare for me.

For almost two weeks I was in heaven. I loved my part of a ditzy girl who flirts with Peter even as the dead body of her friend lies drowned in the bathtub, and being able to react to "Columbo's" strange moves as he investigates was delicious. His wife, Shera, who I had worked with on *Starsky and Hutch*, visited the set one day. I told her if Peter and I both weren't already married I'd run off to Mexico with him in a New York minute. He couldn't have been a more considerate actor to work with.

When the glow of having worked with Peter Falk faded and I once again began looking for work, the reality of my relationship with Don became unavoidable. While I was working on *Columbo*, I had allowed my friend Porter to shoot a short film in our house and had also recruited my actor friends to act in it. One of the actors told me that during the filming, my husband had spent hours alone in the bedroom with an acquaintance of mine who was very attractive and flirtatious. I didn't even bother asking him about it. Unless he agreed to go to counseling, I was done.

Counseling is always a horrible ordeal of he-said, she-said, and trying to convince the therapist that you are right and the other person is a complete jerk. Somewhere in there is the whole purpose of going to counseling; trying to make a relationship work. After a few sessions, we decided it was best to live apart and see what happened.

I rented a little house in Tarzana, and my cats and I had yet another home. I went on long walks with Brownie up in the hills and contemplated the end of yet another marriage. After Rob, I really never wanted to get married again. All I had ever wanted was to live in my little apartment on Moorpark in Studio City with Kitty and work as an actress until I died. That was it. Instead, my life had wandered around like it had a life of its own and I just went along for the ride. I thought God had directed me to my soul mate. Instead I had found another man who couldn't be trusted. My mother used to tell me, "Oh, you're just like your father and your grandfather! You believe everything people tell you and trust everybody!" I don't know what happened to my father in this regard, but I know my grandfather was a kind, generous man who co-signed a loan for a friend who proceeded to default on his loan and my grandfather lost his farm and everything he had and was forced to move to town with his wife and many children. That is how my mother saw me – too trusting, and losing every time I take a chance on someone. I vowed that from now on, I would never get married again and the only beings I would love were my family, my true friends, and my animals.

The Actors Co-op, every year, celebrated the Oscars with a huge banquet. We invited friends, family and people in the business to a dinner and live screening of the awards on a giant screen. The Co-op members acted as waiters and attended to everyone's needs. I invited my mother to attend and she was happy to fly down and stay with me. We went to the banquet and she was thrilled to actually get to talk to the famous Dr. Ogilvie and decided, after meeting my friends in the Co-op, that actors weren't necessarily drug addicts and lost souls doomed to hell. I also arranged for her to go to a taping of *The Price is Right* where Bob Barker, who I had met before at a Fund for Animals fund-raiser, put us in VIP seats up front. He announced our names to the audience and made a big fuss over her and the fact that I had just guest-starred on a *Columbo*. At every commercial break, Bob would do a hilarious stand-up routine. Now I understood why his audience was always in such a raucous good mood. Afterwards, we went backstage and met with Bob and the models on the show, and everybody treated my mother as the biggest VIP guest they had ever had. Then April invited us to lunch at Universal and we visited the stage where Peter was filming. As we tip-toed toward the set and over the big cables my mother got nervous and said, "Maybe we shouldn't be here. Maybe we'll get kicked out!" April assured her that Peter knew she was coming and everything was all right. He, of course, treated my mother like a queen and looked at her face and said, "Now I know where Britt got those blue eyes!" She was overcome; first her idol Bob Barker and now Peter Falk acting like she was the most important person in the world.

Erika loved her grandmother and would do anything to make her trip enjoyable. We drove her up to the Hollywood sign where she could look down on the lake and see the whole city spread out below us. She had no idea that Los Angeles could look so beautiful. The last time she had been down she and my father worked the whole time on our house so she didn't get to see much of anything. This trip was all for her.

My father had healed himself of prostate cancer a few years before by juicing, but now he had some sort of problem with his lungs that my mother totally blamed on doctors. She didn't trust hospitals and doctors very much. I flew up to visit with my father who was home in bed and when I saw him I was shocked that he looked so old and frail. He wasn't able to communicate very well but one day as I sat by his bedside, he was reminiscing about when he was a young boy in Stavanger, Norway and he was explaining something to me I didn't understand. I asked him a question about it and he replied in Norwegian with as much anger as he could muster, "You are so stupid!" and then turned away and went to sleep. Those are the last words he ever spoke to me. I flew back down to LA and in a few weeks he was gone.

After my father died my mother decided to visit Norway, and while she was there called and asked me if I wanted to fly over as well. I was over the moon excited that I would see my homeland again and reunite with my family. I flew to Oslo where my aunt Anna, and uncle Fredrik, met me at the airport and, after a brief stay with my cousin, Inger, and her husband, Svein, my mother and I drove over the mountains to my hometown of Sauda.

All during the trip, Fredrik entertained us with jokes and songs and kept us all in stitches with his stories. I was amazed that someone who looked exactly like my father could be so completely different from him. It made me wonder again why my father chose the path of embracing a dour, hell-threatening religion and leaving Norway instead of choosing to enjoy life and all the opportunities Fredrik had obviously taken advantage of after the war.

At first sight of my hometown I cried. I felt a yearning so strong to never have left Sauda, to still be only Norwegian and have lived my whole life in Norway. It would have been so different had we stayed: going to the university would have been free, there would have been the possibility of working in the theater in Oslo, and the small films made by Swedish and Norwegian directors would have been so much more conducive to the intimate, realistic acting I enjoyed. But no use in looking back. My parents had moved to America where my life had gone all to heck.

We stayed in Sauda with my Aunt Serina and my cousin, Hilde, and, after getting all of our things settled in our room, I met up with my other cousin, Berit, and her husband and two daughters. I spent days exploring my old childhood haunts, visiting the people who now lived in "my" house, enjoying my river, my waterfall, my candy store, my bakery and everything else in Sauda I considered mine. I was traveling back in time and it made me feel happier than I had been in decades. But there was an ugly spot on my beloved country. Why was Norway killing whales? I did not under- stand why Norwegians would support murdering these beautiful, majestic animals. Norway is rich. What is the purpose in being one of only three other countries (Japan, Iceland and Denmark) who are involved in that grisly business? I asked my family members and they were and are dead set against it. Whenever people protest the killing in Norway, the whaling industry sends people to talk to school children and tell them what an important thing it is for the country to murder whales. What can they possibly say? What excuses do they give? Everyone I know in Norway admires Paul Watson and his fight to save whales. That the slaughter continues makes no sense to me and it is a terrible black mark against our country.

After a few days of reliving my childhood, reality knocked on the door and we had to leave our family and friends and fly home.

During my time in Tarzana, I lost both my cat, Hughes, who I had found abandoned in Hughes Market, and Millie to cancer, and my precious Penmar disappeared. My neighbors said there was a chance she might have been taken by a hawk but I never did know how that could have happened. She wore a tag in case she got out, but no shelter or friendly rescuer ever called me to say they had her. It was another blow to lose these three, and now I only had Gilbert, Maude, Rocky and Squeeky left. Don and I decided on an amicable divorce. I had tried to find the trust I used to have in him but it just wouldn't happen. I gave custody of Shell and Brownie to Don. Shell loved riding on Don's shoulder when he puttered around the house and slept close to him every night. I couldn't take that away from either one of them. And Brownie was Don's faithful companion when they went hiking in the mountains. I visited both of them when Don wasn't home and knowing that they were happy was a comfort to me.

When my lease was up, I briefly stayed in Orange County with friends and then Alan, who seemed to have gotten control of his addictions, offered to have me stay in a large house he was renting for both a living space and office. He had formed a production company with two friends and was trying to get some television projects off the ground. My cats would have a nice home in Valley Village and Alan wanted me to write presentations for his production company. Even though I did write two pilots and a television proposal for them and we all had our privacy, it was not a happy situation. Erika was still at times very hostile towards both Alan and me and was going through a difficult period with her boyfriend. Nevertheless, we made the best of it because I knew living there was only temporary. I had a very productive period writing my own scripts during that time and Alan's company produced infomercials while trying to get his pilots produced. One infomercial was a huge fundraiser for Childhelp, cast with well-known stars, and Alan hired many of my friends at The Actor's Co-op to act in the production. He featured me in two of his info-mercials, one of them included my friend Victoria Boa, which was filmed in Las Vegas for a brand of golf clubs. We all enjoyed our time working together.

Whenever I didn't have an acting agent, I would submit myself for roles I saw in the Breakdowns. One day I had a call from a man who was shooting a music video and he thought I was exactly what he was looking for. Wonder of wonders, when he met me it turned out I was. We immediately hit it off, and I was cast in the part. I was playing an older married woman who would not leave her husband for her very handsome young lover, which was the plot of the country song we were filming the video for. The group was made up of talented singers and musicians and the video turned out great, but the best thing about the shoot was getting to know Jesse Escochea, the director. He worked for the police department and, as a sideline job, often filmed cops on dangerous calls. When he found out I was a writer, he told me about his idea of creating a dramatic show that would combine the exploits of paramedics and police. He arranged for me to do ride-alongs with both cops and paramedics, and after I felt comfortable with what I had experienced and learned, I wrote the pilot. Jesse took it to one studio where the development people seemed extremely interested and then, after a few conversations back and forth, didn't hear back from them. Next thing he knew, a friend of his took the same idea, sold it to the same studio, and the show went on the air. Jesse could never prove his friend stole the idea and ran with it, but it was a tough loss for both of us.

Years of struggle, betrayal and bad decisions had worn me down and worn me out. I worked hard, had talent, prayed and meditated every day, was attractive and a nice person but it wasn't enough to get me where I so badly wanted to go; earning my living as an actor. I was headed beyond self-pity into a dark despondency. Then Gilbert, my precious, gray cat who was also known as "Gilbert the Greeter" because he insisted on sleeping on a bed on the front porch during the day and getting up to say hello to every person who came to the door, died. It wasn't long after that that Rocky passed away of cancer and I became so depressed I was not fit to be around other people. I stayed briefly in an apartment with Maude and Squeeky, then headed north. My mother had told me she wanted help getting the house ready to sell so she could move into something smaller and I agreed to help her in any way I could. She was finally going to have me all to herself up in Marysville, which is what she had wanted since I left with Rob. And I was more than willing to be there, because, as far as I was concerned, it was all over for me in Hollywood. I might as well be dead. And what better place to be dead than Marysville, Washington, up in the middle of nowhere and where I had sworn I would never return? Haul out the hemlock. I was going to have a whale of a pity party!

CHAPTER 16

Giving up...But Maybe Not

THE DRIVE UP NORTH WAS grueling. By that time, I was driving an old clunker that could barely make it up the I5 freeway. The air conditioner stopped working going up the Grapevine and Maude and Squeeky were suffering terribly. By the time we got to Oregon, Maude was acting strangely; climbing up and down the seats, crying almost croaking sounds. Panicked by her behavior, I held her on my lap as I drove. I was relieved when she quieted down in the motel room, but her breathing became more and more labored, and just over the border into Washington, she died in my arms. I pulled into a rest stop and broke down and cried. My very best friend in the world for sixteen years was gone. I had put her through hell – moving from place to place, forcing her to adjust to new houses and new people while she stayed ever faithful, never complaining, always loving and talking to me to the very end. I held her close all the way to my mother's house and buried her next to my father's favorite rose bush. Now the only cat left of my entire brood was Squeeky and I hoped he wouldn't leave me for a long, long time. He was all I had left.

Adjusting to life in Marysville was like a dead person adjusting to purgatory. I saw myself as a pitiful failure and didn't much care about anything. I was breathing but my existence bore no resemblance to life. I went through the motions of living: spent time with my sister and family, signed with a temp agency and went to my various jobs and spent my days feeling like a zombie. But, being a good actress, I made sure no one knew how I felt and that no one suspected that I was really no longer alive. At night, I would hold Squeeky and cry and face the horror of possibly having to stay up there for the rest of my life.

Eventually, the acting sickness that had plagued me since I was in the third grade started showing signs of life again. No! No! No! Why can't I just forget about acting?! Get an agent? Oh, what was the point?! What kind of work could there be in Seattle anyway? I need to forget acting and keep on making that agonizing trip down the freeway toward my office jail, wishing I'd get hit by that proverbial truck that never seemed to find me. My destiny had been to fail no matter how hard I tried, so why even think about acting anymore? Boo hoo, poor me. Wah, wah. I was really wallowing in it. It was over! Over! I contacted SAG Seattle and asked them to send me a list of agents in Seattle.

I interviewed with a few agents and ended up with Topo Swope, one of the best in Seattle. To my complete surprise, I started going out on auditions for independent movies. I also kept track of Equity play auditions and went on "generals," where you do monologues for theater groups and hope you get called in later for an actual role. There are two kinds of actors: those who go to New York or Los Angeles with stars in their eyes wanting to be rich and famous, and those who seem to be cursed with some sort of disease, that inexplicable *need* to act and to attend classes and learn to be the best we can be, whether we do it in a multi-million dollar Hollywood production or on a small stage in Nowheresville, USA. Unfortunately, I seemed to find myself in the *needy* category whether I liked it or not, so here I was yearning yet again to act and bring to life the lines on a printed page, doing my best to make them real.

Nothing was coming my way in Seattle acting-wise and my friend Michael Simms, who had moved to Vancouver from Los Angeles where he hadn't been getting enough work and now was working practically non-stop in Canada, told me I should get an agent up there and give it a shot. So I sent my pictures and resumes to a few agencies in Vancouver, interviewed with the two best prospects and picked one who seemed the most interested in me. They immediately sent me out on an audition for a role in a television show in which I was cast, and then an old friend from Darryl Hickman's acting class, Bob Saget, came up to Vancouver to direct a movie and he cast me in a small part as well. Going up and down to B.C. for auditions became a normal part of life and I came to know Vancouver as well as I did Seattle.

I was sitting on my bed in the middle of a familiar daydream imagining myself in the mountains of Norway in my cousin's cabin hiding out from the world, having mercifully lost every shred of ambition when my agent called and told me I had an audition for a film being shot in Seattle. I made up my face, dressed for the part and got into my ancient clunker for the drive into the city. I passed the University of Washington and crossed the bridge going over Lake Union, looking at the breathtaking views of Seattle and the car started making funny noises. I was almost to the Union Street exit when it died. I steered it over to the tiny triangle that separated the freeway with cars going seventy miles per hour from the cars entering the freeway at sixty miles per hour and stopped. Cars were whizzing by me and no one gave me a second glance, including two highway patrol cars that I tried to wave down. I sat in the car hoping that no one would hit me, even though a few weeks ago, when I was feeling sorry for myself, this would have seemed like a really good opportunity to get smashed up and killed. Now that I was there where it was a distinct possibility, it didn't seem so appetizing. I hoped and prayed that the car was merely overheated and that after awhile it would cool down and I would make it to the exit and down the hill. I figured I would be so late to the audition they would assume I wasn't coming and that was the end of that.

I waited until I thought it was safe to start the car again and after a few tries it did. It chugged out of the little triangle, barely made it over to the exit and down the hill where I pulled over to the curb and stopped. It was more obvious than ever that I was never going to make it to the audition. I went inside a store to call Triple A and, after what seemed like an eternity, a truck came, the driver looked under the hood, made some adjustment and told me I better take it to a garage right away to fix whatever it was. I barely heard him because now that my car was good to go, my audition was foremost on my mind. I drove up to Pike's Market where the audition was to have taken place, parked and walked down to the restaurant they had taken over for the auditions. Ironically, the name of the movie was *Nowheresville*, just where I had ended up.

To my happy surprise, no one cared that I was late. There were several other actors there and I just signed in and waited my turn. Thank you, God! I was called in, read my lines and left. I was up for the part of an annoying mother to a young man who just wanted her to leave him alone. I could easily identify with that role.

Since there seemed to be a lot of women auditioning, I didn't hold out much hope for getting the part but I knew one thing for sure, somehow, I had to get myself a better car. My mother was thinking the same thing. She suggested I have my sister's husband drive my car to an empty lot on a busy street next to their church and put a big for sale sign in the windshield. My sister's husband said it was a sure-fire way to get it seen and sold, and he was right. I felt sorry for the elderly couple who bought the car, but they said they only needed it for short errands to the store and they didn't mind an old clunker. So with that money, and with my ever-generous mother chipping in, I bought a not-so-new but good-running white Mercury Cougar and figured if I ever got another audition it would get me there.

My mother wanted to sell her house and move into a smaller house or a condo and I did my "carpenter's daughter" work to spiffy it up, patching up holes in the wall, spackling, painting walls inside and out, and with the help of my sister, painting the entire fence that ran around the property. My mother had started her own drapery business after she retired and now was ready to give it up. She was as strong and fit as ever, but she deserved to enjoy her retirement. She missed my father terribly but had close friends from Norway and friends from church and, even though she worried about everything constantly, me included, she was always accepting of me and loved me unconditionally. Ever since she had met Lloyd Ogilvie, she had more or less accepted that I was an actress and always would be whether I was working or not. She never pressured me anymore to "become a lawyer." After all, it now seemed certain I would not end up in the gutter in L.A. since I was safely ensconced in Marysville.

Two times while living in Marysville I had hope of something happening with my scripts. Michelle Lee, who had been on *Knots Landing* with Kevin Dobson, had read my script, *Home Run*, and very badly wanted to do it as a movie for television. She tried very hard to get CBS interested, but they didn't think it was the right vehicle for her. Then someone from the production company that had produced *Navy Seals* called and said they had read *Sub-Level Four,* the same script that had interested Bob Barker, and told me they wanted to take it to the next level. I didn't know what they meant and wished I had an agent to follow up on this lead. I kept calling and they kept saying they were still interested, but it died in the trying.

I had wanted to find a church to attend, but there was nothing like Hollywood Pres in Marysville, so I drove all the way into Seattle to go to a Presbyterian church in the University District. Seattle is a very beautiful city when it isn't raining and for some reason I found it fascinating driving by my old neighborhood and high school and thinking about Dave and me and how my life had turned out so differently than I thought it would. I had sacrificed and worked so hard to be an actor and here I was, back where I started, with (according to my rigid measurement code of success and failure) little to show for my efforts. But I still had managed to cling to a tiny amount of faith as small as "a mustard seed" – which is what the Bible promised is all I need – and even though I had severe bouts with depression, I was determined to go forward with my life. I constantly repeated another Bible verse that assured me, "Seek and ye shall find, ask and ye shall receive, knock and it shall be opened unto you." I was determined to keep on seeking, asking and knocking no matter how dismal my present circumstances and how hopeless my future might seem, and just keep playing it one day at a time.

Again, out of the blue, when I wasn't thinking about it, my agent called and told me I had the role of the annoying mother in *Nowheresville*. I was going to film a movie in Seattle! Okay, it wasn't a major feature with big stars, but working as an actress in my hometown was something I hoped would happen but never really expected and here it was – car breaks down, bad – get cast anyway, good.

We shot my scenes in a picturesque little town a little north of Seattle called Edmonds, which I had never seen before. This had been here during my youth? Why didn't I ever come here? The little village is situated by the water at the bottom of hills where the houses above looked out over a view of the sound and the Olympic Peninsula beyond that. The whole scene was breathtaking. Every few minutes a ferry would dock, disgorge its cars, load up with more cars and head back across the water. We had beautiful weather for our shoot, and on sunny days, the Seattle area makes everybody want to live there. Then it rains for three months straight and visitors say, never mind, and head back to the sun.

I loved my role, and the actor portraying my son played his part of the frustrated, annoyed son to perfection. As always, the job was over much too soon and I went back to temping. I found a Lutheran church near my mother's house and liked the pastor and his low-key preaching. But still, it didn't prevent me from almost every day having a moment of panic when I would ask myself, "Is this it for me, then? Is this all there is?" Then I would calm myself down, meditate and pray for several minutes and go on with life. It seemed that nothing could kill my hopes and dreams. I just kept asking, seeking and knocking, knowing that one day, sooner or later, that door would open. I didn't know how I was going to find my way back to the anti-vivisection movement. In Seattle, there were several animal groups all espousing the cruelty argument and feeling comfortable with that. I attended protests for the Sea Shepherd and anti-fur demos but there was no organization that was making any attempt to spread the truth about animal experimentation and that is what I was looking for.

While I was up in Marysville, changes were taking place in the anti-vivisection movement in Los Angeles. Chris De Rose had decided to focus less on anti-vivisection and more on shutting down puppy mills. Another group with much more money than PRISM was now espousing the same philosophy as us – the connection between vivisection, human health and the environment – and had members from all over the country. They seemed on their way to growing exponentially and accomplishing everything that we had wanted to accomplish. Debbie moved to Florida to open up a chiropractic office, and Sandra was working on her own, while other members disseminated PRISM literature and spread the message of the scientific fraud of vivisection. I was disappointed that PRISM wasn't more active, but I understood that having two groups exactly the same operating in the same city, with one able to do much more than the other, it made sense for one group to take the lead. I ordered their excellent material and sent it out when I wrote to newspapers, magazines, politicians and celebrities. My leaders in the anti-vivisection movement had essentially abandoned me, but at least Paul Watson was still at the helm of the Sea Shepherd Society and was fighting the good fight for whales and seals. At one point, someone called from the Sea Shepherd office and asked me to drive up to Vancouver to do a presentation for the Sea Shepherd for a high school class. The presentation went well, the students were amazingly receptive and I told the lady at the Sea Shepherd office I was eager and available to do more presentations.

I was faithful in going to general auditions for theater groups and, even though Seattle is a theater town, there was, at that time, a core group of working Equity actors which was very exclusive and cliquey and incredibly difficult to join. After one of these cattle calls, I was called in to the Bathhouse Theater to audition for the lead in a play called *Someone's Knocking*. The title sounded like it was written for me and the role fit me well: an agoraphobic housewife is completely under the thumb of her husband, who completely controls her, and she willingly submits to his every whim and is terrified of even going out of the house. It was a comedy with a little slapstick thrown in, and comedy is my forte.

The director had me read my part with several men who were up for the role of the husband. After awhile it became obvious that he was trying to fit the husbands to me and I knew I had the part. Doing that play was one of the most satisfying jobs I ever had. The entire cast was brilliant, and Lori Larsen, who played my sister, was beyond funny. I had to think of tragic scenes like my entire family dying in a car accident to keep from laughing every time I had a scene with her.

There was a line from the play that I clung to – "Random good fortune is an inherent inevitability of life." To me that meant, no matter where I lived or what I was doing, there was a chance of something good happening to me. And in the final lines of the play I say to my husband as he disappears out the door after I tell him I can't go back to living the life of a fearful, trapped housewife, "I exist, Jack! I exist! And when I see how far I've come and how far I'll never go, all I wish for now, all I wish is *to live life as alive as I can in the ruins of my fears*." I chose those words to be my guiding light for whatever I did from then on.

When I had finished the movie and the play and I again had to start working as a temp, the letdown was severe. I had to take stock of my life and decide where I was going from here. I couldn't stay with my mother indefinitely and had to decide where I was going to live. I felt that there was nothing left for me in Los Angeles; my daughter was estranged from me, Debbie had moved to the other side of the country, Chris De Rose, the man who convinced me to be an anti-vivisectionist had moved on to include many other animal issues, and the other anti-vivisection group that was doing so well did not seem to need any help from me.

I had given my all to become an actress and had reached a dead end. That young girl who lived in a small apartment on Moorpark in Studio City who wanted only to work as an actress for the rest of her life had been through several kinds of hell. I refused to allow depression to overwhelm me. Going back to L.A. was out. There was nothing there for me anymore. I could move to Seattle and throw myself into trying to become a part of the theater community, but the one thing I knew I couldn't do was stay in Marysville. I decided to move to New York.

CHAPTER 17

On My Own

Now THAT I HAD PLAYED the lead in a play in Seattle, I felt fully prepared to take on the New York stage. I didn't know anyone there, I had very little money, I had no work prospects and didn't have a place to stay. It seemed the logical choice. I loved New York and had wanted to live in Manhattan on my own since the debacle of my time there completely dependent on another person. This time I would have me and only me to depend on and I was ready for that. I needed to get away from everything safe and secure and be on my own. I felt that I absolutely *needed* to do that. I could stay at the YMCA when I first arrived, get a job, and, after I found an apartment, my mother could send Squeeky to me. After I came to the conclusion that I was going to move to New York, I took a drive north, then west through the Tulalip Indian reservation to the rocky beach where I liked to sit and meditate. I asked God for direction and guidance and didn't feel a moment's apprehension or fear. I drove to Seattle and bought a few books on getting settled in Manhattan and was ready to make the move.

By this time, nothing I did surprised my mother. She didn't approve of my decision but soon realized I was determined to go. She promised she would take good care of Squeeky and send him to me as soon as I found a place to live. So I packed my clothes and belongings into several big suitcases and flew to New York. I landed, hauled all my suitcases out to a taxi, and we drove into Manhattan. The first sight of the city was an even headier experience than when I came to be with Steve. I was excited at the prospect that I was actually going to live here by myself and enjoy the city without anyone telling me what to do, how to do it, how to dress, or control me or complain about me or make my life miserable in any way. As soon as Squeeky was with me, every time I came home, all I would get would be love, acceptance and understanding, and comfort if I needed it. What a concept! I had been waiting for that since I lived alone in my apartment on Moorpark.

The cab drove through the streets of New York and I drank in all the sights as if I had never seen them before. I felt I couldn't get enough of every single thing that added to the atmosphere of energy and life that emanated from every person, car, building, street and sidewalk we drove by. We pulled up in front of the YMCA on the Upper West Side, I paid the driver, and he unceremoniously dumped all my suitcases on the sidewalk. He sped off and I lugged the suitcases one by one up the stairs, into the lobby and over to the desk. I was told I would have to put them in a store-room for now until they were ready to have me check in, so I did that and went outside and walked around, getting reacquainted with my old neighborhood, had a bite to eat, and went back to the Y.

My room turned out to be the size of my mother's bathroom with a view of a brick wall. The closet couldn't hold much of my clothes so I only hung up what I figured I would need right away. I had saved enough money for a few days at the Y and for first and last and deposit on an apartment, so first order of business would be to try to find a place to live, then go to Kelly Services and get a temp job.

The payphone was on the far end of the floor several hallways away where the showers were. The next morning, I headed in that direction and was relieved to see a Yellow Pages phone book was hanging by the phone. I planned on calling real estate agents to find an apartment the next morning. But first I had to call my mother and let her know I was okay and check up on Squeeky. My mother sounded slightly hysterical and I assured her no one had mugged me so far and I didn't expect that to happen any time soon. I went back to my room exhausted, a little frightened and excited about finding a new home and sending for my Squeeky. I lay down on the bed and prayed for guidance and blessings on my new adventure.

The next morning, I went out for breakfast at a fast food place then headed back to the Y and started making calls. "Hello, this is Britt and I'm new to the city. I'm looking for a rental on the Upper East Side or Westside for around $800 a month....hello?" Try again. "Hi, my name is Britt and I just arrived in New York and I'm trying to find an apartment for about $900 a month. Can you help me?...no, I'm not from any kind of farm. I'm from Seattle...hello?" After about ten hang-ups I started to worry that the book I had read about New York rentals might have been a bit out of date. But I persisted; "Hello, I'm sorry to bother you but I don't suppose you have any rentals for $900 a month or under? If not, I can call someone else."

The man at the other end of the line hesitated, then,
    "You sound like you're new in town."
    "Yes, I just flew in yesterday."
    "You sound awfully young."
    "No, not really. It's just my voice I guess."
    "I don't know if I have anything for you but meet me at Broadway and 51st in an hour. Do you know where that is?"
    "Yes."
    "See you then."

I hung up relieved, but with my mother's warnings ringing in my head; what if he was some kind of pervert planning on getting me alone in an apartment and doing God knows what? What if he does something really bad to me? He knows I'm alone. Maybe I shouldn't go. Maybe if I do I'll never be heard from again. I shook off the paranoia and clung to the hope that maybe this man would actually help me. I hurried out of the Y and headed for Broadway.

I had described myself over the phone and when a middle-aged man in his forties wearing a tan overcoat came walking towards me with a worried look on his face, I knew it was him. He was shaking his head and sighing as he introduced himself. He had thought from the sound of my voice that I was about 16, but knew at first sight that I didn't have a clue what was going on in the rental market or how naïve I was thinking I would find anything for $900.

"My first reaction was to hang up on you but I couldn't live with myself if I did. You need help and I'm about the only agent in town who will. First let's look at a place that goes for $1700 a month so you can see what something that cheap will get you."

Yikes! That was too rich for my blood! He turned on his heel and began walking fast and I hurried to catch up. We walked to a brownstone a few blocks away that looked pretty nice. As I followed him in the door and walked up the stairs and saw how well maintained the building was I thought, wow, for $1700 you can get something incredible! He unlocked a door and we walked in. I saw a bed and a counter with a sink, a tiny refrigerator beside it and a tiny stove. What was the kitchen doing in the bedroom? I waited to see the rest of the apartment and looked at him expectantly. He just looked right back at me.

"Can we see the other rooms?" I asked.

"This is it. There are no other rooms."

"Oh."

"Yes, oh."

I swallowed hard as reality set in. His face softened when he saw the look on my face.

"I know it's a bit of a shock but I'll keep my eye out for something. You never know. I'll keep looking until I move back to Cleveland in a couple of weeks."

"That should be enough time for me to find a place."

"Yeah," he said, not very convincingly.

The next day I took the subway to Kelly Services on Lexington Avenue. The first time I lived in New York, I never went on the subway alone. Ever. It was too scary. All those different lines on the map going a million different ways. I could end up anywhere. But it was time to suck it up and become a real New Yorker. I picked the right train and ended up where I wanted to go. At Kelly, I gave them my name and told them I had been working temp in Everett, Washington. Where? Never mind. She looked me up on the computer and found me there. I told her I needed to start work right away because I have to rent an apartment. The girl behind the desk didn't look optimistic. I told her I would sit in the lobby and wait until a job came along that I was right for. Her expression told me she thought that was weird beyond words but said, okay, and I sat down with my book and waited for the right job. By the end of the day a job for me had not come in so I told the receptionist I would come back on Monday.

My friend David from The Actors Co-op had told me the church I should join in New York that was a lot like Hollywood Pres was Marble Collegiate Church on Park Avenue near the Empire State Building. I figured out on the subway map how to get there and planned to attend the next Sunday. But I was starting to worry about finding an apartment. I only had a few days left on my reservation at the Y and had to have a place to move to or be homeless. I called my real estate agent every morning and every night to see if he had found something. When Sunday came I certainly had something to pray about.

Marble had a lot of the same atmosphere as Hollywood Pres but the service was even better, as if it had been produced and directed by the best production team on Broadway. Pastor Arthur Caliandro preached a gentle, inspirational sermon, there were moments of quiet prayer and meditation, and when the choir sang they sounded like angels (not surprising since many of them were professional singers). As I left the church, after shaking Pastor Caliando's hand, I felt that I could face anything New York had to offer.

I went back to my tiny room at the Y and looked at my checkbook. My funds were stretched to the limit. I decided I needed a little talk with the man upstairs and walked out into the hallway and stood by the narrow window right outside my room and looked out over Central Park and the Upper East Side. No one was around and I spoke out loud, "You know, God, when Squeeky gets here, it's just You, me, and him. We have no one else. Not one single person. But I believe that soon Squeeky and I will be living out there, across the park, in a nice building in a one bedroom apartment in a great neighborhood and I'll never leave New York. Not ever. Let it happen, God. Let it happen."

Monday came and when I called the real estate agent he told me he had found something for me! A musician friend of his was touring in Europe for several months and wanted to sublet his small studio apartment in the New Yorker Hotel. He was willing to rent it to me for $800 a month. I didn't hesitate and said yes, absolutely yes! Living there would give me plenty of time to find a permanent place. He told me where the hotel was and to meet him there. Again, I consulted my subway map and figured I could get there without ending up in New Jersey.

The apartment turned out to be on the same floor as a recording studio and a few other apartments mostly inhabited by musicians. It was small; just one room and a bathroom but plenty big enough for me and Squeeky. The view out the window was of the Empire State Building which seemed so familiar to me I wondered if this was the hotel my mother, sister and I had stayed in when we first arrived in America. Since our ship would have docked nearby, it made sense. I asked my mother but she didn't remember. Nevertheless, I had a strong feeling that I had seen that same view many years ago, and now I was here again after all these years.

I hurried back to the Y, packed up and again lugged the suitcases into a cab as the cabbie looked on disinterested. We drove by the Empire State Building and the famous Macy's on 34th Street and I carried my suitcases into the lobby of the hotel. Somehow, I got them all into the elevator and into the apartment. I had to hurry over to Kelly Services to sit and wait for a job so I could afford to pay next month's rent.

The receptionist briefly glanced up at me as I came in. I reminded her of who I was and she said, "I know," and went back to her computer. I sat down, opened my book and prepared to wait when a lady came into the lobby out of one of the back offices. "You're Britt?" I nodded. "We have a job in Soho at a management company. Starts tomorrow for an indefinite time. Would you like it?" Are bears Catholic?! Does the Pope do it in the woods?! Yes! She handed me the address and I stepped out into the hallway breathing a huge sigh of relief. Thank you, God! An apartment, a job and a home church. I was a real official New Yorker.

My mother was even more relieved than I was and ready to send Squeeky to me. I had been told that Delta Cargo was the best way to ship him to New York and she said my sister would be taking care of all the arrangements and would make sure that Squeeky got to the airport safe and sound. The rest was up to Delta. My mother called me back in a few hours and told me when Squeeky would be arriving on Saturday. I knew I would be a nervous wreck until he was safely in our new home.

The management company I was working for was staffed with several friendly and very busy people. They gave me a desk and not much to do; just answer the phone when it rang and pass it on to the right person. The phone hardly rang and I sat and tried not to look not busy. After a few hours of this, my boss gave me a restaurant menu and said he owned the restaurant downstairs and I should order anything I want and it was on the house. Every day, lunch was on the house. As it turned out, this was one of the best restaurants in Soho and I had no trouble finding something vegetarian. The food was delivered in short order and was delicious. I couldn't believe I was going to get fed as well as paid. Now all I needed was something to do all day.

I counted the hours until Saturday and made a bus reservation to the airport to pick up Squeeky. A bus left four hours before Squeeky was to arrive, and the girl on the phone told me that would give me plenty of time to get there. Wrong. I thought the bus would go straight to the airport. It didn't. It made one stop after another, taking so long that it became obvious that I would never make it to the airport on time. So I jumped off the bus and frantically started flagging down cabs, none of which were available. I ran down the street waving at cabs like a demented person, desperate, terrified of being late and Squeeky getting lost. Finally, a cab stopped, I hopped in and said "Kennedy Airport!" and we took off. By the time we got to the airport, Squeeky's plane would have landed and, to add insult to injury, the cab driver was confused as to where exactly Delta Cargo was. Eventually, we found it and I got out and ran into the terminal. No one was behind the desk and I called out, "Squeeky! Squeeky!" And I heard a loud meow answering me. I followed the meows and found him behind the counter in his carrier. I was so relieved I could have fainted. I didn't dare open the carrier. If he ran off I'd never forgive myself. I'd already been through that once with Shell. I found somebody who worked there, showed my ID, picked up the carrier, took him out to the waiting cab, and we were off to the city. Now I could breathe again. I talked to Squeeky all the way into the city and The New Yorker Hotel. I'm sure the cab driver thought I was insane but I didn't care. Up in the room I finally could take Squeeky out of the carrier and hold him close. His purrs were so loud I was sure they could hear him in the recording studio next door. And for the first of many times, I held him up by my face so he could purr right into my ear and whispered to him, "From my ear, straight down into my heart." It became my mantra every time I came back to our apartment and saw him safely waiting for me. What a long and twisted journey we had been on; from Encino to New York City, and all the places in between. He was my best and most faithful friend and when I went to sleep that night with Squeeky by my side I was completely content.

I soon found out that wearing earplugs would be the only way I could sleep at night. Between the music throbbing through the wall from the recording studio on one side and the loud, adventuresome couple banging into the wall on the other, the noise continued for hours. But you wouldn't catch me complaining. Squeeky and I had a base from which to conquer New York and that was all that mattered. I knew I needed to somehow find an agent who would send me out so that was my next order of business. I went to Samuel French, bought a booklet that listed agents and started calling. Eventually, I met someone who said they would represent me. I had no doubt that the people I was working for would be willing to allow me to go out on auditions if they should come up. And every Sunday would find me at Marble Church filling me up both spiritually and physically because they had the best chef and the best brunch in town. Arthur Caliandro was a vegetarian and the brunch had plenty of choices for me. When it was announced that the choir would be accepting summer replacements I immediately signed up and started singing with the amazing professionals who could read music and sing complicated songs instantly, sounding as if they'd practiced them for weeks. I leaned on the second sopranos and did fine. What a thrill it was to actually be a part of the choir that had moved me to tears every Sunday.

One of the few things I absolutely hated about New York was and is the carriage horse industry. The horses are forced to dodge heavy traffic, fall victim to fatal accidents, suffer unbearable heat and freezing cold, and at the end of a long grueling day, go back to tiny stables where they cannot move or lay down. They live a life of hell, while movies and television shows romanticize carriage rides through Central Park. Anyone who lives in New York knows how much those horses suffer.

When I contacted the ASPCA to find out what they were doing about it, they put me off again and again until finally they became angry at my relentless nagging. They obviously had zero interest in ending the suffering of the horses. I suspected that they were somehow involved in perpetrating the ugly business, which was confirmed to me later when they became open apologists for the industry, a fact that Mayor Bloomberg used years later in a press conference defending the carriage horse industry. When I called Fund for Animals, they showed little interest in the plight of the horses as well, which surprised me, as they fund The Black Beauty Ranch, but it seemed that no animal group in New York was going to help me. Once in awhile, a horse-loving celebrity would come to town, call a press conference to talk about the horses, and then leave town never to be heard from again. New York school children had an anti-carriage horse campaign going, but as children have no voice in government, have no money and don't vote, politicians couldn't care less about their opinion. I made an appointment with my councilman to talk about the plight of the carriage horses and the entire time I was sitting and talking to him, he looked at his watch and could hardly wait to end the meeting. I wrote letters to whomever I thought might help, including a supposed animal advocate in the mayor's office. Nothing. The carriage industry owned the decision-makers and the elected officials, and I was a mere gnat they easily swiped away. Now, several years later, there are many groups and activists involved in shutting down the carriage horse industry. Last Chance for Animals is supporting NY Class in their efforts to persuade Mayor De Blasio and all the other public officials who were elected, thanks to the efforts of animal activists, to live up to their promises.

I continued my anti-vivisection work alone as well, always taking every opportunity to talk about the fraud of vivisection. If someone gave me an opening, I would open the door and disabuse anyone who had the mistaken belief that we all depend on animal experimentation for cures to disease. My impact was limited but at least I was fulfilling my life's purpose. Chris De Rose was still focused on puppy mills, the leader of the non-profit that had taken over PRISM's mission had become disillusioned and dissolved that group, national anti-vivisection organizations continued to concentrate on talking ineffectually about cruelty and using heart wrenching photos to raise money and making no progress. It was very discouraging. I longed for another charismatic anti-vivisection leader to appear and revitalize the movement. Until then I would carry on by myself.

My friend, Jesse, who worked for the Los Angeles Police Department, had an idea for another television show, and for awhile we worked together long distance on that project. We came very close to selling it but at the meeting in Las Vegas where he was to finalize the deal, other people who he had gotten involved in the project antagonized the producers and the deal fell through. After months of work, it was a severe disappointment.

At the same time, my friend Tony Eldridge made a development deal with Tom Cruise's company and called me and told me to send him all my scripts. He had high hopes of making more deals and wanted my scripts in his arsenal when he went into meetings to pitch projects. It took Tony a few more years of hard work, but he finally had his big breakthrough as one of the executive producers of *The Equalizer*, starring Denzel Washington. Nothing makes me happier than when my good friends find the success they deserve.

I auditioned for the casting director of *Law and Order* and did well. How I would have loved to be cast in my all-time favorite show. It would have been worth my poverty-stricken circumstances living in New York just to work one day with actors of the caliber of the regular cast of *Law and Order*.

I also had a general audition for *All My Children* and a small role was offered to me. While the part was not offensive to me, it would have been to my very religious family and I chose to pass, asking them to consider me for something else in the future. I didn't want to hurt my family for the sake of a small part on a soap opera.

But another possibility was looming on the horizon; singing with a gospel group. The Marble Collegiate Gospel Choir had performed at the church once or twice and I loved their energetic, joyful sound. It was the opposite of the sanctuary choir which sang very traditional music. Both choirs were amazing in their own way. When the director of the gospel choir invited people to audition, a friend from church encouraged me to go for it. So I did, was accepted, and, without a doubt, singing in the gospel choir provided me with the most wonderful experiences I had while living in New York.

I knew that my time at The New Yorker Hotel would come to an end sooner or later. Somehow, I had to find a permanent apartment, but by now I had found out how high rentals in New York really were. One day one of the assistant pastors at Marble called to tell me she had seen a notice on the church bulletin board that a girl was looking for someone to sublet her apartment. Could be worth looking at. I called the number she gave me and took the subway across town and up to E. 86th Street. It was a fifth-floor walkup, and by the time I got to the top floor I was exhausted. The girl offering the apartment was moving back home and doubted that she would be back but she wanted to sublet just in case. I found out the apartment was rent controlled, and, when all was said and done, I was accepted as the new tenant and able to rent the apartment for $950 a month. When Squeeky and I moved in I realized I had found a home in the very area that I used to look out at from the hallway at the Y and where I visualized myself living. I had thought that walking up four flights of stairs several times a day would be an ordeal. After only a few days, it seemed like nothing.

Rehearsing with the gospel choir was much easier than with the sanctuary choir. Our director, the hugely talented, incredibly musical, David Brown, handed out our sheet music several weeks ahead of when we would have to perform. Our rehearsals were preceded by a mini-sermon by David, which struck home with me even more than Arthur Caliandro's. The choir was a melting pot of New Yorkers: old, young, black, white, okay singers, and phenomenal singers. I had never dreamed that a white-bread girl like me, trained as a lyric soprano, would end up singing gospel with singers every bit as good as famous recording stars. David emphasized extreme togetherness, staying focused on him and moving as one big, swaying, clapping body. The sound that such a diverse group of people put out was unbelievable.

My first performance with the group was at the Beacon Theater on Broadway. I was singing on Broadway! I may not have been starring in a Broadway musical but I was singing and enjoying every minute. For hours at a time I could forget I had failed to find unending work as an actress in Hollywood. We were invited to sing at a church in Harlem where (okay, it wasn't a competition) we wowed em' and out-sang their own choir. Because David believed in everyone in the choir getting to know each other, he had us go on retreats in the country to bond while we worked on songs and choreography. Still we tended to form friendships with certain people and hang out with them. That's just human nature.

The girl who sublet the apartment to me also passed on to me, her job as assistant to a very rich woman. I regretted leaving my temp job but this seemed to be more permanent with fewer hours but great pay. My employer was John Kerry's ex-mother-in-law. Her daughter, John's ex-wife, lived somewhere in New England, and, from what the housekeeper told me, was not enamored of her mother's lifestyle and preferred a simpler life in the country. Everything I heard about her made me like her very much. My employer lived in a building near the United Nations in the kind of huge, luxurious apartment I had only seen in movies. Apparently, she had been married to several rich men and buried them all. She had a car and driver and spent her days shopping and lunching and dressed to the nines every single day. I was to keep track of her accounts, pay her bills, go over her investment portfolios and open her mail and decide what to keep and what to throw away. I'll never forget when I showed her a desperate appeal from Bangladesh and she retorted with contempt, "Throw it away! What the hell do I care about starving people in Bangladesh!" She also would show distain for princess-so-and-so, prince-what's-his-name and other European "royalty" who called her. She herself was royalty enough and was not impressed. "Tell them I'm not in!" After awhile I thought to myself, "This job cannot last." The best thing about it was that the house-keeper made me a delicious vegetarian lunch every day. New York was feeding me very well.

I wasn't going out on acting auditions for televisions shows, but nothing prevented me from going on cattle calls for Broadway shows. I sang, I "moved," and I acted; I would get callbacks every once in awhile but no cigar. In New York, "moving well" turned out to mean you better be a professional dancer or forget it. But all the rejection was assuaged by the fact that I was singing and performing on stage with an incredible choir with a director who was a perfectionist. Perfectionism was something that I responded to very well. Why do something if you couldn't be the best? If we had been mediocre, it wouldn't have been fun and I wouldn't have wanted to be a part of it anyway.

It was surprising how incredibly airy and free and delightful life was completely on my own. No one to criticize or yell at me and the only person waiting for me when I came home was Squeeky, full of love and purrs and absolutely approving of every move I made.

One day the rich diva and I had a severe disagreement over something trivial and I used it as an excuse to quit and found myself at Kelly Services looking for another job. The diva had been the only fly in my ointment and I looked forward to working anywhere but for her. Kelly immediately sent me to a company where I worked as a receptionist and the two Italian male owners were so loud and rambunctious in their disagreements the walls would shake as feet stomped and doors slammed and I wondered if I would still have a job in the next five minutes. It was a busy office, again in Soho, a district where everyone wore black, or, I guess, would have to go to jail. As I looked down onto the street below at people passing our building, I observed that the rule was obviously strictly enforced. How I avoided arrest, I do not know, since I owned very little black, because I thought it made me look hideous. I met some terrific people working for that company and stayed for almost a year. I think they had a difficult time finding a receptionist who would stay very long because of the constant turbulence and, even though at times I had to stand up for myself against certain antics on the part of some employees, I enjoyed the job because of the variety of my chores, and the fact that the day would go by fast. One day, before Mother's Day, a beautiful arrangement of roses was delivered to the office. It was from Erika, and the card said, "If I sent this on Sunday no one would know you have a child who loves you." I tried to hide my tears from co-workers but my heart was overflowing.

By now, it had been years since Alan first flew Paul Watson down to Los Angeles to make a deal to produce a television movie on his life. So it was a surprise when I heard from Paul, who said the movie was finally going to be made with John Badham as director. He told me to send him my picture and resume, as there would probably be a part in the movie for me. With high hopes, I sent them and knew that with such a quality director, the movie would end up being a blockbuster. I kept waiting for word on when the movie would start casting and production, but I waited in vain. The deal fell through and an exciting, important story that needed to be told was in Hollywood limbo again. Not an unusual place for a story or script to be.

I received another unexpected surprise when my friend Rod Allison from Carmel sent me a card with a huge check enclosed. His mother had died and he inherited some money and decided to share some of it with me, on one condition. He knew how much I wanted to visit Norway again and told me I had to spend the money on a trip there. I was ecstatic. His generosity overwhelmed me. By now I had earned enough credit to get a paid vacation from Kelly Services and I put in for it immediately. My mother was happy too. She said she was sending me some money as well so I could really enjoy my time there.

All of a sudden, good things were happening. What had I done to deserve all this? I arranged with my cousin, Inger Johanna, who lived in Oslo, to meet me in London and we would stay at her flat in the suburbs. She insisted that she would give me a tour of her favorite city and then we could take the Eurostar to Paris and spend a couple of days there before going back to London and flying to Norway. My neighbor, who had a cat that I took care of when she was out of town, would watch over Squeeky and spend plenty of time with him so he wouldn't get too lonely. I knew my trip was going to be perfect, when, on board the jam-packed plane to London, I had an entire row all to myself and was able to lay down and go to sleep the entire flight.

Seeing London through my cousin Inger's eyes was like taking a trip back to historical times when the Tower of London was a fearsome place and heads rolled on a regular basis. Exhausted, after I had been taken by bus and tube to see every important historical site in my cousin's adopted city, we took the Eurostar to Paris and toured the City of Lights, including taking a trip down the Seine past Notre Dame and decades-old buildings, still exquisite beyond anything I had ever seen. We browsed the shops along the Champs-Elysees, ate and had coffee in outdoor cafés, and relaxed and people-watched. My cousin and all Norwegians consider taking long vacations and trips all around Europe a normal part of life. Their vacations last at least a month and they explore the world like our Viking ancestors (without the raping and pillaging). For me, this trip was a once-in-a-lifetime experience and I was soaking up every minute.

We took the Eurostar back to London and I flew on to Stavanger, Norway and took the boat up the fjord to my hometown, Sauda. Every time I come home, at the first sight of Sauda, I am so overcome with wonderful memories of my childhood I can't stop the rush of emotions that remind me of the girl I was when I lived here and the life I could have had if we had stayed. I want to wrap my arms around the entire town and all the mountains and rivers and waterfalls that surround it and take it all with me wherever I am. To my cousin, Hilde, who has made many trips back every year to visit her mother, visiting Sauda is not as special as it is to me. She was visiting her mother when I came and I stayed with her and my aunt Serina in Åbødalen, up in the hills above Sauda. Alone, I walked everywhere and soaked in all the familiar sights and sounds. The hill I had skied down when I was three, which had seemed so immense, now looked miniscule but "hospital hill," which we had ridden down on our bikes hands-free, feeling very daring, was as steep as I remembered. My cousin, Berit, took me up to their cabin in the mountains and we hiked for miles up the hills to an inland lake. I imagined myself leaving behind New York and everything I owned and just living up here with books to read and no worries, no ambitions, no goals, nothing but being. I was sorely tempted.

It was all over much too quickly and when I got on the boat to leave, everyone came to the pier to see me off. I took many pictures of all of them waving at me and I cried buckets. I was heading back to reality and leaving the one place that held my most wonderful childhood memories.

Squeeky welcomed me home with loud purrs and much affection but coming back to my job with the crazy Italians was a rude shock. Norwegians tend to be quiet and taciturn. As a rule, we do not yell (except at ballgames) and we don't like being yelled at. After awhile, I knew it was time to move on to another job, which was a luxury I could afford in New York because there always seemed to be plenty of temp jobs for me. The one great thing about the job was that I had become friends with Helen Di Giovanni, the beautiful, outgoing, wife of one of the employees, and, even though we are now on separate coasts, remain close to this day. I like to start out my day reading her Yiddish jokes that she e-mails me and seems to have an endless supply of.

So it was on to another company whose president, a young woman in her 30s, also attended Marble. They didn't care if I went on auditions or left early for rehearsals. As long as I finished my work, I was free to come and go as I pleased. There were long stretches of time when I had nothing to do and would listen to Gary Null on the radio and call my friends to chat. It all sounds so ideal on the surface but when you're an actor and all you've ever wanted to do since you were young is act, working temp is agony. The feeling of failure has to be faced and overcome every single day. Depression constantly wants to take over your life and must be fought off because no one wants to be around you if you're down and feeling sorry for yourself all the time. Not even I would want to be around me if that's what I projected every minute. Someone has said, "Fake it until you make it" so that's what I did. I smiled and joked and kept "asking" and "seeking" and "knocking" on that door, believing that sooner or later it would open up and I would be a working actor and my dreams would all come true.

One day, our choir director, David, told us that we would be backing up Whitney Houston in a huge venue in New Jersey; her mom, Cissy Houston would be teaching us the song and we would rehearse with her. Cissy had been a member of "The Sweet Inspirations" and had had a long and successful recording career herself, so I felt honored that she had chosen us to back up her daughter, and felt privileged to be working with her. The night of the performance we were back stage waiting to go on when somebody said, "Look at the monitor." It was the monitor that showed who was in the greenroom. We saw what looked like a very thin, elderly woman with a dead fox, head, tail, paws and all, wrapped around her neck. We were shocked to recognize Whitney, barely able to stand, weak and frail, and we knew we would not be singing with her that night. Instead we performed with Cissy, who was still a marvelous singer.

Early morning cattle calls were still on my agenda, even though hope was growing dim that anything would ever come of it, but one day I got a call-back for a musical being workshopped for Broadway. Thank God, I didn't have to "move" for this one and was very excited to be offered the role of a southern country woman. I thought I was very much miscast but I think the writer/producer liked me and I was happy to be there. At the read-through, we all had dreams of this musical being a huge hit and going all the way to Broadway, but slowly but surely, we realized the book was way too long and the plot meandered all over the place and this might not be the vehicle that would propel us to Broadway stardom.

The night that the singing ranges were decided, I was performing with the gospel choir, so at the next rehearsal I found myself singing in my no-man's-land of too high for alto and too low for soprano. I accepted that as a price I had to pay for the fact that sometimes rehearsals might interfere with gospel choir performances, but somehow I managed to juggle the two. I still remember late one night, after a rehearsal, running with other members of the cast and laughing as we tried to catch a subway train that ran underground by the Twin Towers. Never could I have imagined that soon those Towers wouldn't even exist and where we were running would be a deep black hole.

During this time, I did go out with a few men, not many, and none of them lasted very long. One was very controlling, another commitment phobic, one actor, and two musicians. One of them was the spitting image of Rob: same hair, eyes, and the same gawky way of moving. It was uncanny. They could have been brothers. We had some wonderful, romantic moments that I wouldn't change for the world, but I knew there was no future for us and I ended it. I would rather come home to Squeeky, thank you very much. The human males were all aggravating, annoying and demanding; all things I never again wanted in my life.

We performed our musical at the Producers Club to a packed house of a special invited audience. The show was so long we all prayed that people would stay to the end. After intermission, the audience was reduced to less than half. The other half didn't leave because they were sound asleep. It was obvious we had a disaster on our hands. The executive producer, who was also the director, writer and financier, had no choice but to hand over directing chores to someone else, and when he came in he wrote my part out along with a several other roles. So this was not going to be the big break in New York theater that I had hoped for. The production hobbled along for awhile but never made it to Broadway. Better luck next time. I guess it's back to practicing "moving well."

Much more exciting was the news that the gospel choir was going to sing at Carnegie Hall. We had won first place in the McDonalds Gospelfest competition with our rendition of "King Jesus is A Listenin'." Other groups from different parts of the country had competed with musical instruments to back them up. We sang a cappella and were never so together or so totally focused on David as we were that night. We were one person, one voice, harmonizing, soaring, exhilarating. And we won. Next stop Carnegie Hall.

Everyone has heard the old joke, "A tourist asks a New Yorker, how do I get to Carnegie Hall?" And the New Yorker responds, "Practice, practice, practice!" But I had never thought of singing there, either alone or with a group, no matter how hard I practiced. It was so far out of the realm of possibility I never gave it the slightest thought. Yet here we were, scheduled to sing in Carnegie Hall. We had sung at Lincoln Center and Town Hall and The Beacon Theater on Broadway and I thought that would be as good as it got, but David somehow got us this gig and we were happy to oblige. On stage, during rehearsal, the auditorium felt intimate and our soloists sounded fantastic. I could hardly wait to go on, but my young friend, Tiffany, was very nervous so I whispered to her I had a song that had a lovely melody that I sang quietly to myself at times like this: "Turn your eyes upon Jesus, look full in his wonderful face. And the things of earth will grow strangely dim in the light of his glory and grace." I sang it softly to her just before going on and she seemed to relax and feel better.

I always told my friends when I invited them to come to hear us sing that they wouldn't be walking out after the performance, they would be floating out the door five feet off the ground, and that night was no exception. After all the applause and cheers, we all floated out of there as well. A dream I never even had, had come true.

Jogging and walking around the reservoir a few blocks from where I lived was one of my greatest joys. In the spring I would look at the trees with their pink blossoms and the skyline all around and I would say, "Thank you, God. Thank you that I'm here." But always there was that nagging voice telling me, "You are a failure. You are a failure. You are nothing. You are nobody. You are poor and you will have to work in offices for the rest of your life. Sometimes the fear of a bleak future was so intense I felt almost frozen, unable to get up or get myself to the subway and to work. I compared myself to some of my peers who I had started with, who were now rich and famous and I agonized and asked, why, why, why not me? I was talented and a decent person. Why did they make it and I didn't? Some of them were drug addicts and alcoholics. Some weren't nice at all. As a matter of fact, a few of them were mean and selfish, but in spite of that had everything they had ever wanted. The injustice of it ate away at me until I felt I couldn't function. The Libra that I am wanted everything to be *fair*. But I was determined no one would ever know or I wouldn't even have the friends and things I did have. At one point my depression became so bad I had to talk to David and he directed me to a psychologist at the church who understood what I was going through and helped me find a way to deal with it. Enjoy the present, keep on knocking, and it will happen.

Rarely did I appreciate the successes I had achieved through the years – the many roles I had been cast in, the incredible actors and directors I had worked with, the lessons I had learned on how to become a better actor and the hundreds of hours I had spent on stage enjoying the laughter and applause. Once those experiences were in the past it was as if they didn't matter, and all I could think about was my uncertain future and the horrible prospect of being imprisoned in an office for the rest of my life. That's how obsessed I was with "making it." I now realize that only a small percentage of actors are able to work steadily for their entire careers. Even actors who star in major motion pictures or are regulars in TV series have long dormant periods that may last the rest of their lives. But common sense eluded me as I strove to find acting work that would last continuously into the foreseeable future and beyond. Except for a few soap opera actors and a handful of movie stars, there's no such thing.

I did know that I had learned as a Cinderella Complex former victim it was up to me to be the prince charming I was waiting for. A quote comes to mind, which I don't know is my own or someone else's; "I had flown too high on borrowed wings." It was time for me to make my own way, and step by step I was doing it in the most challenging city in the world. I had that to cling to.

Pastor Caliandro used to preach a sermon regarding taking his little boat out into the bay near his summer house in New England. One afternoon, as the sun was going down, he saw that the water ahead of him was drenched in golden sunlight. He became determined to catch up to the gold and be right in the middle of it. So he rowed and rowed but couldn't catch up with the gold. He came back home disappointed and told his wife, "I tried so hard to catch up to the gold but I just couldn't get there. It kept moving ahead of me no matter how fast I rowed." And his wife said, "But Arthur, I was watching you. You *were* in the gold the whole time!" And that was his lesson for us; we are so busy working on our future goals we forget to appreciate and be thankful for everything we have right now. It was a difficult concept for me to accept, since my goal was so incredibly important it was as if my life depended on it.

Our next performance was to be at Madison Square Garden backing up Marc Anthony. On the bill, besides Marc and us, were Beyoncé and Destiny's Child, Ricky Martin, Michael Jackson, and several others. We had a very short rehearsal in the Garden and only sang one song with Marc. For whatever reason, Michael Jackson decided not to sing but came on stage anyway to a big ovation. We were shocked to see him looking so thin and ghostly in person. I wondered why a man who had still been handsome a few years ago, after several plastic surgeries, kept hacking away at his face until it looked even more deformed and bizarre. On the other hand, Ricky Martin was gorgeous and a charismatic performer. All of us females in the choir fell in love with him but since he was gay he was immune to any overtures from us.

A special treat was when my forever friend Georgia came to visit from where she lived in Reno. When I was at work she explored all the places she had read about and seen in movies. One of the men who was interested in me and had his own limo and driver, picked her up at my place, took her gallery hopping, and we all had dinner after I was through with work. The next day, Georgia and I took the Circle Trip around Manhattan and then rode the train up to Mystic, Connecticut, where we stayed over one night and, of course, had to eat at Mystic Pizza. Back in New York, Georgia bought me a beautiful painting of a black cat who looked just like Squeeky sitting on a windowsill, looking out over the city. She couldn't have given me a more perfect or more thoughtful present.

Epiphany

⤜⤏

I was probably the last person in the country to replace my old word processor with a computer. I took some lessons but eventually had to learn by trial and error. My first internet company turned out to be a bunch of crooks and totally messed me up, but I signed with a bigger company and started to learn about the internet. For everyone I knew it was old hat, but for me, who had fought against getting a computer, it was taking awhile to catch up to everybody else. Winter came with lots of snow and at the fall of the first flake I would bundle up and go out and walk in it. I had loved doing that since I was a kid and always figured I better do it right away before it all turned gray with soot.

So on this cold and freezing Saturday as I thought about the poor carriage horses, forced to stand shivering, waiting to take clueless tourists on their "romantic" winter ride through the park, I decided to take a break from my computer and go for a walk. I bundled up until I looked like the Michelin Man, turned on the radio for Squeeky and headed out the door. I loved the look of the snow as it covered the gray sidewalks, making the lights in the store windows even more festive and inviting. The pavement was a bit icy so I walked carefully, but as the light on Lexington turned red I hurried my steps, missed the curb and fell hard on the street, twisting my knee painfully. I cried out in pain and people rushed to assist me. New Yorkers are like that. I don't care what anybody says. A man helped me up but I could only stand on one foot. He volunteered to let me lean on him as I made my way back home and he reluctantly left me at the front door of my building. I assured him I could walk up the stairs on my own. I don't know how I made it up four flights. My knee was throbbing and the pain was excruciating. I opened my door, hobbled into the bedroom and fell on the bed.

I had known a lot of physical pain in my life and this was right up there with the worst of it. I couldn't go to a doctor because I had no insurance. I knew I wouldn't be able to get to work on Monday, and performing was out of the question. I felt a black wave of depression washing over me, worse than any I had ever felt before. It was as if that bottomless pit I had been dreading all my life opened up below me and I descended into hopelessness and despair. I felt completely alone, with no one to turn to, no help anywhere. I covered my face with my hands and cried as all the bad decisions, the betrayals, the disappointments, the losses, flashed through my brain and a thousand knives tore into my heart. My dreams were dead! I was lying to myself that I still had a chance to make them come true. I was pathetic and delusional, with a bleak future and years of poverty and struggle stretching out before me. I had thought I would end up living in a mansion; instead I lived in a fifth-floor walkup with barely enough room for my clothes. I have disappointed everyone who ever believed in me and now I won't be able to get to work and will lose my job and how will I even be able to pay the rent?! I have been knocking on that confounded door for YEARS! Why won't it open?! Why can't my life turn around?! The answers were glaringly obvious – because no one wants you! Your time has passed, it's over! You're DONE!

I sobbed into my pillow, wailing so all the world could hear. This was not a mere pity party. This was the mother of all self-excoriations. All I wanted was for the pain to stop and for me not to exist anymore. I had failed in my passion and failed in my purpose in life. Failure was my most faithful and constant companion and it was never going to leave me alone.

I exhausted myself crying and when the sobs died down I felt empty and dead inside. Squeeky sat on the bed staring at me with big round eyes.

Somewhere on the edge of my consciousness I became aware of the beginning of a song – the exquisite, melodic chord changes of the introduction, then the sound of harps playing. Was I dying? Was the great producer in the sky about to usher me into a new existence free from pain and hopelessness? I kept listening. No, the song was on the radio. Then a gentle gospel voice began to sing. His voice was soothing, plaintive and kind. As I slowly started to emerge from the black cloud of self-pity that had enveloped me, I became aware that the lyrics were completely apropos to everything that I was feeling, I felt the singer was singing directly to me.

I moved closer to the radio so I could be sure I heard every word. At some point in his life, the singer had felt he couldn't go on, that his life had no meaning or purpose. I held my breath as the incredible beauty of the music and the voices of the choir took flight and soared, singing words of freedom and flying and knowing we can accomplish anything we believe we can do; *doors that are closed will open if we just believe.*

I heard the words of the song, words that were directed right at me, piercing my anguish and calming my soul. I had been singing gospel songs about God's love and encouragement for a long time but for whatever reason, this song hit me so hard it was like being overwhelmed by a tsunami. I felt an incredible release. All the insecurities and fears that had bound me up for most of my adult life were unraveling and letting go. Because of a song? Written by who knows who? That didn't matter. The song had cut through the fog of my deep despair and was speaking to me about *believing* and *flying.*

I whispered softly, "Yes, God, thank you, God." The singer continued to share his feelings about giving up, breaking down and feeling alone. He was telling me that miracles happen when we ourselves make them happen and it all starts within each and every one of us.

I leaned back against the bed and sighed, "Inside of me. Yes, inside of me." I thought to myself of the Bible verse the lyrics referred to; *"Seek and ye shall find, ask and ye shall receive, knock and it shall be opened unto you.*" Who but God knew that I had repeated that verse a hundred times for years to keep myself going? He must have been tired of waiting for me to get the message and was now hitting me over the head with it. The chorus joined the gospel singer in a joyous finale and, rivaling the voices of my own gospel choir, exhorted the listener, in beautiful harmonic crescendo, again and again to *fly!*

I didn't care if anyone walked in the door just then and saw me sitting there on the floor with tears streaming down my face. They could have laughed at me, said I was crazy or delusional, but my entire being felt rejuvenated and no one could have told me any differently. Somehow, I will get myself to work, I will pay my bills, and if I miss a rehearsal or two, David would never throw me out of the choir! I may not have any leaders to lean on in the anti-vivisection movement but with the internet I can reach thousands of people with the truth. And I will have faith that I will act again. Erika is coming to visit soon and we will have a wonderful time! I have an apartment in my favorite part of town, the rent is low and I have family and friends who care about me. I am finally relying on myself and no one else, and in New York City at that!

I always believed that if I weren't a successful working actress I would end up existing in a dark pit, a living hell of nothingness, a life not worth living. But now that I am staring down into the depths of that pit, I find that my life has more meaning than standing on a stage or in front of a camera. My life was saved twice and for a better reason than acting. I had a purpose, a cause worth fighting for, clearly led by God. The pit of despair would not claim me as I was sure it would if I didn't end up rich and famous. Yes, I will keep on asking, seeking and knocking, but the door to my purpose in life had already opened up. Like my wonderful Dr. Caliandro, I *am* in the gold.

I pulled myself back up on the bed next to Squeeky. I was totally drained. My leg was throbbing again; funny how I hadn't noticed that as I was listening to the song. I had the whole weekend to heal and would have to hobble to the subway and up and down the subway stairs for the next few weeks, inconveniencing a lot of people. My fellow New Yorkers would just have to understand and be patient. (They did and they were.) Meanwhile, I would drink hot tea, have some soup and enjoy looking at the snow for two days. On Monday, everything would take care of itself. I was one of God's people and, finally, *I was flying.*

THE END

WHERE ARE THEY NOW?

—ç—

Rob Lind, after a career as a Navy pilot, studied film-making at USC, directed dozens of commercials and an award-winning short film, flew several years for USAir and is again playing with the Sonics all over the world to sold-out crowds and rave reviews. He plays the sax better than ever.

Kevin Dobson starred in several television series and lives in Santa Barbara, California.

Billy Vera still performs with the Beaters, sings, plays piano and treats the audience to cool patter at a local club, and has found his true niche singing big band standards in various clubs in the Southern California area.

Tony Eldridge turned from acting to producing and writing, and is one of the executive producers of the world-wide mega hit, *The Equalizer*. He has various films in development.

Kevin Krasny is still a film editor and has worked on many television shows and movies. He is currently editing *ChicagoPD*.

Chris De Rose, who has risked his health and his life many times for the sake of saving animals, is still head of Last Chance for Animals and still fighting for animals around the world.

Captain Paul Watson, founder of the Sea Shepherd Conservation Society, who has survived persecution, imprisonment, false prosecution and starvation by the greedy people and governments who seek to profit from the torture and death of animals, still oversees several, on-going, sea campaigns in various parts of the globe.

Alan Godfrey retired from the television industry and lives in Northern California.

Erika Godfrey works for a publishing company and, in her spare time, works on her martial arts skills. She lives in the San Fernando Valley with the love of her life, her dog Chewy.

Debbie Widel Goldsmith has a successful chiropractic practice in Florida and is on the board of directors of PRISM.

Eric Morris, brilliant teacher and actor, is still helping actors find their authentic selves and teaching them how to accomplish – "No acting, please."

Sandra Bell, who gave up her successful career as a ballet dancer to fight vivisection, is co-director of People for Reason in Science and Medicine and is as dedicated and passionate towards achieving the goal of ending vivisection as the first day she started in the early 1980s.

ABOUT THE AUTHOR

BRITT ALWAYS KNEW SHE WANTED to be an actor and singer, and for several years, she lived her dream. After being cast in *Play Misty for Me*, Clint Eastwood's directorial debut, she had featured and guest-starring roles in shows such as *How the West Was Won*, *Vega$*, *Columbo*, *General Hospital*, *Days of Our Lives*, and *The Young and the Restless*.

Her career brought her into contact with animal and environmental activists such as Paul Watson of the Sea Shepherd Conservation Society and Chris De Rose of Last Chance for Animals. Then, Britt found her true purpose, working to expose the cruelty and fraud of animal experimentation, work she continues to do as co-director of People for Reason in Science and Medicine.

Britt now lives in Thousand Oaks, California, with her screenwriter husband, E. Nick Alexander, and three formerly feral cats.

Contact: britt@peopleforreason.org
brittlind.com
peopleforreason.org
facebook.com/gotoprism
Twitter @gotoprism

www.ingramcontent.com/pod-product-compliance
Lightning Source LLC
Chambersburg PA
CBHW050250110726
47898CB00007B/2353